Also by Ray Hobbs and Published by Wingspan Press

Published Elsewhere

KNIGHTS ERRANT

RAY HOBBS

Wingspan Press

Published in the United States and the United Kingdom
by WingSpan Press, Livermore, CA

The WingSpan name, logo and colophon are the trademarks
of WingSpan Publishing.

ISBN 978-1-63683-040-7 (pbk.)
ISBN 978-1-63683-968-4 (ebook)

First edition 2022

Printed in the United States of America

www.wingspanpress.com

This book is dedicated to the memory of Milly, aka 'Minky', and Phoebe, Aberdeen terriers whose motives were never less than genuine.

Sources and Acknowledgements

Utley, R. M., Custer, Buckskin Cavalier (London, Salamander Books Ltd, 2001).

Hollihan, T., The Mounties March West (Edmonton, Folklore Publishing, 2004).

Denny, C. E., Denny's Trek (Surrey BC, Heritage House Publishing Co Ltd, 2004).

Andra-Warner, E., The Mounties (Surrey BC, Heritage House Publishing Co Ltd, 2009).

Gay, C. W., Traditional Horse Husbandry (Philadelphia PA, J.B. Lippincott Company, 1916. Reprinted Guildford CT, Lyons Press, 2003).

As ever, I wish to acknowledge the assistance given to me by my brother Chris in the preparation of the manuscript.

RH

Author's Note

This seemingly random series of explanations is unlikely to make immediate sense, but as events unfold, you will encounter obscure references in the text. At such times, you are invited to leaf back to this page for clarification.

I should explain, to begin with, my reference to The Dakota Territory. In case anyone is wondering, the states of North and South Dakota were only admitted into the Union in 1889, long after the events described in this story, and when Seth and Henry would have been long forgotten.

The Hindi word *veshaalay* simply means 'brothel', and a *randee* was, not surprisingly, one of the working girls associated with it. These would figure prominently in the lives of a great many soldiers stationed in a nearby cantonment, or garrison, but the heroes of this story, being of upright character, would naturally have no interest in such attractions.

The order *'Jaldee karo!'*, or 'Quickly, now!' would often be heard on the lips of British non-commissioned officers in India, and would become a normal part of their vocabulary. Their subordinates would know what it meant, even if their families didn't.

Char is mistakenly believed to be the British soldiers' approximation to the Hindi word for tea. It actually originated in China, as *tcha*. The distinction would be meaningless to the soldiers of the time, of course, as service abroad was... well, service abroad, and 'abroad', as everyone knows, covers most of the globe.

The Eleventh Hussars are known as the 'Cherry Pickers', but not in memory of any glorious event in their history. The fact is that, during the Peninsular War, they were surprised by the French whilst resting in a cherry orchard. Happily, they have more than made amends for it in subsequent conflicts, and their record is such that they are able to bear the nickname without shame or embarrassment.

The Hindi word *bhagasheph* needs no translation, as its meaning will become apparent from its context, and the part of the anatomy it describes is, I imagine, the same the world over.

Willow bark tea has been used for pain relief for more than three thousand years, containing as it does salicylic acid, the main constituent of a form of aspirin. Unfortunately, in all that time, no one has been able to improve the flavour.

At this point, to avoid confusion regarding the name of the 'Mountie' force, I should point out that the original body, founded in 1873, was called the Police Force for the North West. This unwieldy title was changed a few years later to the North West Mounted Police. In recognition of its remarkable achievements, King Edward VII conferred on it in 1904 the prefix 'Royal', and then in 1920, the force became known as the Royal Canadian Mounted Police. To this day, it remains the best-known police force in the world.

The purple daisy that Wapun used in dressing wounds was most likely the echinacea plant. The Native Americans of the USA and the First People of Canada used herbs widely, knowledgeably and effectively, a fact that must surely tell us something.

Hokey-pokey was a name for ice cream in the 19th Century, when it would be extremely expensive. Seth might have encountered it from docking in London on his return from India. In any case, its popularity was widely known by that time.

Alkaline air, now an archaic, pharmaceutical term, was the name given in the nineteenth century to ammonia. Unfortunately, whilst the name has changed, the aroma has not. If we find it unpleasant, so does the horse in its stable and, as Seth tells his recruits, that is the best reason for daily mucking-out.

I hope that the foregoing has not been too intrusive, and that you enjoy reading the story as much as I have enjoyed preparing and writing it.

RH

KNIGHTS ERRANT

PART ONE

5th July 1876

Bismarck, The Dakota Territory

1

Setback

S eth eyed the buffers and the bare earth beyond them, and said, 'When they told us the railroad ended here, they weren't exaggerating, Henry.'

'No, they weren't,' agreed his companion, 'but isn't it strange, the way they call their railway a rail*road*?'

'Americans have strange words for all kinds of things,' observed Seth, 'but they seem to understand us.'

Physically, the two men were very different. After a long sea voyage and without the benefit of a barber, Seth had a mane of light-brown hair, but he had managed to remain clean-shaven. Henry's dark hair also grew in abundance and was accompanied by a full moustache that gave him a deceptively stern appearance and, whilst both men were powerfully built, Henry was the burlier of the two. Unusually, each wore a military belt from which hung a cavalry sabre.

Taking stock of their surroundings, they caught the eye of an official in a top hat and a frock coat.

'You're lookin' lost, boys. Can I help you with anythin'? The name's Davies. I'm Stationmaster here.'

'That's very civil of you, Mr Davies,' said Seth. 'We're hoping to get to Fort Abraham in Lincoln.'

The stationmaster blinked. 'What d' you want to go there for, for heaven's sake?'

'We want to join Colonel Custer and the Seventh Cavalry.' It seemed obvious to Seth; it had been their guiding star even before leaving India, and he'd imagined that anyone who'd heard of the celebrated cavalry officer would understand that.

Davies shook his head at some mysterious anomaly and said, 'Well, you've sure chose a heck of a time for it. Ain't you heard the news?' He beckoned them into the office that bore his title over the door.

'We don't want to keep you from your work, Mr Davies,' said Seth.

'Don't you worry 'bout that.' Jerking his thumb unnecessarily in the direction of the wheezing locomotive on the track, he said, 'That thing's gonna be there for the next hour, but you boys need to hear the news now.' He reached across his desk for a folded copy of the *Bismarck Tribune* and handed it to Seth, hesitating for a second to ask tentatively, 'You can read, can't you?'

Seth nodded. 'Aye, well enough.' He read the stark headline and the paragraph that followed it, and the news came like a blow from nowhere. 'I just never expected to read this,' he said. Closing his eyes in disbelief, he passed the newspaper to Henry, who read it and handed it back to the stationmaster without a word, but his reaction mirrored his friend's. They'd travelled from Bombay to London and from London to New York in their quest, only to find a headline that read: *MASSACRE AT LITTLE BIGHORN*. Beneath the headline, in smaller type, was the news of Custer's death and the annihilation of the men under his command. The newspaper was dated the 5th of July, and the rout had taken place on the 25th of June, just eleven days earlier, when Seth and Henry were still travelling from the east coast.

'I guess you boys are just as shocked as we are,' said Davies. 'I'm surmising from the way you talk that you're not from around these parts.'

'We're English,' Seth told him.

'You don't say. So, how do you come to know about Custer and the Seventh Cavalry?'

They'd explained it what seemed a thousand times on the journey, but Seth was happy to enlighten him. 'We were coming to the end of a twelve-year enlistment with our regiment in India when we met an American newspaperman, who told us about Colonel Custer, about the kind of man he was, and what he was doing for the natives out here as well as the white folk, and we decided to join the colonel as soon as we could.' Seth looked at the newspaper again and shook his head slowly at the tragedy that still seemed barely possible.

'Whether he was good for the injuns or not, I wouldn't like to say, but they sure showed him how they felt about him.'

'I don't understand it,' said Seth.

'No,' agreed Henry, 'it doesn't make sense.'

'You just don't know where you stand with them injuns, 'specially the Sioux. Just when you think they're tamed, they up and pull a low-down trick like this one.' He took the newspaper and shied it in the direction of the waste paper basket. 'They'll pay for what they've done,' he said. 'The Government will see to that.'

Both men nodded. They'd been involved in reprisals and they understood the process.

'What'll you boys do now?'

'We'll have to find work of some kind. We have some money, but it won't last us long.' They'd been fortunate in their card games with other crew members on the Atlantic crossing; when they weren't working their passage in the engine room, they'd found games of brag and poker readily enough, but they had no intention of depending on gambling for their income.

'What work can you do, apart from soldiering?'

'We were farmworkers before we joined the colours,' said Henry, emerging from his brooding silence.

Davies looked doubtful. 'In that case,' he said, 'you need to go further west. Get on the westbound stage and head for Pentecost. It's the next town on the trail, and you could just find farm work close by. I may as well warn you, though, that some folks might not take so kindly to you, you being British an' all.'

'Mr Davies, we're obliged to you,' said Seth, 'and we can take care of ourselves.' Turning to Henry, he asked, 'How does that sound to you, Henry?'

'It makes sense, Seth.'

Davies surveyed them for a second, still apparently fascinated by these strange men from another continent, and said, 'Just one thing, boys. Are those swords all you have to defend yourselves with?'

'They served us well enough in India,' said Seth.

'I won't argue with that, but the country you're heading for ain't too well acquainted with law and order, and trouble can come at you from too far away for a sword to be of much use. Take my advice and get yourselves some long-range protection.'

'We'll bear your advice in mind, Mr Davies,' said Seth.

'Right enough,' said Henry.

'Just one more thing, boys, before you go.'

'Yes?'

'I don't like to be personal, but there's somethin' I've been wonderin'. How d' you get your teeth so white?'

'We clean them, Mr Davies.'

They took their leave of the stationmaster, having elicited from him the time of the next stagecoach for Pentecost and the whereabouts of the stage office.

In the event, they located the office of the Minnesota Stage Company without difficulty, and Seth asked for two tickets for Pentecost.

'Two for Pentecost,' said the clerk, consulting the document before him. 'Yes, there are three seats left on this afternoon's stage.'

'We only need two,' said Henry, who liked to be clearly understood.

The clerk eyed him nervously. 'Yes, right, two seats. That's three dollars each.'

'Three dollars?' Henry looked scandalised.

'It's nearly twenty miles,' said the clerk, still looking wary.

'It's just as well we only want two tickets,' said Seth, giving the clerk six dollars as if he were handing him a fortune.

'The stage is expected at eleven o' clock and it leaves at noon. What baggage have you?'

'I told you,' said Henry, 'there's only two of us.'

'He means "luggage",' said Seth patiently. 'He's not talking about fallen women.'

'That's right,' said the clerk, 'I meant trunks and cases, because they have to go on top of the coach.'

'We only have hand baggage,' Seth told him. He remembered hearing the term during their train journey.

'Oh, that's no problem, sir.'

'We're obliged to you.'

'And I'm obliged to you, gentlemen. Good day to you both.'

As they left the office, Henry asked, 'Why do folk find me so scary?'

Seth pondered the question and said, 'You look scary, Henry. You can't help it, and not everybody knows what a soft-hearted soul you are. Even I have to remind myself of it sometimes.'

Henry gave a look of acceptance and then, conscious of more immediate matters, looked at his pocket watch, a recent acquisition, and said, 'We've got more than an hour before the coach leaves.'

'Aye, and that saloon doesn't strike me as the kind of place where we can have a quiet drink.' The rowdiness of the place was apparent from the end of the street, where they stood. Suddenly, the swing doors opened, and a man staggered out backwards and collapsed in the street.

'Well,' said Henry, 'that's one trouble-maker out on his arse.'

The noise continued. 'Aye,' said Seth, 'but his mates are still in there. They must be arguing about who's goin' next. Let's see if we can find a brew.'

'What a hope.' They had discovered since their arrival in New York, to their disappointment, that America was not a nation of tea drinkers.

'There's a place here.' Seth was pointing to a restaurant sign. 'Even coffee's better than....' Neither of them was sure what was worse than coffee, but they opened the door of the restaurant, anyway, and waited to be seated.

A pleasant, smiling woman of middle years came to them and said, 'Good morning, boys. What's your pleasure?'

'We wondered,' said Seth, reasoning that it would cost nothing to ask, 'if we could have a pot of tea.'

'Tea?' Not surprisingly, it was an unusual request, but the woman said, 'Of course. If you like to be seated, I'll attend to it right away.' As she turned to leave them, she hesitated and asked, 'Are you Swedish?'

'No,' said Seth, puzzled. 'Do Swedish people drink tea?'

'Not usually. That's why I was surprised when you asked for it.'

'We're English.'

'Oh.' She seemed even more surprised. 'It was your accent that made me think you might be Swedish. I've met a few Englishmen, but they didn't sound like you. What part of England are you from?'

7

'A village near Beverley in the East Riding of Yorkshire.'

'Ah.' She looked like someone who'd never heard of Yorkshire, let alone the East Riding. With that question answered, she said, 'I'm afraid we're fresh out of lemons. They were used in the cooking.'

'Don't worry. Just bring us a pot of tea and two cups, and you'll see two smiles you'll never forget.'

She hurried off to organise the tea, leaving Seth to say, 'I still can't believe the news about Colonel Custer.'

'No, but we look like getting a cup of tea,' Henry reminded him, concerning himself as usual with the immediate situation, rather than the overall state of affairs, 'an' that makes up for a lot.'

'It doesn't take a lot to satisfy you, Henry.'

When the proprietress brought the tea to them, they kept Seth's promise of two happy smiles, and Henry's assertion was proved correct. It really did compensate for a great deal.

⊕⊢ᛝ⊰⊱ᛝᚻ⊕

The journey to Pentecost by stagecoach was uncomfortable and not in the least enlivened by the company of their fellow-passengers, who included a heavily-bearded and fiercely-disposed minister of The Church of the Vengeful Lord, his plain wife and even plainer daughter. The wife and daughter seemed satisfied with merely looking unpleasant, whereas the minister made it his mission to be disagreeable to the two Englishmen.

Two minutes into their conversation, he made the observation, 'England is a godless country.'

Seth couldn't allow that. 'That's not true, Pastor Goodenough,' he said. 'God has not passed us by.'

'Has he not?' It was clear that the pastor would take some convincing. 'What is your church?'

'The Church of England.'

'A dissolute establishment bedevilled by robed bishops.'

'We haven't seen many bishops, have we, Sergeant Fowler?'

'No, Sergeant Campion, not unless you count the bishop who confirmed us.'

8

'Apart from him, Sergeant Fowler, I'd say none at all.'

'I agree, Sergeant Campion.'

'I think that settles the argument, Pastor. The bishops are nowhere to be seen.'

Clearly exasperated, the minister challenged them again. 'Why,' he demanded, 'do you insist on addressing each other by those ridiculous names?'

Both men looked at each other in theatrical outrage. Seth was the first to speak. 'Ridiculous names? I was baptised "Seth Jacob" in the name of the Father, the Son and the Holy Spirit, and my father was Adam Campion.' He gave Henry a nudge. 'Tell him, Sergeant Fowler. Don't let your family be insulted.'

'I was baptised "Henry Caleb", and my father was Nathan Fowler,' said Henry, glowering deliberately.

'Until earlier this year, we were both sergeants in Prince Albert's Own Eleventh Hussars,' said Seth, 'and, in any case, as free men, we have the right to address each other by any name we choose.'

Seemingly at a loss for a suitable and telling argument, the pastor lapsed into baleful silence before transferring his gaze to the passing landscape.

After a while, Seth caught the eye of the homely daughter and favoured her with a slow wink, at which she pursed her lips, gathered her skirts more securely around her and joined her father in admiring the scenery. Her mother looked across at her fellow passengers, initially with the disapproval of an obedient wife, but her expression changed gradually to something almost akin to wistfulness, before she transferred her attention also to the view beyond the window.

Almost four hours after leaving Bismarck, the coach entered the town of Pentecost and the two Englishmen bade farewell to Pastor Goodenough, his wife and his daughter.

'You know,' said Henry as they stood outside the stage office, 'life with the good pastor and his family must be a merry-go-round of jollity.'

Seth asked, 'Do you remember a man called Briscoe in "D" Troop? He was a deeply religious fellow who still felt the normal urges from time to time. He used to go to a *veshyaalay* in the town and pay for the services of a *randee*, and then come back to the cantonment feeling so guilty he beat himself with a knotted rope. I wonder if Pastor

Goodenough indulges in that kind of thing. It could explain why his daughter's an only child.'

'I'd put money on it,' said Henry, but something that's more important is finding ourselves somewhere to stay the night.'

'You're right, Henry, as usual. Let's ask the stage clerk.'

While other passengers were transacting their business, they noticed that the clerk was a man of mature years, possibly forty, and that he attempted to disguise his partial baldness with long strands of hair arranged strategically across his otherwise bare crown. Unfortunately, two of the strands had failed to remain in place and they now dangled obstinately beside his left ear.

Eventually, he came free, and Seth asked him about board and lodging.

'There's the Palace Hotel.'

'That sounds expensive.'

'You're probably right. There's a hotel above the saloon,' he said, 'but I don't rightly know of any place else.'

'We're grateful for your time,' said Seth.

'We are,' agreed Henry.

They left the office and peered along the street, which seemed to represent the whole town. No doubt, its people lived behind the shops, but the street, with its side-turnings was where business took place. There was a livery stable quite close to where they stood, the Town Marshal's office, a bank, and a general store with a horse trough and a tethering rail. A horse-drawn contraption of a kind that was new to them stood beside it. Elsewhere, was a gunsmith's store and a saloon that seemed currently to be hosting a riot.

'I suppose we'll have to try the hotel over the saloon,' said Seth.

'Needs must.' Henry's agreement came with little enthusiasm.

The door to the general store opened, and a woman emerged, carrying several parcels.

'Let's ask this lady,' said Seth. 'She might know of somebody who'll put us up.'

They crossed the dusty street to speak to the woman just as two men burst out of the saloon. They were clearly the worse for drink, and each looked as ugly and dangerous as the other. It was evident to Seth and Henry that they were looking for trouble.

2

Rough Justice

Whether the two had been ejected from the saloon, or whether they'd left of their own drunken accord was unclear, because they'd stumbled out of the building hurriedly, but they slowed down readily enough.

One of them greeted the woman noisily, beckoning his companion. What they had in mind was clear enough, and it was equally obvious that their attentions were unwelcome, especially when one of them seized her by the waist, causing the parcels to fall from her grasp.

'No! Leave me alone,' she protested. 'Somebody, help me, please!'

Stepping up and on to the sidewalk, Seth and Henry each took a handful of hair and hauled the men backwards, forcing them to release the unfortunate woman.

'The lady said, "No",' Henry reminded them quietly.

'You both heard her,' said Seth. Then, changing direction, they both swung their captives headfirst against the tethering rail, ignoring their cries when their heads made contact with the stout timber structure.

'Do you know what these men really need, Sergeant Fowler?'

'They need sobering up, Sergeant Campion.'

'Agreed.' Together, they thrust the two heads into the horse trough, holding them under until the last second before hauling them out again, their owners choking and gasping for breath. It was an established routine for the two Englishmen. Every payday, soldiers became drunk and violent, and it was the sergeants' task to make them docile.

'When a lady says, "No",' said Seth....

'She means, "No",' explained Henry. Then, as one, they drove their

11

fists into the offenders' bellies and left them to collapse, bent double and gasping desperately for air.

The woman, understandably still in a state of distress, had picked up most of her parcels and was stacking them on the utility. Seth asked, 'Are you all right, ma'am?'

'Yes, thank you. I'm very grateful to you both.' She was tearful but understandably relieved.

Henry lifted the two remaining packages and placed them with the others. 'Is there anything more we can help you with?'

'No, but I'm very grateful. You've both been very kind.'

The miscreants were beginning to stir, having partially regained their breath, but a meaningful look from Seth dissuaded any thoughts of retaliation, and they stumbled sourly on their way.

'We wondered,' said Henry, 'if you might be able to tell us where we could find a room for the night.'

'Other than the Palace Hotel,' she said, eyeing their modest appearance, 'there's only the saloon, and you've seen what just came out of there.'

'Beggars can't be choosers, ma'am,' said Seth. 'We've just arrived here, and we're looking for work, but first we need somewhere to stay until morning, when we can make a start.'

Mention of work triggered a response. She asked, 'What kind of work are you looking for?'

'Any kind, really, but farm work, by choice. We're both experienced farm workers.' Honesty made him say, 'It was some years ago, but we haven't forgotten anything.'

'My husband and I need help on our farm. He's injured, and we were already short of a man. Are you interested?'

'We're more than interested, ma'am. I'm Seth Campion, this is Henry Fowler, and we're both at your service.'

For the first time since the ugly incident, she smiled, and said, 'I'm Mrs Norton.' When they'd shaken hands, she said, 'Climb on the buckboard and I'll take you to the farm.'

On the way, they learned that Mr Norton had slipped a disc and was obliged to remain immobile until it was healed. The farm grew vegetables as well as wheat, and the family also kept chickens. It was a lot of work for a woman on her own.

Mrs Norton was fair-haired, slim and, now that she was in a happier frame of mind, it became apparent that she was quite attractive, a fact that might have prompted her two assailants to behave the way they did, although Seth and Henry later agreed that alcohol and parental example of the wrong kind were the most likely culprits.

The farm was about two miles from the town, a journey of only half an hour. When they arrived, Seth and Henry unloaded the buckboard, and Mrs Norton introduced them to her husband, who greeted them from his bed. Her two sons of eight and ten were openly curious about the newcomers' white teeth.

'We clean 'em,' Henry told them.

After scolding her sons and apologising for their lapse of manners, Mrs Norton told her husband about the incident outside the general store. 'Two drunks tried to get fresh with me,' she told him, 'but these nice Englishmen came to my assistance. They were looking for farm work, so I brought them home.'

'English, huh?' Whether his surprise was because Englishmen were rare in that locale, or because two of his country's erstwhile enemies had gone to the rescue of an American woman was unclear. At all events, he was grateful. 'I'm glad to meet you, boys, and I'm obliged to you for what you did. I feel so helpless when something like this happens.'

'It was no trouble,' Seth told him.

'No trouble at all,' echoed Henry.

Matthew, the elder of the boys, had been studying them since they arrived, and curiosity finally made him ask, 'Why are you carrying swords?'

'These are cavalry sabres,' Henry told him. 'A gang of bandits took them from two British soldiers, so we took them back. That's why the Colonel let us keep them as our property.'

Both boys were now looking at them with new interest. James, the younger of them, said, 'Bandits? Where was that?'

'On the Northwest Frontier of India,' said Seth. 'It was our job to protect the innocent Indians from the bandits.'

'Do you have injuns as well?' The naïve and innocent question came from the same child.

'Yes,' said Seth. 'They're called that because they live in India. They're not like your Indians.'

After supper, Mr and Mrs Norton invited the newcomers to join them for coffee. British cavalrymen were exotic and therefore so fascinating that the Norton boys were allowed to stay up late so that they could hear about the exploits of the British Army in India. Their parents were also keen to be enlightened.

'There have always been outlaws in India,' Seth told them, 'and it was our job to uphold the law. Criminals have to be caught and punished.'

'The trouble was,' said Henry, 'the Army weren't always kind to the innocent natives, and that went against the way we'd been brought up.'

'That,' said Seth, 'was why, when we'd done our twelve years with the regiment, we didn't re-enlist.'

'As well as that,' said Henry, 'we met a reporter from an American newspaper, who told us about Colonel Custer. He said the colonel was a fair-minded man who protected both the natives and the white people, and we decided to travel to America to join him.'

At that point, Mrs Norton decided that the boys had been up long enough. 'Off to bed with you, boys,' she said.

'Oh, Ma, do we have to?'

'Yes, you do. Henry and Seth will still be here in the morning. Off you go.'

The boys bade everyone goodnight and went reluctantly to bed. It was as well, because something was puzzling Mr Norton.

'I don't know how true that is about Custer,' he said, 'but what I don't understand is why you've come here for work instead of going off and joining him right away.'

Seth looked across at Henry, knowing that he was thinking the same thought. They'd only heard that morning about the massacre, so it was no wonder these people were still ignorant of it.

'You haven't heard the news, then,' said Henry.

'What news?' They were apprehensive already.

'We're sorry to be the ones to tell you this,' said Seth. 'Colonel Custer and, as far as we can make out, more than two hundred men were slaughtered nearly a fortnight ago. It happened at a river called the Little Bighorn.'

Although she seemed as stunned as her husband, Mrs Norton asked, 'What do you mean by a "fortnight"?'

'Two weeks. I'm sorry. Don't you call it that here?'

'No, this is the first time I've heard the word.'

Mr Norton was still trying to come to terms with the news. 'I just can't believe it,' he said.

'Neither could we.'

'How did you come to hear of it?'

'We got off the train in Bismarck,' said Henry, 'and the stationmaster told us. It was in the *Bismarck Tribune* this morning.'

'We're sorry to bring you bad news,' said Seth, now embarrassed.

'It's not your fault, boys, but if you're still feeling kindly disposed towards those red devils, I don't think you'll find anybody hereabouts who feels the same way, leastways, not after the news gets out.'

It was difficult to see how the conversation could develop after that, but Mrs Norton avoided further disagreement by changing the subject completely.

'Boys,' she said, 'I can't thank you enough for what you did this afternoon. I must say, I was more scared than I can ever remember.'

'It was no trouble, Mrs Norton, honestly,' said Seth, grateful to her for changing the subject, 'but I think you'd better let one of us go into town instead of you, at least for a while. Either that, or let us give you an escort.'

'That's good of you, boys,' said Mr Norton. 'I just hope you haven't got yourselves a whole heap o' trouble already.'

⚜

The first task Mrs Norton set them in the morning was to mend the fences that had been neglected since her husband's injury. The job was easy enough for them and, by the end of the first hour, they'd made substantial progress.

Seth stopped to survey the work so far. 'We haven't lost our old skill, Henry. It's a very pretty fence indeed, that one is.'

'Prettier than what I'm lookin' at.'

15

'What's that, mate?' Seth turned to see where his friend was looking, and saw two men approaching on horseback.

'It's the two we caught pestering Mrs Norton,' said Henry.

'I do believe you're right.'

The two horsemen rode up to them and stopped. They both wore tangled beards that appeared to be home to the remains of at least one meal, and what teeth they still possessed were dark-brown and uneven. Now that they were close up, the stench of their unwashed bodies and clothing was also starkly apparent. One of them asked, 'You two workin' here now?'

'It's looking that way,' said Seth, holding up his hammer as evidence. 'What's on your mind?'

'We been lookin' for you two, an' somebody told us they'd seen you come up here with that there woman.'

'Well, now you've found us, what do you want?'

'First of all,' said the spokesman, because that seemed to be his role, 'we have a score to settle with you both, an' when we've done that, we've a mind to visit that there farm.'

Seth nodded to show that he'd understood the man so far. 'What business have you at the farm?'

The spokesman turned to his companion and said with a leer, 'He wants to know what business we have at the farm.'

In a similar aside, Seth said to Henry, 'He's quick on the uptake, you know. You've got to give him credit for that.'

'We want to visit that farm because we've heard that the man's flat on his back with sump'n, and he can't get up, an' that purty wife o' his can't have had any fun in a long time. We're gonna give her a little fun, an' just to be fair, we're gonna let her man watch while we do it.' They both laughed as if it were the funniest thing of all.

'It's not as easy as that,' said Henry.

'Why not?'

He put his hammer down to explain. 'To get to the second part of your plan, you have to get through the first part.'

It seemed that it was too much for the spokesman to take in. 'What are you sayin'?'

'I'm sayin' you've got to settle your score with us first. That's what makes it harder than what you think.'

'We'll soon see 'bout that.' They both began to dismount, unaware that help was at hand in the shape of their intended victims, who each grabbed the nearest item of foetid clothing and helped them on their way. Both men hit the ground hard, and the noises they made confirmed that their fall was a painful one. Seth looked at Henry and nodded. They kicked simultaneously, and the two lay writhing and groaning, with their hands belatedly shielding their private parts.

'They were going to teach us a lesson,' said Seth.

'I haven't learned a thing,' observed Henry.

'No, but they have.'

With a look of blind fury, first one, and then the other, reached for his revolver.

'Oh, naughty,' said Seth as he and Henry drew their sabres. Two blades flashed in the sunlight, and the two reprobates screamed as what remained of their trigger fingers spurted blood.

'You'll have to find another way to settle your differences,' said Seth, 'because them pistols aren't going to be much use to you now.'

Howling and clutching their bloodied hands, the two reprobates managed to mount their horses. As they did so, they hurled fresh threats of revenge, which Seth and Henry dismissed with light-hearted laughter.

As they watched the sorry pair ride away, Henry said, 'I suppose we should take the stationmaster's advice.'

'We already did,' said Seth. 'That's why we're here, isn't it?'

'I mean his advice about getting ourselves better armed.'

'I suppose so, but it seems a shame. I mean, we dealt with them two, and they only lost the ends of their fingers. If we have to start shooting, somebody might get killed.'

'That's right enough.' Henry sheathed his sabre. 'Let's get on with these fences.'

***

That evening, Mr Norton raised the subject of the two men again. It was evidently of some concern to him.

'It's all right,' said Henry. 'They came to see us this morning, while we were working on the fences, and we persuaded them to find another interest. They won't be a problem again.'

Mrs Norton asked, 'But can you be sure of that?'

'As sure as anyone can be, but we'll be around here for a while. Don't you worry.'

Looking discreetly at Mrs Norton, Seth saw a devoted wife and mother, and a fair and trusting employer. She was the best kind of person, and when he thought of those villains and what they had in mind for her.... On reflection, he preferred not to think of it. Maybe Henry was right, and they should follow the stationmaster's advice after all.

3

In The Wash

When Seth and Henry returned from the town with the goods on Mrs Norton's list, she was surprised to see a stone jar on the buckboard, and she asked what it contained.

'Beer, ma'am,' said Henry. 'We bought it ourselves.'

'I should tell you, boys, that we don't hold with strong drink on this farm.'

'It's not for drinking,' said Henry, deliberately omitting to mention that they'd already relieved their thirst at the saloon.

'Well, what else can it be for?'

'It's to wash our hair, ma'am. There's just two of your American pints of beer in that jar, but it's enough for both of us to wash our hair and feel clean again. When we've done that, we'll rinse our hair with water and it'll be as if the beer had never come to your notice.'

'Well, I never heard of that, and now you mention it, your hair always does look clean and shiny.'

'It'll be cleaner and shinier after this,' said Seth, taking the jar from the buckboard.

'You boys sure keep yourselves clean an' tidy.'

'That's because we served in one of the smartest regiments in the British Army, ma'am. The Tenth Hussars like to call themselves "The Shiny Tenth", but they're no smarter than the Eleventh. They just talk about it more than we do.'

Mrs Norton seemed to be struggling with something. 'Are you saying,' she asked, 'that your regiment has had more book-learning than the others?'

'No, ma'am.' Seth had an idea of where the confusion lay. 'When

I say "smart", I'm talking about being smartly turned out, with a clean uniform, polished buttons, spurs, boots and tack, and a perfectly-groomed horse.'

'Oh.' Realisation was evident. ' "Smart" means something different to us.'

'I can see that. now. You mean "clever", don't you?'

She laughed. 'We don't say, "clever", but you got the idea.' She pointed to the supplies on the buckboard and said, 'Bring those things inside and I'll make us some coffee.'

Coffee was no inducement for either of them, but they were prepared to be sociable, so they put everything away according to Mrs Norton's instructions, and joined her and Mr Norton for coffee.

'Ma'am,' said Henry when they were seated, 'do you know who owns the lake beyond the white rock?'

'Lake Leconseh?' She frowned in thought, and said, 'I don't know as anybody owns it. Do you know, Frank?'

'No,' said her husband, 'I guess it's public property. What's your interest in it?'

'We thought we'd go for a swim when we have the time.'

'So you can both swim?' Mrs Norton was impressed. 'Is there anything you boys can't do?'

'There must be lots of things, ma'am,' said Seth, 'but we learned to swim when we first started work on the farm. There was a lake close by, and we used to swim in it after a day's work in hot weather. It was one way of getting a bath.'

'As well as that,' said Henry, 'the Reverend Nicholls used to say that cleanliness was next to godliness, so us two swimming in the lake kept him happy an' all.'

Mrs Norton was evidently thinking about their proposed swim. 'I guess it's far enough away from town that you're not likely to offend anybody,' she said.

'That's the last thing we want to do,' Seth assured her.

'I thought you boys must be godfearing, the way you came to my rescue that day. What's your church?'

'The Church of England, ma'am.'

'Oh, well,' she said, evidently giving the matter some thought, 'I don't think we have one of them. Not close by, anyway. We're Baptists. At least, we are when we can get there safe an' sound.'

'We'll be happy to take you to church, Mrs Norton,' said Seth, 'and keep you from harm.'

'But Sunday's your day off.'

'We don't mind giving up Sunday morning, do we, Henry?'

'We don't mind at all,' confirmed Henry.

'Boys, you're so good to me.'

'We're not perfect,' said Seth. 'I don't suppose anybody is, but we like to be helpful when we can be, isn't that right, Sergeant Fowler?'

'Right as ever, Sergeant Campion.'

The next Sunday, Mrs Norton drove the boys to church in the governess cart. Seth and Henry rode beside them, as promised. It was a fine, hot day, and the two men were almost relieved that they had no dark Sunday clothes. They would attract the notice of others in church, who were more appropriately dressed, but Mrs Norton had said she didn't mind that, and therefore, they certainly didn't.

Having parked and secured the governess cart, Mrs Norton led the children to the church door, where the minister was greeting his congregation.

'Good morning, Mrs Norton,' he said. 'How pleasant it is to see you again.'

'Yes, it's not been easy, coming to Sunday Service recently. I've been attending to my husband.'

'Of course. How is he?'

'He's improving, and I thank you for your concern.'

The minister was eyeing Seth and Henry doubtfully. He asked, 'Are these men with you, Mrs Norton?'

'Yes, they work on the farm and they've very kindly escorted me here today.'

'Seth Campion, sir,' said Seth, removing his hat.

'Henry Fowler, sir.'

'Your accent is strange to me, gentlemen.'

'We're English,' Seth told him.

'Ah, well, English or godfearing American, if you're going to join us, I must insist that you leave your weapons in the porch. They have no place in the house of the Lord.'

'No need to insist, Reverend,' said Henry, unbuckling his belt. 'We respect God's house as much as you or anybody else.' He and Seth were placing their sabres and their new gun belts beside the seat in the porch, when a voice behind them said pettishly, 'English, and so soon after the Centennial.'

Seth turned and smiled disarmingly at the disapproving harridan, who leant impatiently on her walking cane. 'Greetings from across the sea,' he said. 'God bless you, ma'am.'

She snorted, but the two girls who were apparently with her beamed at the Englishmen with undisguised friendliness, their brown curls and ribbons making them even more inviting than nature, or their cross-grained parent, had possibly intended.

'Come along, you two girls,' said the woman, 'and remember where you are.'

Mrs Norton, the two boys, Seth and Henry took their places on an empty pew and bent their heads appropriately. From the pew opposite them, the two girls, unknown to their mother, kept glancing across at the newcomers.

The service began with a prayer and then a hymn that neither Seth nor Henry knew, but they did their best to sing it.

The service wore on, with the longest and most boring sermon they'd ever heard, but not even Morning Worship at Pentecost Baptist Church could last forever, and it drew eventually and mercifully to a close.

As they took their leave of the Reverend McEvoy, he asked, 'What is your church in England?' Suddenly, it seemed, everyone wanted to know that.

'The Church of England, sir,' Henry told him.

'Ah, then you would find this morning's observance somewhat different than that to which you're accustomed.'

'We did,' they assured him. They had no recollection of either the Reverend Nicholls or the succession of Army Padres they'd known ever preaching for more than ten minutes, and the morning's epic had been a test of their staying power. They could only sympathise with the two children and, for that matter, the two pretty girls in the opposite pew.

They buckled on their belts and then helped Mrs Norton and the children into the governess cart before mounting their horses and raising their hats to the two friendly girls and the sour woman as they departed.

When they reached the farmhouse, they helped Mrs Norton and the boys out of the governess cart and unhitched the horse.

Mrs Norton asked, 'Will you join us for coffee?'

They were eager to go to the lake, but some things were worth the wait, so they accepted her invitation whilst resolving, somehow, to find tea as soon as they could.

⚜

From the angle of their approach, the lake was almost obscured by the wooded hillside that sloped downward almost to the water's edge, but they'd ridden further and seen the extent of it. They tethered their horses and, seeing no one around, undressed. They'd been looking forward to the occasion for some time and in their keenness to get into the water they failed to notice the two horses concealed in the trees only fifty or so yards away.

They walked down the slope, looking warily for any creature that might be lurking in the undergrowth, until they reached the shallows, where they soaped themselves luxuriously. Then, when they were satisfied with their efforts, they waded out to where the water quickly deepened.

'This is just perfect,' said Henry.

'Perfect,' echoed Seth, swimming further out and ensuring that all the soap was rinsed from his body.

They swam for a while, occasionally treading water to appreciate the glorious extent of the blue lake.

After a while, Seth stopped swimming to listen more closely to an unusual sound. At first, he wondered if what he'd heard was birdsong of an exotic kind; it had been difficult to tell when he was swimming,

23

but now he recognised the sound of female voices. As he listened, he heard giggling. 'Hey, Henry,' he said, 'can you hear it?'

'Hear what, mate?'

'Voices. We've got company.'

They listened, and Henry said, 'Women's voices. You're right.' They swam towards the cover of the trees and heard the voices again. They sounded much nearer.

'Hello,' said a voice that sounded very close indeed, 'you've found our secret swimming place.'

Seth turned to where the voice seemed to be coming from, and a girl materialised from the cover of the overhanging trees. Only her head showed above the water. He asked, 'What's secret about it? It's too big to miss.'

There was the sound of someone emerging from an underwater hiding place, and another voice said, 'We've been coming here for ages. Well, two weeks, anyway.' Like the other girl, she was submerged up to the neck, but only feet away from where Henry stood. She asked, 'Don't you recognise us? We saw you in church this morning.'

'Of course,' said Seth. 'Your mother wasn't happy about us coming to America so soon after the independence celebrations. To be honest, we didn't have any choice.'

'She's not our mother,' said the girl. 'She's our mother's cousin, and she's awful. She can't follow us up here, though. She can't ride horseback because of her hip. That's why it's our secret place.' She looked at Henry and asked, 'Why doesn't your friend say something?'

'He's just not used to going for a swim and finding two pretty lasses where he doesn't expect them.' He added, 'It's no surprise to me. It happens all the time.'

'What are your names?'

'I'm Seth.'

'I'm Henry, and I do talk, but you surprised me, just as Seth said.'

'Oh, Henry,' said the other girl, 'what a lovely, deep voice you have. I'm Ida.'

'And I'm Katherine,' said the girl nearer to Seth, 'and in case you're wondering, it's all right for us to talk to you here like this, because no one can see anything with the sun reflected on the water.'

It was probably true from the girls' angle of view, but they were standing in the shade of the trees, and Seth could see, without difficulty, Katherine's well-formed breasts, their upturned nipples now proud in the cool water, and the dark, triangular shadow below that had enticed mankind since the human race began.

'You're right,' he said, vaguely aware that Henry was having a similar conversation with Ida, who had persuaded him to swim along the shoreline with her. 'I can't see a thing.'

'We come here a lot,' said Katherine, adding with a look of regret, 'but only until we have to go home.'

'Where's home?'

'Boston, Massachusetts. It's in New England,' she prompted, 'on the East Coast. We're at a school for *ladies*.' She pronounced the last word with a flourish.

'School?' Suddenly, Seth had an awful feeling. There were taboos and laws about girls below a certain age, and for all he knew, the same strictures might apply in America. As if that were not enough, his conscience was also aroused, tediously ready as ever to throw down the gauntlet to temptation.

'It's what I think you English call a "finishing school",' she explained. 'The idea is to prepare us for marriage to wealthy husbands. In case you're wondering, we're both of marriageable age, so it's okay for us to talk with men like this.'

'That's one way of looking at it,' he agreed, realising that he was currently looking at quite a lot. He transferred his gaze deliberately to her face, which was as attractive as he remembered it, especially now that the warm air had partially dried her hair. 'How old are you, Katherine?' He had to know.

'We're nineteen. We'll be twenty in October.'

'Twins?'

'That's right. We're not identical, as you can see, and we're different in other ways, too, but we like the same things.'

'That's nice.' He couldn't think of anything more to say, although it seemed that Katherine was at no such disadvantage.

'You can kiss me if you like,' she said.

It seemed a good idea. He took a step closer to her and cupped her narrow waist with his hands. Even under water, she felt smooth and inviting. He ran his hands slowly and appreciatively over her hips and then her thighs, and back again before drawing her closer to kiss her.

If her attitude had left him in any doubt, her lips confirmed her lack of innocence. They kissed enthusiastically, but all too briefly, because she broke away, glancing across the lake to her sister, and said, 'It's time for us to go. Will you stay here until we're gone?'

'Of course,' he told her.

'Good.' She kissed him again. 'When shall we see you here again?'

'The only time we have free is Sunday afternoons.'

'Oh, what a pity. Still, next Sunday?'

'I wouldn't miss it for anything.'

She gave him a final kiss. 'Mm,' was all she said, but the soft consonant seemed to linger in the air as she and Ida waded out of the lake, turning briefly and tantalisingly to wave before disappearing into the trees.

4

Arson and Affection

Mrs Norton kept Seth and Henry busy for the next few days, and they were quite happy with that; they were there to work, and working for Mrs Norton was no hardship. They naturally looked forward to seeing Katherine and Ida again, but that would be on Sunday, and they had much to do in the meantime. They hadn't bargained, however, for the events of Thursday night.

It was unusual for Seth to wake up during the night, but he was hurried into wakefulness in an unusual way. He was dreaming that he was filling a lamp, and the odour of the lamp oil, the stuff the Americans called kerosene, was particularly strong. In fact, it was so strong that he could still smell it when he opened his eyes in the darkness of the bunk house. Then realisation jerked him into life. 'Wake up, Henry, quick,' he urged.

'Wassamatter?'

'*Jaldee karo!* The place is on fire!'

In the meagre moonlight, they found their boots and sabres. As an afterthought, because the practice was new to them, they grabbed their gun belts as well, and hurried outside in time to see the rear wall of the log-built bunkhouse burst into flame. They heard running footsteps in the yard, and when they looked in the direction the sound was coming from, they saw two figures running towards the farmhouse. Seth and Henry set off in pursuit and, being fit, they soon gained on the two men. One carried on running, but the other turned towards them. He was holding something that looked like a rifle, and their suspicion was confirmed when they heard a gunshot, and a bullet passed dangerously close to them with the noise of an angry insect. They were also

27

uncomfortably aware that they were silhouetted against the blazing bunk house, thereby presenting a clear target, although the man with the rifle fared no better with his next shot. It turned out to be his last, however, when a bullet from Henry's revolver found its mark. There was a scream of pain and a clatter as he dropped his rifle.

'Guard him, Henry,' said Seth. 'I'm going after the other one.' Crouching low, he ran towards the homestead and flattened himself against the side wall, working his way to back of the building, which was where he expected to find his quarry hiding.

As he turned the corner, he found him crouched against the rear wall. The bunk house fire was now illuminating everything around it, and the fire raiser was clearly visible. Again, there was the ominous and overpowering stench of lamp oil. Seth lifted his revolver and said, 'Hands on your head! Now!'

The man's response was to pick up a rifle, but with one hand heavily bandaged, his movements were clumsy. Seth shouted, 'Drop it!' He could now see him plainly, and he wasn't surprised when he recognised him as one of the two renegades they thought they'd dealt with for good.

The man continued to fumble with the rifle, most likely trying to insert one of his uninjured fingers into the trigger guard. He raised the rifle to fire, but Seth fired first, hitting either his shoulder or his arm. It was difficult to tell, but the noise he was making was no less rewarding for that.

'I warned you,' Seth told him. 'Leave that oil where it is, or I'll put the next bullet between your eyes. Now, stand up and walk.'

By this time, the gunshots had alerted the Norton family, and Mrs Norton called from the front of the house, 'Who's there?'

Seth was about to tell her, but Henry spoke first. 'It's the two troublemakers, Mrs Norton. They've burned the bunk house to the ground and they were going to do the same to the farmhouse, but we got to 'em in time. We'll take 'em to the Town Marshall, but there's a little problem in our way.'

'What's that?' She'd brought a rifle to the door, but she lowered it, still in a state of alarm.

'Our clothes were in the bunk house,' Seth told her as he marched the other villain to the front of the building. 'All we have is what we're wearing now.' In the firelight, it was plain for her to see that he was clad in nothing but his woollen underwear and his boots.

'Oh, that's terrible. You'll have to borrow some of my husband's clothes.' As an afterthought, she said, 'Don't worry about money for new clothes. You've earned it tonight.' She was clearly and understandably tearful when she said, 'I don't know where we'd be without you boys.'

'That's very kind of you, Mrs Norton,' said Seth, 'and don't worry about that. You've got us, and we're happy to go on looking after you and your family. It's just a pity we couldn't save the bunk house.' Then, surveying the two arsonists, he said, 'I suppose we'd better bandage these two before we tie 'em up. They're lower than the rats in the chicken feed, but we have our standards.'

'I'll get something to tear into bandages,' said Mrs Norton, disappearing into the house.

One of the men, still moaning, asked, 'You gonna' take us to the marshall?'

'What else d' you expect?' Seth wasn't in the mood for answering silly questions.

'They hang fire raisers 'round these parts,' he whined.

'You'd have been happy enough to see all of us, including two children, burned to death.'

'We didn't mean no harm to the family.'

'Tell that to the judge. He's paid to listen to lies.'

<hr/>

They transported the felons on the buckboard, with Henry driving, and Seth riding alongside, watchful and ready to shoot if necessary.

Eventually, they drove into town and woke up Marshall Higgins, who resented the intrusion at first, although when he learned the reason for it, he became quite amenable. They made arrangements for a return visit so that they could make legal depositions, and were about to take their leave, when Seth remembered something else that was important to them.

'Have you any idea, Marshall, where we can buy tea?'

'Seth,' said Henry, 'that's not the kind of question you can ask of an important man.'

'Well, being important, he's more likely to know the answer than anybody else. Isn't he?'

The marshall answered for himself. 'Tea? There's no call for tea in this town.'

'We were afraid of that.'

The marshall thought for a moment and said, 'You could try speakin' to one of the Chinese miners. You might just be lucky there.'

It seemed an odd piece of advice. 'Where will we find a Chinese miner?'

The marshall regarded him with amusement before answering. 'Anywhere where they're prospecting for gold, an' they say the Black Hills is the place to be.'

'What's the nearest town?'

'I'd say it's Deadwood, but that's a journey of two hundred and fifty miles or more.'

'I'm obliged, Marshall.' It was bad news, after all. They would have to look elsewhere for tea.

———※———

Until they could build a new bunk house, they slept on the parlour floor, which was no worse than a tent in Kashmir or some of the barracks they'd known, so they made the best of the situation.

On Sunday, they took Mrs Norton and the children to church for the second time, although neither Seth nor Henry could see the attraction of Reverend McEvoy's interminable sermons. Neither could they understand why a kind woman like Mrs Norton subjected her children to the ordeal. In the end, they agreed that it was all she and the children had ever known, and with nothing for comparison, maybe it didn't seem so bad to them.

The Morning Service provided one benefit that would not have won Mrs Norton's approval, and that was renewed contact, albeit of the visual kind, with Ida and Katherine, who showed unmistakable signs of being as welcoming as ever.

When they arrived at the wooded slope, they went straight to their previous place, tethered the horses and undressed.

With no one else around, they washed and rinsed themselves unhurriedly in the tepid shallows before striking out into deeper water, where they revelled in their new freedom. There was added pleasure in being able to relax after the turmoil of the week, and it seemed to Seth that, even if the girls didn't turn up – and that was a possibility, given their free-spirited ways – the visit to the lake was still a fitting reward for the week's labours. He was about to communicate his feelings to Henry, when something burst out of the water beside him and, a second later, a similar phenomenon occurred at Henry's side. Turning to his personal newcomer, he said, 'Katherine, you crept up on us.'

'Yes, you hadn't a clue. Admit it.'

'I'm not denying it. Have you just arrived?'

'Yes, we'd have been here sooner, but Aunt Emily wanted us to do a chore for her.' Her expression betrayed her resentment.

Now some distance away, Henry and Ida were having their own conversation. Seth returned his attention to Katherine, who was looking speculative. She asked, 'Have you ever kissed under water?'

He trod water while he pretended to ponder the question.

'Surely you can remember,' she protested.

'No,' he said thoughtfully, I don't think I have. Have you?'

'No. Shall we try it?'

If kissing games were all she wanted, he was prepared to accommodate her, and he was about to tell her that, when she suddenly duck-dived beneath the surface, apparently taking his compliance for granted.

He followed her, confident that in the clear waters of the lake he would find her easily, but there was no sign of her at first. He looked from left to right and saw nothing, but then two arms encircled his waist from behind. He turned, taking her in his arms and meeting her lips in what, in normal conditions, would have been a kiss, but that was as far as the experiment ran. Together, they came to the surface, coughing and spluttering. When she could speak, Katherine said, quite unnecessarily, 'No, it doesn't work.'

'All right, let's go into the shallows.'

'Now, that's interesting,' she said, swimming a gentle breast stroke beside him. 'You say, "Let's go into the shallows", but I would say, "Let's head for where it's shallow".'

'Do you really find that interesting?'

'No, I just say the first thing that comes to mind.'

They reached the overhanging trees where they'd met on the previous Sunday, and put their feet to the bottom. Only Katherine's head and shoulders showed above the surface, although her other charms were still visible in the still water.

Seth looked around him and said, 'Henry and Ida have disappeared.'

'Are you surprised? Anyway, are you going to kiss me again?'

His previous suspicion seemed to be correct. She really did want to play kissing games. 'All right,' he said, 'turn around.'

'What?'

'You heard me. Turn around so that we're both facing the same way.'

'All right, but no funny business.' She turned her back to him.

'No funny business,' he agreed, smiling at an expression that was new to him and running his hands slowly over her hips and thighs as he had the previous Sunday. They felt as smooth and firm as he remembered them.

'Do you like stroking me?'

'Yes.' He moved her hair to one side and kissed her neck and shoulder softly.

'That's really nice,' she murmured as he repeated the action. 'You haven't seen me naked yet, have you?'

He thought of the previous occasion and their brief underwater experiment, but gave her the answer she no doubt wanted to hear. 'No, I haven't. That's a treat in store.' Cradling her breasts with his hands, he kissed her neck again. 'Listen, Katherine,' he said. 'Now you've had time to think about it, if you don't want to do the whole thing, I'll understand.'

'You know, Seth, you're just too good to be true, but now I've had time to think about it…. What the heck? Let's dry ourselves and then

32

get friendly.' She led the way, with Seth making a quick detour to pick up his things, and soon they came to a glade not far from the edge of the wood, where he did his best to answer the torrent of questions she put to him about his past and his home life.

'This is a good place,' she said, drying herself on a large towel. 'If there are any snakes, it'll be too hot for them. They'll stay underground until it gets cooler. In any case, most of them stay south of the Missouri River.'

Seth unsheathed his sabre and laid it on the ground, close at hand.

Katherine asked, 'What's that for?'

'It's just in case a snake fancies a day on this side of the river, and doesn't want to waste it all underground. One of the important things I learned in India about snakes is that you just can't trust the unholy things one inch.'

Katherine stopped drying her hair to ask, 'Do they have snakes in India? I didn't know that.'

'They've got cobras, swamp adders, kraits, pythons…. You name whatever evil kind you will, and they have 'em. Anyway,' he said, 'let's not talk about snakes.'

'No,' she said, spreading her towel on the grass to dry.

'Is this a good time for you, Katherine?'

She looked up in surprise. 'I guess it's as good as any,' she said.

'I mean, is it a safe time for you to… do it?'

'Oh, I've got something a whole lot more reliable than that, but you'll have to excuse me for one minute.' She took something from her pack and disappeared with it momentarily into the wood. As promised, she returned less than a minute later and sank down beside him. 'It's all taken care of,' she assured him. 'It's illegal in most states to buy and sell such things, but you just have to know the right people.'

'Things have been invented while I've been in India,' he concluded, taking her in his arms, 'and, by the way, now that I've seen you naked, I can tell you that you're a glorious sight.' He drew her into a long, sensuous kiss.

When she could speak, she said, 'I knew you'd be a great kisser.'

'I had to be, to qualify as a sergeant. It's one of the tests they set.'

'Don't be silly.'

'I'll show you. Corporals only have to kiss on the lips, but this is the sergeants' test.' He kissed her neck and shoulders, moving downward to her breasts. 'I like to kiss your... these things,' he told her.

'Breasts,' she prompted a little breathlessly.

'I couldn't remember the polite name for them.' In truth, he derived a strange and secret kind of pleasure from hearing the word on a woman's lips.

'Neither can most men. At least, that's what they say. Anyway,' she said, humouring him, 'what do the ordinary soldiers do?'

'The troopers? They're always in a hurry, so they don't concern themselves too much with the preliminaries.' He kissed one nipple with exaggerated gentleness before moving on.

'Like I said, Seth, you're a great kisser.'

He accepted the compliment by returning to her lips, at the same time stroking downward with his hand and lingering for a while on her abdomen preparatory to venturing into the forest.

After a few seconds, she began to moan excitedly. 'How did you know... about that thing?'

'I found it just now, by accident,' he said. Do you like it?' He'd actually learned the secret from an Indian girl of precious memory, but he knew better than to mention previous encounters at such a time.

'Like it? I *love* it, and you're so gentle.' She continued to enjoy it until impatience got the better of her and she whispered a breathless and urgent request, gasping with delight when he obliged her.

After some time punctuated by a spell of unbridled excitement, she said, 'Please stop. Just for a minute.'

Startled by the novelty of hearing her use the word 'please', and ready as ever to oblige, he came to rest.

'Seth,' she said, 'You're not just a great kisser.' Her face was glowing with pleasure.

'It takes two,' he assured her, raising himself so that he was resting on his elbows and inadvertently flexing his loins as he did so.

'When you do that, you make it twitch inside of me,' she complained, 'and I can't concentrate.'

'What do you want to concentrate on?'

'I want to know about you being a soldier. How did it happen?'

'The usual way. I took the Queen's shilling, and they gave me a pill-box cap, a blue coat and red breeches.'

She appeared to be studying him. Eventually, she said, 'I've met Englishmen in Boston, but they didn't talk like you.'

'In that case, they didn't come from the East Riding.'

'Where's that?'

'Yorkshire.'

She tried the accent. 'Yahksha.'

'That was a good try,' he told her, 'but you really need to be born there.'

'Anyway,' she said impatiently, even though she was the one who'd digressed, 'why did you join the Army?'

'For adventure. We were farm workers, Henry and me, but that was too quiet for us, so we joined the local yeomanry, the East Yorkshire Hussars, and then, a year later, we joined the Army full-time, and they put us in the Eleventh Hussars and sent us to India.'

'What did you do there?' She gasped as he flexed again.

'Sorry, I'll try not to do that too often.'

'Just for now, anyway.'

'All right. We had to defend the people of India against the bandits – India's full of them – and we did that well, but we weren't happy, Henry and me, with the way the Army sometimes treated the law-abiding Indians. It went against our principles, and that was why we came here to join Colonel Custer, only to find he'd been killed.'

'You told me before that you thought he was the answer to the trouble between the settlers and the red men. Did you really believe that?' She gasped again. 'You keep on twitching inside of me,' she complained.

'I'm sorry. Try to ignore it, and yes, we did.'

She gave a sigh of disbelief. ' "Try to ignore it", he says. Anyway, what happened after that?'

He went on to tell her about meeting Mrs Norton and about the other incidents.

'You know,' she said, when he'd finished, 'that Mrs Norton must spend her life giving thanks that you two came along when you did.'

'We only did what was right, the way we were taught.'

'Where did you learn that?'

'At Sunday school, where we learned the five R's.'

'What are the five R's?'

'Reading, 'riting, 'rithmetic, right and 'rong.'

With a mischievous smile, she asked, 'Did they teach you about the lusts of the flesh?'

'No, we must have been absent that Sunday.'

'Okay, how did they teach you about right and wrong?'

'I can't remember exactly. As I recall, they just hit us when we misbehaved. One thing I do remember, though, is the way the Reverend Nicholls used to dismiss us after a grown-up service, such as Matins or Evensong. It went like this:

' "Go forth into the world in peace. Be of good courage. Hold fast to that which is good. Render to no man evil for evil. Strengthen the fainthearted. Support the weak. Help the afflicted. Show love to all mankind.Love and serve the Lord, rejoicing in the power of the Holy Spirit."

'Then he would ask for one of the usual blessings.' Summing up, he said, 'I can't remember hearing any other reverend dismiss us that way, and I've known quite a few Army padres, but we've never forgotten it, and it's all we've ever tried to do.'

Usually so self-possessed, Katherine seemed quite affected by his disclosure. She blinked several times and sniffed before saying, 'I'll tell you what you are, you and Henry. You're nineteenth-century knights errant.'

'What does that mean?'

'You should know. You had them in England.'

'I don't recall seeing any.' He flexed his muscles and apologised hurriedly.

'That's all right.' She proceeded to enlighten him. 'In centuries gone by,' she explained patiently, 'knights in armour would ride for miles, looking for wrongs to put right. They protected the weak and the poor, and they rescued damsels in distress. Sometimes they went on the Crusades to fight the infidel and search for the Holy Chalice from the Last Supper.'

'That doesn't sound like Henry and me,' said Seth, shaking his head.

'You don't recognise yourselves because you're too modest, but the two things aren't so different. Your quest isn't the Blessed Chalice, it's your *ideal*. You didn't find it in India, but you thought you saw it in Custer, so you came to join him, and now that he's dead, you're still searching. The wonderful thing is that, while you search, you go on righting wrongs, protecting the weak and helpless, but the only… Seth, you're twitching again.'

'I'm sorry.'

'You're forgiven.'

'You mentioned protecting the weak, and then you were going to say something else when I twitched,' he prompted.

'Yes, I was going to say that no knight is complete without his lady.'

'I can see that.'

She sighed heavily. 'I'd like to help you with that one, but you and I have a limited future together.'

'We should make the most of it.'

'We— You're twitching again.'

'I have to twitch to keep him awake.'

'Would he really go to sleep inside there?' It seemed a genuine question.

'Why not? There are worse places to lay his head, and he's not as excited as you are about the knights of old and the Crusades.'

'In that case,' she said, encircling Seth again with her arms, 'maybe he's waited long enough, and it's his turn to get excited.'

5

Tea And Toothpaste

Building a new bunk house was hard work. First, trees had to be felled, cut into logs of exact length, and transported to the homestead. All that took much time, as there was a limit to the number of logs the horses could be expected to haul in one load.

'I've never known anybody care as much about horses as you two boys do,' said Mrs Norton after she'd fed them at the end of one arduous day.

'Horses are decent animals,' said Henry, 'more decent than some of the human kind we've known, and they deserve kindness as much as anybody. When we worked on the farm, we depended on the horses for our living.'

'And when we were in India,' said Seth, 'we depended on them sometimes for our lives. You know, when an animal does all that for you, it's only right to be grateful and treat him well.'

'We knew some in the regiment who forgot that, those who'd grown up with horses and should have known better.' Henry spoke matter-of-factly, but there could be no mistaking the strength of his feelings. 'If you beat an animal, it'll do what it has to do and no more, but our horses would do anything for us, and that was just as well, because when you're knee-deep in bandits with murder in their hearts, you need friends, both two and four-legged ones.'

'You're right, boys. I agree with everything you've said.' She checked that the outer door was locked, and asked, 'Do you need anything more before I leave you for the night?'

'We thank you, ma'am,' said Seth, 'but we have everything we need.'

'In that case, I'll bid you both goodnight.'

'Goodnight, ma'am.'

'Goodnight, ma'am.'

Seth turned down the lamp, and they sat in the firelight.

Henry had taken lately to smoking a pipe, and he lit his now, using a taper from the fire. When it was going well, he asked, 'Did you know Ida and Katherine were going home soon?'

'Do you really have to smoke that stuff, Henry? It smells like dung.'

Henry considered the comparison and found it inappropriate. 'No,' he said, 'it smells better than that. Did you know that, though, about Ida and Katherine?'

'Next week,' confirmed Seth. 'They have to be back at that rich-wives' school of theirs.'

'I wonder what they learn there.'

'Most likely, they teach 'em not to smoke baccy that smells like fox dung. Anyway, you'll be able to ask Ida about it on Sunday. It'll be your last chance, mind.'

'Aye, it's been too good to last.'

'An' all the time,' said Seth, adopting a mischievous look, 'it's been going on under that cross old Aunt Emily's nose.' He was reminded of a question that Katherine had asked. 'Henry, do you recall learning about the lusts of the flesh at Sunday School?'

'No, I don't remember that.'

'We seem to have missed that day. Maybe it was harvest time.'

The thought had them both chuckling, and they sat in easy silence until Henry gave his pipe a final puff before knocking it out against the flue and saying wistfully, 'There's just one thing missing at this time of the day.'

'Char.'

'You were thinking the same, Seth. It's best not to think about it, because I don't know where we're going to find any in this country.'

'We'll be saying that about the other thing next week.' Tantalising memories of Katherine, nude and nubile, came unbidden to mind.

'It really is best not to think about that,' said Henry, laying his bedroll on the floor and removing his boots, 'but a spell of hard work tomorrow will drive it from our minds.'

Hard work wasn't the only distraction the next day, and particularly for Henry, who had to go into town to buy chicken feed, oil and flour.

He was leaving the feed store when he heard shouting and swearing outside, so he opened the door to see what was happening, and found several people, mainly women, gathered on the sidewalk. A man was shouting at his dog, and the women were complaining about his language.

One of them said, 'The man's a disgrace. He shouldn't be allowed near decent folks.' Others agreed, but were seemingly reluctant to challenge the offender.

Putting his purchases on the buckboard, Henry asked, 'What's going on?'

The woman who'd just spoken said angrily, as if the fault were Henry's, 'Moses Pitchforth's dog slipped its tether, and now it won't come back to him.' She pointed out the offender, and Henry saw that he was wielding a stock whip.

'Well, the dog's not going to come back while he's waving that thing.'

'In that case,' said the woman, 'somebody needs to tell him.'

'Excuse me for one moment, ma'am.' Henry edged past her and addressed the man with the whip. 'Hey, you.'

The man turned and saw him. 'Who, me?'

'Yes, you. That's no way to get a dog to come to you.'

The man glared at him, apparently affronted by his intervention. 'He's my dog, and I'll call him how I like.'

'Lay one finger of chastisement on that dog,' said Henry, 'and I'll give you the beating of your life.'

Pitchforth eyed him speculatively, no doubt deciding, as others often had, that a fight with this powerful-looking stranger could have only one consequence. 'You don't know what he's like,' he said. 'He's self-willed and downright ornery when he has a mind.'

Henry wasn't sure what 'ornery' meant, but he knew it had a lot to do with the way Pitchforth had been treating the unfortunate dog. 'I've worked with animals as long as I can remember,' he said, 'and I know that to make a dog obedient you have to win his trust. You don't do that by beating and terrifying him.'

'Tell him about his cursing and swearing,' said the woman, who seemed to be spokesperson for the bystanders. 'This is a godfearing community, and I don't know what you're used to, wherever you're from, but we don't hold with blasphemy.'

'Neither do I, but his swearing's a matter for him and his conscience,' said Henry. 'It's his cruel and ignorant ways with one of God's creatures that concern me.' He looked up the street, but could see no sign of the animal. 'Where is the dog?'

A man on the edge of the crowd pointed up the street and said, 'He's hiding in the doorway of the hardware store.'

Henry wasn't surprised. 'What's his name?'

'He ain't got no name,' said Pitchforth. 'He's a cur, and curs don't have names.'

'In my book, a man who whips his dog is worse than a cur, Pitchforth, and I've got a name for you, only I'm not going to use it in front of these ladies. Listen, will you sell the dog to me?'

'You want my dog?' He sounded incredulous.

'That's what I said. What will you take for him?'

Pitchforth appeared to give the question some thought. Eventually, he said, 'Well, he's no damn' use to me, an' I gave a dollar for him.'

'I don't believe you. Nobody gives a whole dollar for a mongrel.' It was sheer bluff, but it made sense.

'Okay, I paid a quarter for him.'

'In that case, I'll pay you a quarter, and then you'll be no worse off.' He took some loose change from his pocket and counted out twenty-five cents.

'Okay, he's yours, but don't say I didn't warn you.' Pitchforth took the money and went on his way.

The man who'd spoken earlier said, 'The dog's still there, mister. You can see him now.'

Henry looked to where he was pointing and saw a small, black-and-white terrier of some kind, still with its ears back and no doubt expecting Pitchforth to return and exact his usual punishment. 'I need to visit the feed store again,' he said. 'I'll be back.'

Thankfully, the feed store was empty of customers. The proprietor recognised Henry and asked, 'Did you forget somethin'?'

'No, I need some dried meat and sheep dip, if you have it.'

'Sheep dip? There ain't no sheep 'round these parts. You have to go further south for sheep.'

'All right. What do you use to get rid of dog fleas?' It stood to reason that a dog as badly treated as Pitchforth's would be infested.

'Why, dog dip, of course.'

'I'll take some of that, then.'

He took his purchases to the buckboard, cut off a small piece of pemmican, and started up the street towards the hardware store. Hearing his footfall, the dog turned and saw him, backing off uncertainly. Henry slowed down and said in a coaxing voice, 'Don't be scared, you daft dog. It's only old Henry, and I'm not goin' to hurt you.' The dog backed away again, its ears still folded back in fear and doubt. 'Look, I've brought you some meat. Come on, lad.' He saw the dog's ears twitch. Evidently, he was undecided. Henry tried again. 'See what I've got here? Come and get it.' It seemed only right that the dog should have a name, and the first word that came to mind was the price Henry had paid for him. 'Come on, Quarter. There's a good lad. Come on, Quarter.' The dog came forward uncertainly, and Henry saw the rope around his neck that Pitchforth had used to tie him to the tethering post. 'Come on, Quarter. Come to Henry and get some meat.' He held the pemmican at arm's length, and the dog inched towards him, finally taking it. Henry picked up the end of the rope and said, 'Let me take you to your new home, Quarter. You'll find it's an improvement on your old one, an' you'll meet a better kind of folk an' all.'

❧❦❧

Mrs Norton had been waiting for the flour, and she came into the yard when she heard Henry arrive. She asked, 'What have you got there, Henry?'

'This is Quarter, ma'am,' he said. 'He's going to guard the farm against intruders and he'll keep the rats out of the chicken feed. We'll build a kennel for him this afternoon and make him comfortable. All you need do is feed him and don't let the boys spoil him.'

Still surprised, she asked, 'Where did you find him?'

'In Pentecost. A man called Moses Pitchforth was callin' him an' threatening to whip him, so I offered to buy him. I think he'll be useful. Just for now, though, I'd be obliged if you'd lend me a washing bowl so that I can dip him. He has unwanted companions.'

'Of course. That Moses Pitchforth's foul of mouth and foul of nature. I'm surprised you persuaded him to sell the dog to you.'

'I can be persuasive, ma'am. Isn't that right, Quarter?' Quarter looked at Henry as he spoke, wagging his tail. It was a new relationship, but he'd already decided that anything his new friend said was right.

That afternoon, Henry and Seth built a kennel beside the site of the new bunk house, where it would be sheltered from the wind. They laid down fresh straw for bedding, and Quarter, now clean and free from vermin, quickly claimed it as his own.

⊸⊷⊰⊱⊹⊰⊱⊶⊷

With the news that the arsonists had been taken to Bismarck to stand trial, Mrs Norton, who was astute enough to realise that the Reverend McEvoy's sermons held no appeal for Seth and Henry, decided she had no further need of their protection. Consequently, the next time they saw Katherine and Ida was when they arrived at the lake. As was their habit, the girls waited until the men had washed and rinsed themselves, before surprising them, whereupon Ida and Henry lost no time in going to their personal trysting place.

Walking up the wooded slope, Katherine said thoughtfully, 'I don't know when we'll be allowed to visit with Aunt Emily again, if we ever are allowed.'

'Why wouldn't you be?'

'This is our final year at the school. After that, we'll be introduced to a lot of eligible men with a view to marriage.' She added gloomily, 'It could happen before then.'

'What does "eligible" mean?'

'It means that they're rich enough to be considered suitable as future husbands.'

Seth gave that some thought, the concept being a new one for him. 'I hope your rich husband's going to treat you kindly,' he said. 'Otherwise, he could find himself answering to Sergeant Campion of the feared "Cherry Pickers".' He considered that possibility and said, 'I suppose I'd listen to what he had to say, and then challenge him to a duel. You will be careful not to marry an expert swordsman or marksman, won't you?'

'Don't joke about it, Seth, but we must keep in touch.'

'I'm game. You have to remember, though, that I'm no scholar, and my kind of letters won't be what you're used to.'

'That's nonsense. They'll be written by you, and that's all that matters.'

When they reached the place they'd used on their last meeting, they dried themselves and laid out their towels before sinking down together.

Seth asked, 'Aren't you going to make the necessary arrangement?'

'Oh, my goodness.' She blinked at the realisation. 'That *would* have been something to remember you by. I'll only be a minute.'

During her brief absence, Seth compared her world, or what he knew of it, with his. From what he remembered of life in England, it seemed to him that people married out of love – either that, or when prompted by pregnancy, which amounted to roughly the same kind of thing – whereas, in Katherine's society, marriages were still arranged. On reflection, he preferred the former, and that just demonstrated that the rich didn't always have the best of things.

Katherine interrupted his thoughts by throwing herself down beside him and asking, 'What were you saying about cherry pickers?'

'I was just saying that, if your husband treats you badly, he'd better watch out.'

'I meant, why did you say "Cherry Pickers"?'

'Oh, that. It's what the Eleventh Hussars are famous for, far and wide.' Moving downward, he kissed each nipple slowly and reverently. 'Picking cherries takes skill, you see.'

'Oh yes, kiss me, Sergeant Campion. Remind me why they made you a sergeant.'

He kissed her softly, her breasts, her shoulder, her neck, her throat, her chin and her lips, and then made the return journey. At the same time, his hand explored her torso, massaging the place between her navel and the temptation that lay beyond it. All the time, she moaned softly until further arousal prompted the ultimate invitation.

❦

As they lay together, she asked, 'Do you ever get homesick for England?'

'Not really, but there are things I miss about it.'

'Such as what?'

'*Char.* Good, black tea, that is. We just can't find any here.'

'It means that much to you, huh?'

'Yes.'

She leaned over him to kiss him slowly. Then, she said, 'There's no shortage of tea in Boston.'

'Isn't there?'

'There was so much at one time,' she assured him, 'they threw it into the harbour.'

'That was criminal.'

'That's what King George the Third and the British Government said at the time.' She smiled at his innocence. 'Didn't you do history at your Sunday school?'

'There's a limit to what you can fit into one afternoon a week,' he reminded her.

'Well, don't you worry. I'll send you some tea when I get home.'

'Katherine,' he said, kissing her repeatedly, 'you are a wonder.'

'Not only that.' She propped herself up on one elbow to ask, 'What do you use to wash your teeth? They're very white, but there's no cleansing paste or brushes to be found in Pentecost.'

'We use a frayed stick. We dip it in powdered charcoal and brush them with that,' he told her, looking puzzled. 'What is cleansing paste?'

'It's a new thing the Colgate corporation have started making. It's a paste for teeth. It tastes really nice – better than charcoal, I'm sure – and they sell it in jars. There are special brushes for teeth as well. I'll send you some paste and brushes. What's your address?'

45

'The Norton Farm, Pentecost, I suppose. Mrs Norton always collects any mail from the town.'

'Okay, the tea, the paste and the brushes are as good as yours.'

'That is very kind of you, Katherine. Let me know how much I owe you.'

'You owe me just one more time before I have to go.' She kissed him to tempt him, even though it was quite unnecessary.

'You drive a hard bargain, Katherine.'

'That's just what I want you to do, right now.'

⊷⊲⊱⊹⊱⊰⊷

Eventually, Katherine stood fully-dressed beside her horse. Her eyes were wet and her distress was unmistakable. 'Goodbye, Seth,' she said. 'Write to me, won't you? I'll write to you, and I'll send you those things.' She clung to him at length and they kissed for the last time. When he'd given her a leg up into her saddle, she said, 'Just keep on doing all of those things the reverend told you about. Remember to do your duty as a knight errant.'

'Goodbye, Katherine.' He threw her a kiss as she turned and rode off to join Ida. He'd never done that before, but neither had he met anyone quite like Katherine.

6

Pastures New

S eth straightened up to ease his back, and surveyed their joint handiwork. 'It's not bad so far,' he said.

Following his example, Henry nodded and said, 'Considering it's our first log building, it's not bad at all.'

Busy and inquisitive as ever, Quarter inspected the latest log to be pegged in and apparently found that it met with his approval.

Seth watched him thoughtfully. 'Mrs Norton needs to make herself his gaffer,' he observed.

'Aye, we won't be here forever, and he's her dog, when all's said and done.'

Agreed on that point, they worked on until Mrs Norton came out to them with two mugs of coffee.

'There you are, boys,' she said. 'I know it's not tea, but it's all I can offer you.'

'And we're grateful, ma'am,' said Seth. 'As it happens, there's some tea on its way to us. We're expecting it to arrive very soon.'

'Now, however did you arrange that?' As ever, she seemed amused by their resourcefulness.

'The girls who were staying with Miss McKendrick are sending it from Boston, ma'am.'

'And just how did you get to know those two?'

'We met them when they were out riding,' said Henry, opting for something fairly close to the truth, 'and we got talking. That was when we told them we were missing the blessed herb, and they said they'd send us some.'

'They'd have been in severe trouble if Miss McKendrick had known they were passing the time of day with two strange men.'

'Englishmen, too,' said Seth, actually thinking of the trouble they'd have been in if Miss McKendrick had known just *how* they'd been spending their time. The thought still kept him amused.

'Yes, she's a devout Republican.'

'Each to her own, ma'am.'

'I agree, and I'll let you boys get on with your work. It's looking very promising.'

'Thank you, ma'am.'

Seth sipped his coffee and grimaced. As a distraction, he asked, 'What were the chances, would you have said, of you and me going up to the lake and finding two friendly water nymphs the way we did?'

'I wouldn't have put money on it, Sergeant Campion, so I reckon we were lucky.'

'We were very lucky, Sergeant Fowler.' It was a blissful memory, and that, Seth decided, was well worth having.

Over the next week, they put the roof and door on the bunk house and installed two bunks, having explained to the disappointed Norton boys that their place was still in the farmhouse. Mrs Norton inspected it, Quarter gave it his wholehearted approval and, to make the occasion complete, Mr Norton, walking with the aid of crutches, echoed his wife's satisfaction.

'It's good to see you up and about, Mr Norton,' said Henry.

'I can't tell you how it feels to be walking again, even with these things,' he said, standing unsupported for the first time, but using his crutches again to move around the new building.

'It won't be long before your back's as strong as ever,' said Seth.

'Maybe it won't, but we're going to need you boys here for a while yet.'

'We're not going anywhere soon,' Seth assured him. There was still work to be done on the farm and it wouldn't wait for Mr Norton's back to heal.

The two actually stayed until mid-August, when Mr Norton, now moving easily, came to the field where they were planting the last of the summer vegetables.

'That sky promises rain,' he said.

'Just as well we got this lot planted,' said Seth.

'As a matter of fact,' he said seriously, 'I've come to talk to you boys about something else.'

Seth and Henry stood upright to listen to him, but said nothing.

'Now that I'm able to do a whole lot more around the place, we don't need quite so much help.' He seemed to find the subject difficult to broach.

'We always knew the work was temporary,' said Henry. 'It was on account of your injury that Mrs Norton hired us.'

'I know that, boys, but this is far from easy, what with all you've done for us. What I'm saying is that we're only going to need one of you from now on.' With the words finally spoken, he looked almost relieved

'Ah well, there's a problem with that,' said Seth. 'You see, we've been a pair for as long as we can remember. We played together, we went to church together, we started work on the same day, and we enlisted on the same day. Whatever we do, we do as a pair, so if you don't need us any longer, that's the way we'll leave.'

Somewhat downcast, Mr Norton said, 'I was afraid of that.'

'Hang on a minute,' said Seth. 'There is something we could try. Suppose one of us stays on while the other sets about finding work for both of us. I don't know how long it'll take, but it'll give you a chance to find the man you want.'

'That's a good idea.'

'Seth does most of our thinking for us,' said Henry. 'He doesn't always get it right, but nobody's perfect, I say.'

Now relieved, Mr Norton leaned on Seth's spade to say, 'I'm grateful to you both for taking it like this, and to you, Seth, for your idea. Let's give it two weeks and see what happens.'

'The only question now is which of us is going and which one is staying.'

'You're the one who usually does the talking, Seth,' said Henry.

'Now, how did I know you were going to say that?'

―――――――――

In fact, the two weeks were almost up before Seth had any success. He'd tried the livery stable first, as it called for the kind of work they'd done for twelve years in the Army, but without initial success, and he was about to call at the stage office next door. Vacancies occurred with the Minnesota Stage Company from time to time, and it was as well to keep checking. Driving a stagecoach wasn't an inviting prospect in the current weather – it had already been the wettest August most people could remember – but they weren't in a position to pick and choose. He was about to enter the office, when the proprietor of the livery stable called him.

'Hey, you.'

'Are you talkin' to me, Mister?'

'Yes, you.' He rolled his tobacco to one side of his mouth to speak. 'You were lookin' for work a while back.'

'I still am.'

'Maybe I can offer you sump'n.'

Trying not to look too keen, Seth turned away from the stage office and approached Ernie Hesketh, the owner of Pentecost Livery Stable. 'I'm looking for two jobs,' he reminded him. 'My mate's as skilled in equestrian husbandry as I am.'

'What in hell's eques… what you just said?'

'Carin' for horses.'

'Whyncha say so, then, 'stead o' talkin' a whole new language?' He spat out a stream of amber juice and shifted his tobacco again.

'What are you payin'?'

'Sixteen dollars a month.' He made the offer with an air of finality, which didn't impress Seth.

'Is that all?'

'You want two jobs. Take 'em or leave 'em.'

Seth shook his head at the proposition. 'You've got the chance to employ two first-class grooms, both experienced cavalrymen, and you want to pay sixteen dollars a month? That's an insult.'

'It's all I can afford. Sixteen dollars and you pay two dollars each rent for livin' over the stable.'

'That's ridiculous. Make it twenty a month and I'll be interested.'

Hesketh's unkempt beard seemed to quiver at the suggestion. 'I'm not the rich man folks think I am,' he said. 'Sixteen dollars is reasonable.'

'How about sixteen dollars a month and accommodation all in?'

'What are you sayin'?'

'The place over the stable,' he translated.

'You're askin' a lot.'

'Sixteen dollars a month and the living quarters. That's more than fair, Mr Hesketh.'

'You'll be the ruination o' me. I'm too generous for my own good, an' that's a fact.' He fidgeted for a few seconds and said, 'All right. Sixteen dollars a month an' the place over the stable.' They shook hands on it.

'O' course, you'll have to fend for yourselves up there, but there's everythin' you need.'

Seth was relieved to find a job for them both, but he wasn't about to lose face. He asked, 'What's the story? What happened to the last two who worked for you?'

'I had to fire 'em both for drunkenness. Same 'll happen to you if I find you drunk on the job.'

'That won't happen. When we work with horses, we take the work seriously. Now, will you hire me two horses so that I can tell my mate an' bring him back with me?'

'Let's see your money first.'

Seth took out a handful of banknotes, and Hesketh took half of them.

'What's the extra twenty for?'

'Deposit, to make sure I see my horses agin.'

'All right.' Seth wanted to be away to make the return journey before dark. He hadn't time to look at the living quarters, but almost anything would be acceptable after the cheap accommodation at the saloon. He could do well without the noise from below as well as on his floor, where the 'hookers', as the Americans called the women of opportunity, took their clients.

⊕⊦⦙⧖⦙⧗⦙⧖⦙⊦⊕

Taking their leave of the Norton family was as difficult as they'd anticipated. The children were naturally sad to see them go, Mr Norton had long-since realised how grateful he was to the two newcomers, and Mrs Norton was openly distressed. 'I truly wish we could keep you, boys,' she said. 'You came like the answer to a prayer, but it's just not possible.'

'If you ever need us,' said Seth, 'you'll know where to find us. We won't see you in difficulty.' They shook hands with them both.

As they went to their horses, Seth asked, 'Did you pack the tea, Henry?'

'It's in my carpet bag, safe and sound, with the teeth-cleansing paste.'

'It's just as well,' said Seth, swinging himself into his saddle, 'or we'd have been back sooner than any of us expected.'

They rode away in silence, until Henry said, 'We keep saying goodbye to folk. There must be something unhealthy about that.'

'Everything happens for a reason, Henry. That's all I know.'

⊕⊦⦙⧖⦙⧗⦙⧖⦙⊦⊕

They made their way past the horses and climbed the ladder to their quarters, which consisted of a bedroom and a scullery with an oil stove. They would have to use the privy behind the stable. The whole place needed cleaning, but they would attend to that later. For the time being, they laid out their bedrolls, confident only that nature made them immune to any vermin the visiting horses had brought with them.

Seth had with him a letter from Katherine, which he read for the fifth or maybe the sixth time before turning out the oil lamp. It was a new experience for him.

52

7

Animals Come First

They were up early in the morning, mucking out and then cleaning the stable scrupulously before starting work on their living quarters, which were equally in need of attention.

When Hesketh arrived, he called up the ladder, 'Hey, you two!'

Seth came to the doorway. 'That sounds like us.'

'Huh. At least you're up an' about.'

'Since six o' clock,' Seth told him. 'We've mucked out, and cleaned both the stable and the living quarters. Where do you keep your salve?'

The tobacco Hesketh had been chewing came to rest. 'What are you talkin' about?'

'Ointment for saddle sores. Where do you keep it?'

'I don't know. Take a look in the toolbox, there.'

Henry, who had just come down the ladder, opened the toolbox and searched inside it, finding an old and grimy tin of salve. When he opened it, he saw it was almost empty. 'We're goin' to need more than this,' he said.

'Waddya want it for, anyway?'

'The roan mare has saddle sores,' Seth told him. 'They should've been treated before now, an' they're goin' to need a lot of salve.'

'You're gonna be the ruination o' me.'

'Oh, aye? Five cents for a tin of salve? I'm heartbroken for you, Mr Hesketh.'

Hesketh spat out another stream of tobacco juice, possibly to add strength to his protest, and took some coins from his pocket. 'Here's a nickel,' he said, picking one out. 'See to it that you don't spend no more 'n that.'

'You're the soul of generosity. What is he, Sergeant Fowler?'

'He's the soul of generosity, Sergeant Campion, as well as everything else folk call him.'

'Well,' said Hesketh, shuffling his feet self-consciously, 'I won't stand by an' see an animal suffer.'

'That's the spirit, Mr Hesketh.' Seth stopped at the doorway to say, 'I'll be back in two shakes, Henry. Do us a favour, mate, an' put the kettle on.'

He crossed the street and walked into the General Store, where he was obliged to wait. When the two women in front of him had been served, he said to the storekeeper, 'I want some salve for saddle sores.'

'Salve,' said the storekeeper, taking a tin from a shelf behind him. 'That's five cents.'

Seth handed the coin over, saying, 'Mr Hesketh didn't know what I meant by "salve".'

The storekeeper was unimpressed. 'It's been so long since he bought any, I'm not exactly surprised.'

'Good day to you,' said Seth, taking the tin.

'Good day, friend.'

Seth stepped out of the store and straight into the path of two young women. At a first glance, they were both quite attractive, with dark, well-kept hair, which they wore pinned up.

'Hi,' said one of them. 'You must be one of the new stable hands.'

'Word evidently gets about quickly,' he said. 'I'm Seth.'

'I'm Marie,' said the one who'd spoken first, 'and this is Carrie.'

'Pleased to make your acquaintance, ladies.' He shook hands with both of them.

The girl called Carrie said, 'We haven't seen you in the saloon yet. You must be new to the territory.'

So they worked at the saloon. 'No, we were at the Norton Farm until yesterday. At least, my mate was. I've been here longer, trying to find us a job.'

Marie said, 'You stayed at the saloon, didn't you? I do recall seeing you there, now I think of it.'

'That's right.'

'Maybe we'll see you and your friend in there some time.'

Seth decided to clear things up straight away. 'The thing is, ladies,

I appreciate you both greeting me in such a friendly and welcoming fashion, but I have to tell you that we don't make a practice of purchasing favours.' He touched the brim of his hat. 'I wish you both well, though.'

They were looking at him open-mouthed, and then they looked at each other. First Carrie, and then Marie, gave way to hearty laughter.

'I don't see what's to laugh at,' said Seth. 'As I see it, it's a man's choice whether he does business with—'

'We're not hookers,' Marie told him, 'we're singers, part of the entertainment. It's true that some of the chorus girls swell their income by doing that, but it's not for us.'

Seth closed his eyes in painful embarrassment. 'I'm truly sorry, ladies,' he said, opening them again. 'I got the wrong idea.'

'That's all right, you're not the first man to do that. Living and working at the saloon, we find it happens all the time.'

'Anyway,' said Carrie, 'where are you from? I can't place your accent.'

'Yorkshire, England.'

'You don't say. Well, maybe we'll see you around.'

'So long, Seth,' said Marie, apparently as unruffled by his gaffe as Carrie evidently was. They made for the door of the General Store.

'Goodbye, ladies.'

He returned to the stable to find Hesketh gone and Henry drinking tea.

'I thought you must have bought all the stock in the store by now,' he said.

'No, but I met two nice lasses who work in the saloon.'

'The saloon?'

'It's all right. They're not whores, they're singers.'

'Both of them?'

'That's what they said.' He dropped tealeaves into a tin mug and poured hot water over them. Then, instead of sitting down to drink the tea immediately, he took the tin of salve to the roan mare. 'You poor old lass,' he said, opening the tin and scooping out some of the ointment. 'If old Hesketh had seen to this when it first started, you wouldn't have been in this state now.' He massaged the stuff into the sores and left them to absorb it while he returned to his tea.

'I gave her what there was in the old tin,' said Henry. 'I hope it was all right.'

'It would be. She'll need the same every day for about a week, I reckon.'

To make sure they hadn't missed anything, they examined all the horses in the stable and, short of walking them up and down, found them sound.

'It's the biggest wonder,' said Henry, 'when they're at old Hesketh's mercy.'

They saw nothing of Hesketh for the rest of the morning and, at twelve o' clock, they hung up the 'CLOSED' sign and crossed the street to the saloon, where the first person they saw was Hesketh. He was lounging backward in a chair and, if he wasn't already drunk, that appeared to be his intention. He saw them, and his reaction was predictable.

'What 're you two doin' here? I warned you 'bout drunkenness when I set you on.'

'We haven't had a drink yet,' said Seth, 'but you seem to be ladling it back.'

'I've every right to.'

'An' we've every right to a break at mid-day. We're going to have a quiet drink, an' then we'll go back to the stable. All right?'

'Just you see that you do.'

The saloon was in the shape of a music hall, just as they'd expected, with the floor given over to tables and chairs, where men sat playing card games in a haze of cigar smoke. In front of the stage, a man sat at a piano whilst another nursed a banjo.

While Seth and Henry were waiting to be served, the Master of Ceremonies walked on to the stage to a loud chord from the musicians.

'Gen'lemen,' he announced, 'Give a hearty Pentecost welcome to the *Chanteuses* from Baltimore, Maryland. Here are Carrie and Marie!'

Seth had never heard of *Chanteuses* – it sounded like "Shantooses" – but his brief meeting with the girls told him it was probably an American slang name for singers. Seeing that the bartender was free, he ordered two beers just as the girls came on stage to a lively introduction by the pianist and the banjo player. The song began with both girls singing sweetly but plaintively in harmony.

'The ideal man is hard to find, and some girls never find him.
Sometimes, the kind of man they find leaves a trail of woe behind him.'

Then, in a more upbeat mood, came Marie's solo:

'I met a man from Delaware with fancy whiskers and curly hair;
I'd never seen a man so cute as he.
He was rich and oh, so handsome, his place was worth a sultan's ransom;
There was just one little thing he kept from me.
When, inside his shaded carriage, he offered me his hand in marriage,
He didn't tell me 'bout the other three!'

Both:

'He didn't tell me/her 'bout the other three.'

The song continued in the same fashion:

Carrie:

'I knew a man from Philadelphia, no man in Penn state was wealthier;
He was the perfect match, so I believed.
He would whisper words of love that touched me like a velvet glove,
How could I know I was being deceived?
When he took me on his knee and spoke those honeyed words to me,
'Twas but a tangled web that bluebeard weaved.'

Both:

''Twas but a tangled web that bluebeard weaved.'

Marie:

'I met a man from Blaine, Kentucky. How could a girl be quite so lucky?
He had horses, real estate and charm.
I swore my love would never falter, dreamt of standing at the altar,
Never did I see cause for alarm.
He stood upon the grass so blue and said, "I see a place for you,
Not at home, but working on my farm."

Both:

'Not at home, but working on my/his farm.'

Carrie:

'I met a man from Laramie, who said, "My darling, marry me.
I've everything a woman could desire."
He told me of his grand design that one day would be partly mine,
His prospects of success were never higher.
And now the part that's really funny – he thought I had all the money.
How could a man be such a scheming liar?

Both:

'How could a man be such a scheming liar?

'Yes, the perfect man is hard to find; there are so many of the other kind.
We meet the critters daily in our quest.
Poker sharps and two-bit hustlers, horse thieves and cattle rustlers,
Ever since we took the train out west.
But still we mean to go on lookin', movin' on to see what's cookin',
There has to be some class among the rest!'

The act went down well and received loud applause from the clientele, so they sang another song, also mainly in harmony, which pleased everyone again.

Seth and Henry found a table, and were discussing the act, when Carrie and Marie suddenly appeared beside them.

'Hello, boys,' said Marie. 'Do you mind if we join you?'

'No, you're welcome,' said Seth. 'Henry, this is Marie and this is Carrie. Ladies, this is my mate Henry. What do you want to drink?'

'Don't worry about that,' said Carrie. 'Our drinks are on their way.' As she spoke, one of the bar staff put two drinks on the table. They thanked him and turned again to Seth and Henry to ask, 'What did you think of the turn?'

'The turn?'

'The act, us two.'

'Oh,' said Seth, 'It's champion. We enjoyed it.'

'Champion,' agreed Henry.

Marie asked, 'Don't they call them "turns" in England?'

'We don't know,' admitted Seth. 'We've only been to a music hall once, and we spent the last dozen years in India.'

Her thoughts on that piece of information remained a mystery, at least for the moment, because an unkempt, unshaven man had detached himself from his group and was now whispering something to Marie with his hand on her bare shoulder.

'No,' she said, pushing his hand away, 'we're singers. We don't do that.'

'I can make it worth your while,' he assured her with a leer that revealed two rows of uneven, brown teeth.

'You heard,' said Seth. 'These ladies are not for hire.'

'Not by you or anybody else,' confirmed Henry. 'Go and play cards. It'll take your mind off it.'

The man looked at Henry and made a quick decision. 'My mistake,' he said. 'No offence meant.' He hurried back to his table.

'It's really nice to be called "ladies",' said Carrie.

'In our world, all women are ladies,' Seth told her, 'until they prove otherwise.'

Not for the first time, Henry asked, 'Why do folk find me so scary?'

'I don't know,' said Carrie, ''cause I think you're really nice, an'

I love that deep voice of yours. Have you ever thought of taking up singing?'

'He only sings in the bath,' said Seth. 'That's when he can find one.'

'Well,' said Marie, 'thank you, boys. That was noble of you, an' if you're looking for the bathhouse, it's at the end of the street.' She pointed in the general direction.

'It's safe enough for men,' said Carrie cryptically. 'Where have you boys been doing your ablutions?'

'Lake Leconseh,' Seth told her, 'but it'll soon be too cold up there. That's when we'll need the bathhouse.'

Carrie looked across at Marie and asked, 'Why didn't we think of that?'

'I don't know, and it's only September. It doesn't start to get cold until October.'

'Well,' said Seth, getting up from the table, 'we've enjoyed talking with you, but we have to be back at work.'

'Call in again,' invited Marie. We like your company and we feel a whole lot safer with you boys around.'

'We will,' said Seth. They took their leave of the girls, then picked up their hats and left the saloon.

'Did you notice,' asked Henry, 'we were the only men in the place who doffed our hats when we went indoors?'

'They haven't had our advantages, Henry.'

As they approached the stable, Henry spoke again. 'I'm not fanciful as a rule,' he said, 'but do you suppose there might be something special about Lake Leconseh?'

'No, Henry,' he said confidently, 'we couldn't be so lucky again.'

Seth gave the roan mare another treatment of salve, and then it was time to brew tea again. They were waiting for the water to boil, when a man and a woman turned up, asking for Hesketh.

'You'll probably find him in the saloon,' said Henry, 'but you won't get much sense out of him.'

'We want to hire two horses, just for the afternoon,' said the man, 'fourteen-two and fifteen-four.'

'Okay,' said Seth, making his way past the boxes. 'Let's see what we've got. You can't have this one,' he said, 'because he's at livery, but this one is about fourteen-two hands, and that coloured horse over there is fifteen-four.'

'Why do you call it a "coloured horse"? It's skewbald.'

'It's just a difference of language,' Seth explained. 'I call it a coloured horse, an' you call it skewbald, I suppose.'

'Oh, look at this one,' said the man's wife, pointing to the roan mare. 'He's a beauty.'

'She's a mare,' said Henry, and she's not for hire.'

'How many hands is she?' The man's tone was demanding.

'Fourteen-four, but she's not for hire.'

'Now look here, mister,' said the man. 'I don't know who you think you are. As I see it, you're nothing more than a stable bum, and if my wife wants to hire that pony, then hire it she will.'

'I'm sorry to disappoint the lady,' said Henry, 'but that mare isn't for hire. She's being treated for saddle sores.'

'They don't look so bad to me.'

'They're bad enough,' said Seth, that the answer is still "No", she's not for hire.'

'Saddle up the two you showed me,' said the man, but let me tell you, you ain't heard the last of this. I'm gonna speak to Ernie Hesketh an' I'll be surprised if you still have a job tomorrow, either of you. Anyway,' he said, as if it had just occurred to him, 'I can't place your accent. Where are you both from?'

'England,' Seth told him.

'That makes it worse. I'm not gonna be denied by two goddamned Britishers.'

It was a familiar exchange, but Seth still resented it. 'You folk really like to hold on to a grudge,' he said. 'By my reckoning, it's been more than sixty years since we gave you a hiding.'

'That don't make no difference.'

'It does to us. That's thirty dollars,' said Seth, 'five dollars each, and the rest is a deposit.'

With an ill grace, the man thrust thirty dollars into Seth's hand. He waited until the two horses were saddled up, and then left without another word.

The pair returned the horses at a little after six that evening, when the man repeated his threat. Seth returned the deposit, but said nothing. They were hanging up the tack from the two horses when Hesketh arrived.

'You two, come out here, now!'

Obediently, they left the stable and stood before him.

'One o' my reg'lar customers says you refused to hire a horse to his wife.'

'We did hire a horse to her,' said Seth. 'It just wasn't the horse she wanted.'

The tobacco moved across Hesketh's mouth like a shuttle. 'I'm waitin' to know why she didn't get the horse she wanted.'

'Come with me,' said Seth, moving back into the stable.

'What are you sayin'? I want a explanation off o' you.'

'Come and look at this.' Seth led him to the roan mare and pointed to the sores on the mare's back. 'Your friend wanted us to saddle that horse an' put her through more pain an' discomfort.'

Hesketh peered over the box and asked, 'Is she really bad?'

'If you had sores like them on your back, would you want somebody to put a saddle and the weight of a rider on them?'

'She don't look all that bad to me.'

'Maybe that's because you're still three-parts drunk from this afternoon. Look around you.' He pointed to the newly cleaned boxes and the fresh straw smartly plaited at the entrance to each of them. 'That's the work of two ex-sergeants of the Eleventh Hussars. How long is it since this place was as clean as it is now?'

Hesketh shifted his tobacco uneasily. 'I guess it's pretty clean,' he admitted.

'It's cleaner than you've ever seen it. This stable and the horses in it are being cared for now by professionals, and if I say that mare's unfit for work, then that's what she is.' Although he'd only just realised it, Seth's voice had risen in volume, and Hesketh was looking rattled.

'Okay,' he said, 'she's unfit for work. I didn't know how bad she was.'

'In that case, you'll just have to trust Fowler and me, and remember that we know our job. We care about horses and we don't like people who want to hurt them. You can tell that to your mate and his wife.'

'Okay, okay. Calm yourself.'

'If I'm angry, it's not just that I care about the mare's wellbeing, it's because you doubted the word of an ex-cavalryman. As I see it, you've got the best help you've ever had, an' I'll thank you to show some respect. Is that clear?'

'Yeah, yeah, all right.'

'By heck, Seth,' said Henry when Hesketh was gone, 'I thought you might have gone too far just then, talking to him as if he were a trooper you'd caught dodgin' his duty.'

'No, he knows what he's dealing with now. He'll be more careful in future.'

8

Support The Weak

In the days that followed, they saw nothing of the demanding man and his wife, and customers keeping their horses at livery even complimented them on the improved conditions in the stable.

By mid-day on Sunday, they reckoned they'd earned their afternoon off and, after a drink in the saloon, they called into the stable to hire two horses.

'It's been quiet so far,' said Hesketh, taking their money and forgoing the deposit, as he was assured of their return.

Seth asked, 'Who have you had?'

'Just the stage, as usual, an' the man with the bay gelding at livery. He took his out, an' some young women came as well, out for a ride.'

'Okay,' said Henry, 'we'll be back by six.'

'See that you are.'

Even though they had Hesketh largely tamed, he still had to talk tough occasionally, if only to bolster his self-esteem.

They saddled up two horses and rode out to Lake Leconseh, planning to use it as long as the weather allowed. After that, they reasoned, there was always the public bathhouse.

In their usual way, they soaped themselves at the water's edge and then swam into deeper water to rinse the soap away. As it wasn't particularly sudsy, rinsing was easy enough, and they simply enjoyed swimming and relaxing after their labours.

They swam happily for ten minutes or so before Henry said, 'You know, Seth, I think you were wrong about this place.'

'Why do you say that, Henry?'

'Because I think history's repeating itself. Look towards the forest.'

Seth turned and saw two naked figures in the shallows. Although the detail was difficult to make out, their long, dark hair identified them as female and, at that moment, they saw Seth and Henry and made for deeper water.

'Let's go and say, "Hello",' suggested Seth. At that distance, neither could be sure that the bathers were the girls from the saloon, but there was a fair chance that the young women Hesketh had mentioned were those two, and that they'd ridden out to the lake.

When the distance was down to about thirty yards, they were able to recognise Carrie and Marie.

'Hello, boys,' said Marie. 'We see you had the same idea we did.'

'It's our regular Sunday afternoon treat,' said Seth.

'We were just going to dry ourselves,' said Carrie. 'If you like to join us when we're dressed, we'll be on the ridge above the forest.'

'That's very civil of you,' said Seth. 'We'd like that, wouldn't we, Henry?' From where he was standing, the view was more than enticing. If history wanted to keep repeating itself at Lake Leconseh, he had no objection.

'We certainly would.'

'Just one thing, boys,' said Marie. 'Will you turn your backs while we walk up the slope?'

'Of course.' Seth tore himself away from the underwater vista that had held his gaze, and the two turned away.

'Thank you kindly, boys.' There was a swishing sound as the girls left the water, leaving the rest to the men's imagination.

Seth and Henry waited a few minutes before turning and making their way up the slope to the place where they'd left their clothes.

'After that,' said Henry, 'I believe in magic.'

'I have to say, I'm tempted that way, an' all.'

They dried themselves and dressed without hurrying, reluctant as they were to give the wrong impression and create suspicion by turning up too promptly. Then, when they considered that sufficient time had elapsed, they mounted their horses and skirted the edge of the forest.

They found the girls a hundred yards or so further along the ridge, now fully clothed, Carrie brushing out her hair and Marie gilding the lily with an application of makeup.

'Hi boys,' said Carrie, 'come down and join us.'

They dismounted and made themselves comfortable beside their new acquaintances.

'It's good that you mentioned this place,' said Marie. 'We'd begun to think there was nowhere we could take a bath in private.'

'And then we turned up,' said Seth.

'You two are different,' she assured him. 'You know how to behave decently.'

'What's the problem at the saloon?'

'We can get a bath,' said Marie, rolling her eyes upward, 'if we don't mind keyhole peekers making leering comments outside the door. I guess it's not surprising when you consider the kind of men who gather there. They sometimes lurk when they know someone's bringing water, so that they can have a quick look-see while the door's open. Only recently, I was washing my hair and I thought Little Rose, the chambermaid, was bringing hot water. When I looked, it was Harry, the master of ceremonies you saw when you came to the saloon. He thought it was funny.'

Henry asked, 'Weren't you fully clothed?'

'Er, no. When you have as much hair as we have, washing it is a wetting experience.'

They were distracted when one of the girls' horses whinnied and reared up. Seth leapt up, drawing his sabre, and ran towards the horses, which were both in a state of alarm. Then he saw the cause of it, coiled in front of them, its brown patches almost camouflaging it against the fallen leaves on the forest bed. He heard the ominous rattle as its tail quivered, and took a huge swipe with his sabre, severing its head from its body. After a quick look around, he wiped his sabre on the grass, after which he untethered both horses and led them up to the ridge, soothing them and offering the reins to the girls. 'They'll feel safer here,' he told them.

Henry asked casually, 'What was it, Seth? A snake?'

'Aye, a rattlesnake.' He'd heard about them and had them described to him, but the rattle had confirmed it. 'It's likely that the cooler weather has brought them out from their underground hiding places,' he said. 'It's probably warmer above ground.'

Both girls were white-faced and clearly shaken.

'You're in safe hands,' Henry told them. 'I've seen Seth deal with a king cobra before now. He's like lightning with that sabre.'

Marie asked tentatively, 'Aren't rattlesnakes deadly?'

'I don't know, but that one isn't,' Seth assured her, 'at least, not now.'

'And we thought we'd found the ideal place to take a bath,' said Carrie.

'It'll soon be too cold,' Seth reminded her. 'Anyway, if there's no privacy at the saloon, what's the problem at the bathhouse?'

'The problem,' Carrie told him, recovering from the shock, 'is Frank Brunner, the man who owns it. The partition between the men's half and the women's is in poor repair, and Frank likes to keep an eye on his female customers. He's a brainless galoot, but that doesn't excuse him.'

'It seems to me,' said Henry, much surprised, 'that Pentecost is full of Peeping Toms. Is there nobody you can complain to?'

'Not since Marshall Higgins died, and nobody knows how long it'll be before we get a new town marshall.'

'But we saw Marshall Higgins not long ago,' said Seth. 'We took the two who'd tried to burn down the Norton Farm, and handed them over to him. It was only a few weeks ago.'

'He's only been dead less than two weeks,' explained Marie. 'He collapsed in the street and died suddenly, and now there's no law in Pentecost.'

Seth recalled a conversation with Katherine in that same place, and her parting words to him. He said, 'If you're agreeable, ladies, we're going to offer you our protection. We'll find a way of spoiling Frank Brunner's game until we can get him to repair the partition.' The situation at the saloon could take a little longer.

'You two boys are something else,' said Carrie. 'First you warned off that warthog in the saloon, then you killed a rattlesnake, and now you've made yourselves our personal protectors.'

Seth shuffled modestly. 'It's no trouble,' he said. 'Nuisances, rattlesnakes, peeping Toms.... It's all in a day's work for us, isn't it, Sergeant Fowler?'

'Just a normal day's work, Sergeant Campion.'

Purchasing the necessary equipment was embarrassing, but Seth brazened it out with the owner of the general store and was able to pass it to the girls that same day at noon. All they had to do then was wait for events to develop.

The roan mare was now healthy and ready for work. As far as Seth and Henry could see, they had a stable of healthy, contented horses, which was just as it should be. Also, Hesketh was preening himself because of the compliments he was receiving from customers about his immaculate establishment.

❦

Eventually, the girls were able to report back to Seth and Henry about their experience in the bathhouse.

They'd gone along in the afternoon, between performances, and each requested a bath. Frank Brunner was delighted to welcome two young and attractive women into his premises, and he ushered them through the women's entrance. They waited until their two tubs were half-full, and dismissed the attendant, telling her that everything was to their satisfaction. Having done that, they spent some time making the water very soapy indeed.

While they were doing that, Marie heard a faint noise coming from the men's compartment and alerted Carrie. They were agreed that it sounded not unlike heavy breathing. Glancing in the direction the sound was coming from, through a crack between the boards, Marie saw an eyelash flicker. Keeping her back to the aperture, she filled the enema syringe that Seth had given her with hot, soapy water and flattened herself against the wall so that Brunner couldn't see her. Then, in one swift movement, she pointed the syringe at the offending eye and squeezed the bulb hard.

There was a howl on the other side of the partition, and a door clashed as Brunner no doubt went in search of fresh water to rid his eyes of their stinging. Marie and Carrie then undressed and enjoyed a bath free from the eye of prurience.

❦

When Seth and Henry saw Brunner in the barber's shop during their mid-day break, his eyes were still red, and he wore dark glasses.

'That's a nasty thing you've got there,' said Seth.

'Horrible,' agreed Henry. 'What have you been doing to get that?'

'I was in my bathhouse,' growled Brunner, 'gittin' on with cleanin' an' all o' that, an then hot, soapy water come squirtin' through a crack in the wall. I asked the two women who'd been in there if they knowed anythin', an' they said they didn't know nothin' 'bout it.'

'Nasty,' observed Seth, 'an' it could happen again. Hot water has a will of its own when it's set in motion.'

Brunner almost howled. 'I can't be doin' with that happenin' agin.'

'Well,' said Seth, 'it seems to me there's only one remedy.'

'What's that?'

'You've got to mend that wall so that there's no more cracks in it.'

'You bet,' said Brunner. 'I'm gonna do that this very afternoon.'

Seth and Henry paid him a visit later, to check on his handiwork, and they found the partition free from cracks and pinholes.

<hr>

'We're more grateful than you can imagine,' said Marie, when they next visited the saloon. A hot bath makes all the difference in the world, even when it's in his moth-eaten bathhouse.'

Seth asked, 'Now that he's been dealt with, do all the girls have the same problem here at the saloon with lack of privacy?'

'For most of the chorus girls it's as good as advertising, so it's not a problem. The only other girl who's vulnerable is Little Rose, the chambermaid.'

'She's about twelve or thirteen,' said Carrie. 'No one really knows, and she's a half-breed, so she gets a hard time from some people.'

He wondered about this vulnerable child. 'A half-breed, you say. What are her parents?'

'Her father was a white American and her mother was a Sioux squaw,' said Carrie, 'so she's not welcome in either camp, not that it excuses the saloon owner for paying her as little as he does. Being an orphan, as well, she's at everyone's mercy.'

69

'Where she can find any mercy,' said Marie. 'No one around here feels at all friendly towards the Sioux, particularly after the Little Bighorn, and then, of course, there's the other danger.'

'What's that?' Seth thought he knew already.

'The worst kind of men.' She left the rest unspoken.

'Has the worst happened yet?'

'We don't think so, but it's only a matter of time.' She said wistfully, 'If only this town had a marshall.'

'Or, for that matter,' said Seth, 'some kind of law.'

Marie smiled fondly and said, 'There has to be a limit to what you boys can do.'

9

A Show Of Strength – And Tenderness

Katherine's most recent and, it seemed, final, letter served to confirm to Seth something he already suspected, that women were an unnavigable maze of contradictions; in fact, he reckoned that, in some cases, they didn't know, themselves, what they wanted.

Dear Seth,

I'm sending you some more tea and teeth-cleansing paste because this is going to be my last letter to you.

I'll soon be leaving this school, because my father has introduced me to the son of one of his business acquaintances. His name's Lester and he's a politician, but he seems okay. I guess I could do a whole lot worse, but he'll never do for me what you did. I can tell that just by the sight of him. I just have no idea how I'm going to teach him anything about bedroom manners without him realising I'm not the virgin he ordered. I can blame the physical irregularity on horseback riding, but I'll have to be mighty careful not to give the game away by knowing too much.

I'd better tell you, also, that my father has similar plans for Ida, so Henry is likely to get a letter like this one very soon. It's up to you whether you warn him or let it come as a great big shock.

I wish the news could be better for all of us. I'll never forget the times we spent at Lake Leconseh, loving, talking and twitching. I hope you don't mind me mentioning the twitching, because it had never happened to me before I met you, and it was really cute.

At all events, we have to stop writing, now, and I'll have to find a way of erasing those times from my memory so that I don't go through life wishing it was otherwise.

At that point, Seth gave up trying to understand her. He read the rest, taking it at face value because it was the only way.

Don't reply to this letter. I shan't be at this address much longer, and I think a clean break is necessary. I hope you go on to find some really nice girl who appreciates everything about you, even though right now, I'm as jealous as heck of her, and I haven't even met her.

I hope you have a happy life and find that ideal you're searching for very soon. Meanwhile, good luck with all your chivalrous deeds.

Yours tearfully and with unbounded affection,
Katherine.

It was sad news, although Seth hadn't been counting on seeing her again, so his sadness was for her and for Ida. He resolved that he would warn Henry as an act of friendship.

⊕⊢ᛒ⊹ᛕ⊹ᛖᚺ⊕

The next three weeks passed almost without incident; it seemed that the absence of a lawman in Pentecost now made little difference to people's lives, and they were content to wait for the appointment of a new marshall.

Meanwhile, the newspapers that arrived with the stage brought news of events in the Dakota Territory and Montana. It seemed that the 7th Cavalry were permanently in action, herding the natives into reservations and punishing them when they left those boundaries. It was impossible to find out more, and opinions regarding the rights and wrongs of the situation varied, although most voices were raised in condemnation of the Sioux and Cheyenne tribes. That prejudice was amply demonstrated when three fur trappers from the southern part of the territory stopped over on their way north. They were unwashed, clad in stinking buckskin and their attitude was loud and belligerent, especially on the subject of an incident at a place called Slim Buttes.

'Them red varmints had it coming to 'em,' one of them said.

Henry asked, 'What happened? We never get to hear about these things.'

'The cavalry rode into their village and taught the red fiends a lesson,' said a man with wild hair and a bushy beard. 'Anyways,' he said, eyeing Henry's sabre, 'what are you toting them toothpicks for?'

'They come in useful sometimes.'

'Did you two used to be soldier boys?'

Henry nodded.

'You talk kinda strange. Where are you from?'

'England.'

The trapper seemed to find that a cause for laughter, as did his companions. 'Hey, you two,' he said to them, 'here's two o' them there redcoats. They just don't know where they're not wanted.' The others joined him again in unrestrained laughter. Henry took a pull at his beer, causing the one with the heavy beard to ask, 'Is that what you drink in England, redcoat? In case you didn't know it, men drink whiskey.'

'They're welcome to it.'

'So you don't like our whiskey?'

It was clear to Henry and Seth where the conversation was heading. Seth asked, 'Do you find that surprising? I imagine the rats enjoyed relieving themselves of it.'

It was too much for Bushy Beard, who lashed out at Henry with his right. Even as Henry blocked and countered it, nervous drinkers and gamblers pulled their tables back out of harm's way, unintentionally creating an arena.

Bushy Beard staggered and then came back at Henry with another punch that also failed to connect. Henry drove his right fist hard into the trapper's solar plexus, causing him to jack-knife, fighting frantically for breath. Hauling him upright by his beard, Henry dealt him another blow that sent him staggering backwards so that he hit the far wall before subsiding in a semi-conscious heap. 'That's for calling me a redcoat,' he said. 'I wore a blue tunic and I was proud of it.'

The other two trappers had been watching the fight, seemingly startled by the sight of their companion defeated and slumped on the floor, and now they confronted Henry, which was Seth's cue to join his friend.

In a matter of seconds, Henry despatched his opponent to join Bushy Beard on the floor. Meanwhile, Seth and the third trapper, a huge man with a face filled with malice, circled each other warily. Suddenly, Seth feinted with his left and kicked hard at the same time. The trapper collapsed, nursing his most intimate parts and howling in agony. 'That's for calling British cavalry sabres "toothpicks",' he said. Both men returned to the bar and finished their beer in one well-earned swallow.

'I don't think they're finished yet,' said Henry, looking over his shoulder.

Seth turned his head to see Bushy Beard get to his feet. He was panting and almost recovered, but with hatred in his eyes. He confronted Henry and, in one practised movement, pulled out a skinning knife. Almost as he did so, he screamed, dropping the knife and clutching his hand, which was bleeding freely.

'Some folk will only learn the hard way,' said Seth, wiping his sabre on Bushy Beard's shirtsleeve. Having done that, he took a glass of whiskey from the bar and poured it over the bleeding hand, provoking another howl of agony. 'I'd get a bandage on that if I were you,' he said dispassionately, 'before you bleed all over the floor.'

'One of you said something about not being wanted,' Henry told the trappers. 'You three had better get on your horses and start riding, because I can tell you without fear of being told I'm a liar, you're not wanted here.'

The trappers slunk out of the saloon, and Theo, the bartender, rose from his crouching position behind the bar. 'I was expecting trouble from them three,' he said, sounding like a man who'd seen it all before, albeit from a safe hiding place.

'It was just as well they weren't carrying pistols,' said Seth, looking down at his waist, where he carried his sabre, but no revolver.

'Don't you boys ever carry guns?'

'Not usually, Theo,' said Henry. 'Guns are too dangerous for our liking. In any case, we're not violent men.'

❦⊱✦⊰❦

That Sunday, Henry and Carrie rode up to the white rock together on the mutual understanding that they would give the lake a miss. Marie and Seth rode instead to Red Wolf Creek, where no such agreement was necessary. In any case, it was warm enough to sit in the sun, but too cold for swimming.

They dismounted beside the Creek and found a flat boulder to sit on.

'After all the noise and fuss at the saloon,' said Marie, 'it's good to sit here and listen to the water flow past us.' After a minute or so, she surprised Seth by changing the subject completely and asking, 'Why did those men want to set fire to the Norton Farm?'

'Revenge, I suppose.'

'Revenge for what?'

Seth told her the story of how they'd gone to Mrs Norton's assistance, and about the events that followed that incident. 'They were sent to Bismarck for trial,' he said. 'They've probably been hanged by now. I don't like the idea, but there's nothing I can do about it.'

'You don't approve of hanging?'

'No.'

'Even for murder?'

'I don't think it's for any man to decide that another man should die,' he said. 'As a soldier, I had to kill or be killed, and that was hard enough, but I couldn't make that decision in cold blood.'

She looked into his face, as if for the first time, and said, 'That's quite a conscience you've got, Seth.'

'It works for me.'

'Was it your folks who shaped your conscience?'

'No, mine weren't around all that long. I learned those things at church.' He told her about the Reverend Nicholls and his memorable dismissal. 'We see it as a kind of guide through life,' he said.

'You could do a whole lot worse. Do you know what you fellows are?'

'Are you going to tell me we're like the knights in the olden days?'

'Yes, I was. How did you know I was going to say that?'

'Somebody else told me the same thing some time ago.'

'A woman?'

'A girl, really.'

'Is she important to you?'

'She was, for a short time.' He decided to be honest. 'I only knew her for about three weeks. She lives in Boston, Massachusetts, and she'll most likely be engaged to be married very soon.'

'Are you likely to see her before that happens?'

'As likely as I am to ride with Colonel Custer, which was our aim when we came out here.'

'You're an unusual man, Seth.'

'And you're an unusual woman, Marie.' He studied her face carefully.

'Why are you looking at me like that?'

'I'm only wondering what you'd do if I kissed you.'

'Oh, well.' She hesitated before saying with sudden boldness, 'I guess you could try, an' then you'll maybe find out.'

Taking her in his arms, he kissed her very gently on her lips.

'You're well-practised,' she remarked. 'I hope you're not a libertine.'

'No,' he said seriously, kissing her again, 'Church of England.' He teased her upper and lower lips alternately until she joined him in a wholehearted, sensuous way.

'Of course,' she said when she could speak, 'I'm new to all this.'

'In that case, you're learning very quickly.' They kissed again, and he reached the conclusion that she was indeed a quick learner.

10

A Good Night

On their return, Seth and Henry visited Brunner's bathhouse and immersed themselves in soapy water of a less turbulent kind than that which had caused Brunner so much discomfort, before dressing in clean clothes. Each had an idea of where his friend was bound, but neither said a word. Eventually, however, they took the identical route to the saloon hotel and climbed the same staircase to the second floor, where they parted awkwardly, Henry going to room twenty-five, and Seth to room twenty-two. Hopefully, the embarrassment would soon wear off.

Marie had forsaken her riding clothes for a full, pleated blouse and brown skirt. She held out her arms in welcome. 'Hi,' she said, 'you look a little careworn.'

'Henry's only three doors away,' he whispered.

'And you were both keeping it a secret from each other.' Her brown eyes teased him.

'We try to be…. What's the word? Dis… something?'

'Disgraceful?'

'No.'

'Disreputable?'

'No. He remembered the word. 'We try to be *discreet*.'

'Have a drink to calm your nerves,' she said, handing him a glass. 'It's gin. I've nothing else.'

He accepted the gin gratefully, still conscious of her amusement. 'Dash it all, Marie,' he said, 'when we sat on that rock this afternoon, you behaved like a shy virgin.'

She smiled at his description. 'Good, wasn't I? Anyway, what makes you think I'm not really a virgin?'

'Let's stop playing guessing games,' he said, joining her on the bed.

'Right, you'll find out soon enough whether I am or not.' She joined him in a luxurious kiss, after which she said, 'Excuse me for one second. May I take your vest?'

For a moment, he wondered what she had in mind, but when she helped him out of his waistcoat, he remembered that Americans called the garment a 'vest'. He watched her drape it over the wooden doorknob so that it obscured the keyhole perfectly, and he remembered what the girls had said about the voyeurs in the building.

They kissed again before and during the course of undressing, and Marie eventually stood before him as he'd seen her fleetingly in the still waters of the lake. The sight was no less captivating.

'Marie, you're… lovely.' It was the first time he'd used the word – he'd always thought of it as a word women used – but it described her gentle curves and smooth, ivory flesh tone better than any other word he knew.

'You're very kind.' She turned back the covers and beckoned to him.

'Have you…? I mean, what are we doing about preventing… accidents?'

'It's all in place,' she assured him, and he was relieved once again that things had developed during his time in India. He joined her between the coarse sheets, revelling in the contrast of her softness and the new intimacy between them.

'It's my first time,' she said, adding mischievously, 'with an Englishman.'

'We're no different from Americans,' he assured her, 'except… downstairs.'

'Downstairs?'

'Englishmen tend to be smaller.'

'Smaller?'

'About half the size,' he told her with a look of hopelessness, 'if that.'

'Ah well, we must be thankful for small mercies.' She carried out her own reconnaissance and gasped. 'Do you call that thing *small*?'

'I was being modest.' As he saw it, one leg-pull deserved another, but he kissed her before she could berate him for it. In his experience, no woman liked to be outdone.

'Seth,' she said when he allowed her to speak, 'you're a great kisser.'

'Thank you,' he said, moving downward and pausing when he reached her neck. 'I practise whenever I can.'

After a while, she said, 'Hey, that's really nice. No one's ever kissed them until now.'

He was surprised. 'I like to kiss your... these things.'

'They're called "breasts",' she told him helpfully.

'Thanks. I can never remember their proper name.'

'You're not the only man with that problem, but feel free to carry on.'

He worked his way minutely around one areola, favouring the proud nipple with his lips before distributing his kisses more widely.

'Seth,' she moaned, 'you're something special. Do you know that?'

'You're being kind.'

'No, I'm not. Just the fact you weren't inside of me in the first minute makes you different from other men. What you're doing now puts you in another class again.'

He decided that her life had been woefully lacking, but he kept that to himself. Instead, he said, 'Marie?'

'What?'

'Stop talking and just enjoy it.'

'Oh, I shall.'

While he continued to kiss her, he explored her with his hand, traversing her flat midriff and then advancing slowly through the enticing grove that lay beyond it.

Suddenly, she gasped. 'Seth, you've uncovered my secret.'

'Yes, I don't know what it's called in English, but I think it deserves a special name.'

Her next utterance was lost as she reacted repeatedly until she could wait no longer.

In response to her demands, he joined her, and she wrapped her legs around him to hold him in blissful captivity. Thereafter, her excitement was seemingly limitless and, whilst she expressed it in ways that were neither articulate nor coherent, the message they carried was clearly the same.

Eventually, she subsided, breathless and exhilarated. As soon as she could speak, she said, 'Please stop.'

He obliged, concluding that it must be an American custom to do it in instalments.

'Seth— Aah.'

'I know, I twitched. I'm sorry.'

'I'd suggest you do missionary work, except that I want you all to myself.'

He arranged himself more comfortably on his elbows whilst trying not to make unnecessary movements. After some thought, he said, 'If I could use words better than I do, I'd write a book about it, because I think there's a need for it in this country.' His theory was based on his experiences with only two American women, but it was an encouraging start.

'You'd never get it into print. There's no shortage of puritans in this country, believe me. I think the Pilgrim Fathers only came here to spoil everyone's fun. All the same,' she mused, 'a book like that would be a marvellous thing, if it only existed.'

It seemed an odd thing for her to say. 'There is one,' he told her.

'What?'

'It's called the *Kama Sutra*—'

'Aah. You twitched again.'

'I'm sorry. Sometimes, it just happens without any help from me.' He went on. 'Indians swear by the *Kama Sutra*. They say it's the oldest book of advice on… what we're doing now.'

She was staring at him as if he had magical powers. She asked, 'Have you read it?'

'No, I can't read Indian writing, but I've had some of it explained in English.'

She listened with childlike fascination. 'Did it tell you about the thing you found?'

'What thing was that?'

'Down there.' She pointed unnecessarily to her middle.

'Oh, that. Well, it was the person who read to me who told me about that.'

'But you don't know what it's called?'

'Not in English. In Hindi, it's called the *bhagasheph*.'

'You remembered that, but you can't remember "breasts". I find that strange.'

'So do I, but memory is a strange thing. Let's call it your "rosebud".' He kissed her in a leisurely way and, when she tried to speak, he kissed her again.

'Seth?'

'No more talking,' he told her, moving gently once more.

⚜

'Do you have to leave?' It was no more than an expression of regret. Marie knew that Seth had to return to the stable. Not even the promise of a night of ecstasy could keep him from giving the horses the care they needed.

'I'm not going to run away,' he assured her, unhooking his waistcoat from the doorknob to complete his attire. 'I'll see you tomorrow.' He kissed her and left the room, walking as quietly as he could along the bare passageway to the stairs that led past the first floor, where the noises from the chorus girls' rooms suggested that business was being conducted at a lively tempo.

As he stood at the door that led to the saloon proper, he heard the sound of movement behind him. He turned and saw Henry. 'It's noisy tonight, Henry.'

'Aye, they're a rowdy lot.'

They let themselves into the saloon, where a dozen games, at least, were in progress, and that wasn't all. Henry pointed up to the audience boxes above the empty stage, where every curtain was closed.

'I can't see the attraction of doing it in one of them things,' said Seth. 'There's nothing between them and us but a flimsy curtain.'

'Happen that's the attraction,' observed Henry in his quiet way.

They left the saloon and crossed over to the stable, where a close inspection told them all was well.

81

After a little thought, Seth said, 'We could take turns to keep an eye on things.'

'We could,' said Henry. 'We could work out a rota.'

'Just like the old days.'

'That's right,' agreed Henry.

Seth smiled and said, 'Military training's a wonderful thing.'

'It is an' all.'

The two undressed and went to bed.

'Goodnight, Sergeant Fowler.'

'Goodnight, Sergeant Campion.'

Seth smiled to himself again. It had been a very good night.

11

A Word of Warning

The two men had mucked out the loose boxes and put fresh straw down, and were about to make a brew, when they received a visitor. He was elderly, and he spoke with a high-pitched voice in a dialect that Seth and Henry found almost unintelligible. They learned the reason for it when he told them he'd come from Montana.

'I'm just passin' through,' he told them, an' I need stablin' for my burro.'

Henry asked, 'What's a burro?'

'What's a burro?' The old man's squeak went an octave higher.

'Aye, what's a burro?'

'D' you mean to tell me you don't know what a burro is?'

'That's what he means,' confirmed Seth. 'That's why he asked you.'

'You two work in a stable an' you don't know what a burro is?'

'Let's do this the quick way,' suggested Seth. 'Just tell us what a burro is.'

Just then, a *hee-haw* from the nearest tethering rail broke the suspense.

'We know what you mean now,' said Seth. 'A burro is a donkey.'

'I ain't never heard of a burro bein' called a one o' them,' said the irritating man. 'In Bible times, they called 'em "asses", an' that's downright funny when you consider what an ass really is, but they're burros now, an' I want stablin' for mine.'

'Sorry,' said Henry, 'we can't do that.'

'What for can't you do that? Are you full up or sump'n?'

'No, we just can't stable a donkey.'

'Whyivver not, for gosh sakes?'

'We have to protect the horses,' Seth told him. 'The man who keeps the general store has an empty stable. You could ask him if he'll let you keep your donkey there.'

'If you won't oblige me, it seems I'll have to.'

'No offence,' said Henry, 'but donkeys an' horses don't mix.'

'First I've ivver heard of it.' He turned and walked back across the street, muttering to himself. 'Burros an' horses don't mix. Horse shit. That's what that is. Them two greenhorns don't know what they're talkin' 'bout.' He disappeared inside the general store, emerging a few minutes later to untether his donkey. It seemed that he'd been more successful at the store.

They thought no more about it until mid-day, when they visited the saloon as usual. Before they could order two beers, they heard Hesketh's voice.

'Hey, you two. Waddyer mean by turning custom away?' The old man was seated beside him.

They ordered their drinks and waited until they'd arrived, before answering him.

'You're an ill-mannered man, Hesketh, isn't he, Sergeant Fowler?'

'He's that all right, Sergeant Campion.'

'Never mind all that,' said Hesketh, more irritated than ever. 'Waddyer mean by refusin' to stable a burro? Ain't this fella's money as good as anybody's? What've you got against burros, anyway?'

'His money's probably as good—'

'D' you think I can afford to pick an' choose my customers?'

'Be quiet, Hesketh, an' let your ears give your tongue a rest for once.' Seth put his beer down with studied patience. 'Now listen. In Europe, donkeys, burros, or whatever you like to call them, are born with lungworm, an' they're so generous with it, they give it to the first horse they can find. Now, as I see it, the donkeys in this country must have been brought over from Spain when the Spaniards were in charge of things, so there's a good chance they'll have lungworm too. Do you want your horses and the stage company's horses to die of lungworm? Ask your livery customers if they want their horses to get lungworm. Let's ask 'em now.'

'No!' Fearful that any of his customers might get wind of the danger, Hesketh signalled Seth to be quiet. 'Just leave things as they are.'

'Bear in mind what I've said, Hesketh. For an old man, you're surprisingly ignorant about horse husbandry.'

'All right. Keep your voice down.'

'What's happening here?' Marie touched Seth's arm in greeting, clearly intrigued by the raised voices.

'Hello, ladies. This tight-fisted old so-and-so pays the wages, but he needs to remember who's running that stable.'

The girls' drinks arrived, borne by a waitress the two men hadn't seen before. The girls were also surprised to see her.

'Little Rose,' said Marie, 'what are you doing in here?'

'Mr Forsberg told me to help in here,' she said quietly. She was clearly the half-Sioux orphan the girls had mentioned. She looked at Seth and Henry with the diffidence of an habitual victim.

'These men won't hurt you, Little Rose,' said Carrie. 'They're friends of ours.'

'That's right,' said Seth. 'Pleased to meet you, Little Rose. I'm Seth.' He shook her hand as well as he could, hers being very small.

'I'm Henry. Glad to meet you, Little Rose.' Henry held out both hands to envelope hers. She was a fetching little thing, with a hint of her Indian parenthood in her features, although her father's influence was also apparent. She appeared to be about twelve. The girls had said possibly thirteen, but Seth doubted it. He remembered the girls voicing their worries for her safety in an establishment populated by unscrupulous men. She was scarcely out of childhood, and first appearances offered no evidence that she was remotely nubile.

She left them to answer a shouted order for drinks, but the customer saw her approaching and said, 'Don't let that half-breed papoose near my table.'

'No,' said his companion, 'git her outta here.'

'Come away, Little Rose,' said the bartender. 'I'll do it.'

Seth looked away, sickened. 'Do you remember the way the Shudras used to treat the Dolits, Henry?'

'I was thinking the same thing.'

Carrie asked, 'Who are you talking about?'

'The Hindus in India. The Shudras are the highest in rank. They give the dirtiest jobs to the Dolits and treat them like animals.'

One of the men was shouting again. 'Don't you come near my table, half-breed!'

Little Rose cowered by the bar until Marie hurried over to her and said something in her ear before bringing her back to the table.

'Listen, Little Rose,' said Seth. 'People like that man who just shouted at you are the lowest kind of life there is. He's got no right to treat you like that, but you've no need to be scared anymore, because we're going to look after you.'

'Relax, Little Rose,' said Marie with a half-amused smile in Seth's direction. 'You're under the protection of the Eleventh Cavalry, just like Carrie and me.'

'Eleventh Hussars,' Seth corrected her.

'It's all the same to Little Rose. All she knows is that she has two new friends, and that's always good news in a community like this one.'

The half-hour break was drawing to its close, and Seth was about to advise the girls to take Little Rose somewhere safer, when the loud man and his companion got up to leave. They had to pass the friends' table on their way out, and they both eyed Little Rose with undisguised distaste. With two men at the table, however, they said nothing but walked out of the saloon in silence.

Seth got up, followed by Henry, who said, 'Will you excuse us, ladies?'

They followed the two men outside and grabbed them before they could go any further.

The man who'd been doing the shouting demanded uncertainly, 'What you want with us?'

'We want to tell you something important,' said Seth.

Taking the pair by their shirtfronts, he and Henry slammed them against the front wall of the saloon, knocking the breath out of them. 'Now, listen, you two,' said Seth, 'We know about what the Sioux did to Colonel Custer and his men, but it wasn't Little Rose's fault. She wasn't even there. Being a half-breed isn't her fault either. In case you don't know it, that happened nine months before she was born. In any case, it's time you started treating her like a human being, because if you insult her again, we'll just have to give you both a daily hiding 'til you learn your lesson. D' you understand?'

'Yeah, yeah.' Clearly terrified, the shouter was quick to appease him. 'We get the picture.'

'Good. Go and sin no more.'

They went back into the saloon to finish their drinks. 'Those men won't trouble you again, Little Rose,' said Seth.

'Good,' said Carrie, 'even though I don't really approve of violence.'

'We're not keen on it, either,' Seth told her, 'but it's the only language some men can understand.'

They took their leave of the girls and Little Rose, and made for the doorway, waving a friendly farewell to Hesketh, who'd evidently heard the commotion outside the saloon.

'What is it with you boys? You don't like burros, but you love redskins. I don't get it.'

Seth patted him on the shoulder and said, 'Don't waste time worryin' about it, and don't spend all your money on whiskey, Hesketh. It's payday today, remember?'

⊕⊢<del>3</del>⊶⊢⊱Ɛ⊢⊶⊜

The girls had to sing in the saloon that evening, but Carrie took Henry back to her room afterwards, whilst Seth, who'd lost the toss, returned to the stable.

He was examining one of the stage horses that had come in that afternoon, when he realised he had a visitor.

'Hello, Seth,' said Marie. 'What are you doing?'

'I've been checking the stage horses. This one's about to cast a shoe. I'll have to take him round to the farrier in the morning.' He kissed her in greeting.

'You really care about these horses, don't you?'

'Any horses, really. Most creatures, in fact.'

'Not all creatures, then?' Her friendly eyes teased him.

'I draw the line at things that do us harm,' he explained. 'Some of the officers in India liked to shoot tigers for sport. Now, I'd shoot a tiger if it was a case of him or me, because they're not the friendliest of pussycats, it has to be said, but I wouldn't shoot one for fun, an' I'd only shoot a wild boar for its meat.' He gave the horse with the loose shoe a

87

friendly slap on the rump as he led Marie back to the living quarters. 'I was just going to make a brew,' he said. 'Would you like one?'

'A brew?'

'Tea,' he translated.

'Yes, I like tea.' Suddenly inquisitive, she asked, 'Where do you find tea around here?'

'We had it sent to us.'

They arrived at the bottom of the ladder, and she said, 'You go up ahead of me, Seth.'

'Why?' He'd been brought up believing that ladies went first, at least, when it was safe for them to do so.

'So that you're not looking up when I climb the ladder.'

'I wouldn't, anyway, but I'm not going to argue.' He climbed the ladder and, when she came up after him, extended his hand to help her into the quarters.

'So this is where you live.'

'It's not what you'd call residential,' he admitted, lighting the oil stove, 'but we've had worse billets.'

'Did that girl send you the tea?'

'What girl?'

'You know, the girl who told you that you and Henry were knights in armour.'

He nodded. 'And her sister. They sent us tea and teeth-cleaning paste as well. We'd always used charcoal, you see, but it did the job.' He showed her his teeth.

'Very nice.' She seemed more interested in Katherine. 'That girl,' she said, 'did you do the same things with her that you do with me?'

Seth shook his head emphatically. 'I can honestly say,' he told her, 'that I never got into her bed. In fact, I never went near her bedroom.'

'Good, I'm glad to hear it.'

It was a female characteristic that baffled Seth, that they had to be sure nothing significant had happened before they came on the scene. Then, after a moment's thought, he realised that he was being unfair to them, as most men set great store by virginity, although he'd always thought it was overrated.

He dropped leaves into two mugs before infusing them with boiling water.

'Did you drink tea in India?'

'All the time.'

'But you don't drink a lot of liquor.' It seemed to surprise her.

'What's liquor?' He'd heard of it, but no one had enlightened him.

'Such as whiskey and beer.'

'Certainly not whiskey, and I don't drink all that much beer.'

'In fact,' she said approvingly, 'you and Henry are good-living fellas.'

'We try to be, as I've told you.' He decided to indulge her curiosity. 'We were brought up by our mothers, Henry and me, and they both died at the same time of the same contagion.'

'You poor boys.'

'Well, we were old enough to fend for ourselves, and the farmer we worked for and his wife were good to us as well, but I suppose our mothers had always been too busy to teach us the important things, so the only guidance we got was from the church. It was Sunday school that taught us reading, writing and figuring, and the Reverend Nicholls who taught us everything else. We learned all the things I told you about in that special dismissal of his, and we learned about moderate behaviour, including not drinking to excess. Too many soldiers drink heavily when they have the money, and it usually leads to violence and disorder. There's no future in that.'

She'd been listening to him with a kind of wonder, but now she smiled mischievously and said, 'I'm glad you didn't learn about the perils of lust.'

'We've talked about that, Henry and me, and we reckon it must have been harvest time when the Reverend Nicholls got around to that, 'cause neither of us can remember it. We'd be harvesting seven days in a row at the time.'

'And, in any case,' she said snuggling up to him, 'nobody's perfect.'

She'd set a thought process in motion, and he felt that he had to tell her about it. 'I don't like that word, "lust",' he said. 'Lust is just a physical need that makes men pay chorus girls – I mean the pickers among them – for favours.'

' "Hookers", not "pickers",' she corrected him, laughing at his mistake. 'So, are you telling me you're driven by something nobler than lust?'

89

'Yes,' he told her seriously, 'and, if you're honest about it, so are you. When we met outside the general store, I thought straight away you were pretty.'

'You thought I was a hooker.'

'That was a mistake. I'm talking about after that.'

'Okay, go on.'

'Then we met and talked, and I decided I liked talking to you. I liked it even more when we sat and talked at the lake.' He was careful not to mention seeing her naked in the clear water. 'When we rode out to Red Wolf Creek, I liked you so much, I wanted to kiss you, and it was only then that I began to want more than that. What I'm really saying is that it was affection, not lust, that led to what we did.'

'You've convinced me, Sir Seth, and I agree with you.' She reached up to kiss him.

'Don't let your tea get cold.'

'Doan't let yer tea get coald,' she mimicked.

'All knights talk like this,' he said.

'All of them?'

'They do round our way.'

She kissed him again. 'I could never talk like you,' she said, 'but I love to listen to you, because you always mean what you say.'

12

Welcome and Rejection

Seth and Henry had just hitched four fresh horses to the stagecoach, and were returning to the stable, when a stranger approached them. He stood out from the majority of Pentecost's population in that he was dressed smartly in a three-piece suit, and his grey whiskers were trimmed and clean. He wore a bowler hat, or 'derby', as the Americans called it, and he was smoking a cigar.

'Good morning to you, boys,' he said. 'My name's Edgar H. Silverman. I'm Mayor of this town, and I'd be greatly obliged if you'd spare me a little of your time. I realise you won't have seen me around. The fact is, I've been in Bismarck, transacting a few deals, but now I'm back in town, there's something I'd like to put to you.'

'Good morning, Mr Silverman,' said Seth, shaking his hand. 'I'm Seth Campion and this is Henry Fowler. We're happy to hear what you have to say, but we'll have to talk out here.' He nodded in the direction of the Mayor's cigar and explained, 'We can't allow smoking in the stable, on account of the risk of fire. That, and it unsettles the horses.'

'Well, I never knew that, about the horses, I mean. It just shows you that we live and learn. As we're safe outside, can I offer your boys a cigar?'

'We don't smoke,' said Seth, 'but we thank you all the same.' He could say that confidently, now that Carrie had persuaded Henry to give up his pipe.

'Well, boys, it's like this. I've been hearin' things about you both, how you apprehended two fire raisers an' delivered 'em to Marshall Higgins, God rest his soul. I also heard how you dealt with a bunch of

91

no-good fur trappers who entered the saloon with evil intent, and I'm obliged to you for that as well.'

'It was no trouble at all,' said Henry.

'I'm glad to hear it, the town bein' temporarily without a marshall an' all.' He adopted the look of a man about to impart good news. 'I've been wonderin',' he said, 'if you boys would consider puttin' on the badge of office an' sharin' the duties of Town Marshall.'

Seth and Henry exchanged looks and came to unspoken agreement. As usual, Seth spoke for them both. 'That's quite an honour you're offering us, Mr Silverman, but we don't see how we can accept it. For one thing, we're not American citizens.'

'That can be taken care of, boys. Nothin' easier.'

'That's not all,' said Seth. 'It seems to us that a town marshall is a permanent kind of official, an' we've no idea how long we're going to be in Pentecost. We honestly don't know what's going to happen next.'

The Mayor made no attempt to conceal his disappointment. He asked, 'In that case, what brought you to Pentecost in the first place?'

'We arrived in Bismarck, ready to join up with Colonel Custer and the Seventh Cavalry,' Henry told him, 'and we learned about the Little Bighorn. We needed to find work, and the stationmaster advised us to try Pentecost.'

Silverman stroked his beard in apparent consternation. 'I just thought,' he said, 'that, you boys always bein' on hand when trouble rears its head, and bein' able to deal with it an' all, you were the right ones to do the job.'

'We're sorry to disappoint you,' said Seth, 'but you can be sure that not having a badge and official powers isn't going to stop us taking action when things have to be put right. If we see unlawful activity, malicious behaviour or any man threatening the weak and helpless, we'll step in, and we'll carry on doing it until Pentecost gets a new marshall, or until we leave the town.'

'Well, I'm grateful to you for that, at least.' He shook hands with them both. 'It's been nice, talkin' with you, boys, even if I wasn't able to persuade you along the lines I had in mind. Of course, you could change your minds....'

'If that happens, Mr Silverman,' said Seth, 'you'll be the first to be told.'

'I appreciate that, son, an' it's "Mr Mayor", by the way. We Americans take official titles seriously.'

'So do we, Mr Mayor. That's right, isn't it, Sergeant Fowler?'

'As right as right can be, Sergeant Campion.'

The Mayor looked unsure for a second.

'Goodbye, Mr Mayor.'

'Goodbye, Mr Mayor.'

'So long, er, boys.'

—⊕⊣⋺⋇⊂⋹⊢⊖—

Seth waited until the girls were seated, and Little Rose had served them with the drinks supplied by the management, and said, 'We had a visit, this morning, from the Mayor of Pentecost.'

'You were lucky to catch him,' Marie told him. 'He doesn't spend a lot of time here.'

'He's usually in Bismarck, doing deals,' said Carrie. 'He only has a home in Pentecost because he's the Mayor, and it makes him feel important.'

'After this morning's meeting, we can believe that.' In fairness, Seth added, 'He did offer us a cigar apiece.'

'Accept a cigar from a politician,' said Marie, 'and he'll have you in his clutches.'

'We didn't. He offered us a job, and we turned that down an' all.'

'What job was that?'

'Town Marshall.'

'What, both of you?'

Henry nodded. 'We share everything.'

'I'm not surprised you turned it down,' said Marie. 'You're birds of passage, like us.'

The description was new to Seth, but he liked it nonetheless. He looked around the saloon and saw Little Rose taking drinks to four men seated at a gaming table. There was no incident, but the atmosphere was less than friendly. He had to ask, 'Has Little Rose had any trouble since we dealt with those two yesterday?'

'No, word's gotten around, but I'll tell you something else I've heard, that I really don't like. There've been murmurs about you and Henry, resentful talk about two Britishers being too big for their boots. Be careful, Seth.'

'Oh, we'll be careful. It's not the first time we've been threatened.'

Under the cover of the table, she stroked his hand and asked, 'Shall I see you tonight? I'm free after nine.'

'I'll see you then.'

'Better make it a quarter after nine,' she advised.

<hr>

It was actually closer to twenty-past nine when Seth knocked softly on Marie's door.

'I had to wait 'til I knew the landing was clear,' he told her as she opened it to let him in. He took off his waistcoat and hung it over the doorknob. 'I don't want to give you a bad name,' he said.

'The reputation goes with the premises, Seth, but it's not likely to be a problem much longer.'

'Why not?'

'Because Forsberg, who owns this place, is going to take over our rooms and give them to newcomers when they arrive.'

'I don't understand.'

She handed him a glass of gin and explained. 'He takes a cut out of every transaction, so it makes sense to have as many hookers here as he can find. He's a very greedy man.'

'Isn't it against the law?'

'There's no federal law against it. Anyway, as soon as his new girls arrive, Carrie and I will have to leave. We'll still be employed in the saloon, but we'll have to sleep elsewhere. At the Palace Hotel, I guess.'

It sounded despicable. 'It'll be very expensive for you.'

'We'll just have to take smaller rooms.' Clearly touched by his concern for her, she said, 'It'll be a whole lot nicer there.' She took his hands. 'Anyway,' she said, 'let's not worry about that now.'

They undressed and climbed into bed, and Seth said, 'Maybe the sheets will be softer at the Palace Hotel.' In truth, sheets of any quality were a novelty to him, his concern being purely for her comfort.

'They couldn't be any rougher, and that's a fact.' She submitted to a long, languorous kiss and said, 'And they'll be changed more often.'

He kissed her again, precluding further conversation, at least for the time being, as she found his attentions substantially more rewarding than a discussion about accommodation and bedding.

'They've been waiting for you,' she said with evident satisfaction.

'Mm.' Her breasts wouldn't have had to wait long, although he was concentrating, for the moment, on the valley between them, an exploration that was providing him with a special kind of reward.

'Can you remember what they're called?'

He shook his head, intensifying the reward.

'Breasts,' she reminded him.

As a reward for the favour she'd unwittingly provided, he turned his attention to one breast and ran the tip of his tongue slowly around the areola, feeling each of its tiny protrusions and then taking the raised nipple delicately between his moistened lips.

'Seth,' she moaned, 'you may not be able to remember their name, but you sure know how to handle them.'

'Hush,' he chided, moving back to kiss her on the lips. As he did so, he ran his hand over her hip, stroking and massaging gently. Presently, he ran his middle finger slowly down the crease between her thigh and her abdomen. She tried to speak again, but he silenced her with a lengthy kiss. Eventually, she managed to say, 'Now, Seth... please.'

ⴰⵀ⵰⵰⵰ⴰ

'Will we still be able to do this after you move to the hotel?' The question had occurred to Seth more than once that evening.

'There shouldn't be a problem. They don't take hookers; in fact, they'll have no dealings with the trade. Otherwise, they're pretty easy-going.' She knelt above him, talking matter-of-factly.

'Have you spoken to them?'

'Yes, when we looked like losing our rooms, it seemed like a good idea to have someplace we could go.' Her eyes suddenly opened wide. 'You twitched,' she said accusingly.

'Sorry, I couldn't help it.'

95

'I don't believe you. You do it on purpose just to tease.' As if the suspicion had just occurred to her, she asked, 'Do you like it when you twitch?'

He lay still, considering the question. 'When we were lads working on the farm and we'd got to the end of a hard day, the farmer used to give us an apple from his orchard.' To avoid misunderstanding, he explained, 'That was on top of our wages, you understand.'

'A kind of bonus?'

'Is that what it's called? Well, a twitch is like a bonus, as well as—'

'Ah!'

'Sorry.'

She settled again. 'As well as what?'

'I was going to say it's a reminder of what there is to follow.'

'Okay, far be it from me to keep you waiting.' She began to move repeatedly above him while he stroked her smooth thighs slowly and appreciatively.

<hr />

He let himself out quietly and stepped out into the side street that ran between the saloon and the laundry. Apart from the noise from the saloon, the street was quiet. It was quiet enough for him to hear the crunch of a footstep behind him. He turned and heard a man's voice say, 'Injun lover.' He held out a hand to protect himself against something hard and heavy that, in spite of his efforts, struck him on the head. Thereafter, he knew nothing.

13

Rough Justice and Mercy

He came round on his bedroll in the living quarters above the stable. How he'd got there was a mystery. All he knew was that his head ached abominably.

'Have some willow bark tea,' suggested Henry, holding a tin mug in front of him.

'I'm more obliged to you than you know, Henry.' Seth took the mug and sipped the foul infusion. 'What happened?'

'Two fellas caught up with you when you left the saloon. By the time I got to you, they'd whacked you over the head with a pick handle.' With a smile of satisfaction, he said, 'Now, they know how it felt.'

'Did you deal with 'em, Henry?'

'I had to. I wasn't goin' to let 'em get away with that.'

'I'm ever grateful, mate.' Seth drank some more of the willow bark tea, grimaced at the awful taste and handed the mug back to Henry. 'I think it's beginning to work,' he said.

'Aye, it's good stuff.'

'What's the time?'

Henry consulted his pocket watch and said, 'The hour lacks a quarter.'

'Which hour?'

'One o' clock. You'll feel better in the morning.'

Seth hoped so. 'Grateful thanks, Sergeant Fowler. Goodnight.'

'Goodnight, Sergeant Campion.' Henry turned down the wick.

In spite of a sizeable and tender bump on his head, Seth did feel a great deal better when morning came. He owed the relief from his immediate pain to the willow bark tea, but he knew he owed a great deal more to Henry, who had clearly been on the lookout when the attack took place. They had been looking out for each other for as long as they could remember, and Seth was determined to keep an eye on Henry.

In view of the previous evening's incident, they resolved to carry their revolvers. They made the decision with some regret whilst also recognising the need for self-defence in a society that accepted violence as a way of life.

When they entered the saloon, they had no difficulty in identifying Seth's assailants; each bore fresh bruises, and they greeted Seth and Henry with a look of mute hatred before leaving the premises, either through reluctance to share the venue with the two Englishmen, or through fear of further reprisal. The latter seemed the likelier of the two.

When Marie and Carrie went off-stage, Henry pointed out a man they'd seen at the bar on several occasions. He was particularly noticeable because of a broken nose and a wall eye that seemed to be covered by a kind of translucent membrane that lightened the iris and gave him a threatening appearance.

'Aye,' said Seth, 'it's a long time since I've seen anybody as ugly as that.'

'He can't help it,' said Henry.

'Happen not, but he could stop at home.'

'Right enough.'

They gave Little Rose a cheery greeting when she brought drinks for Marie and Carrie, and congratulated the girls on another fine performance.

'You get better every time we hear you,' said Seth.

'That's right,' said Henry.

'We're thankful to you, boys.' Carrie, at least, appreciated their compliments. Marie seemed distracted. 'There's been talk of some trouble last night, involving you two,' she said.

'It was no trouble at all,' Henry assured her.

'I worry about you boys.'

'You mustn't do that,' said Seth. 'We can take care of....' He was about to say, '...ourselves,' but, in the light of recent events, he changed it to '...each other.'

'I hope so.'

Carrie interrupted the conversation by saying urgently, 'Nat Fewster's just taken Little Rose upstairs and she didn't look too happy about it!'

Henry and Seth got up from the table and dashed to the stairs. They weren't familiar with Fewster's name, but it sounded as if he was up to no good.

There was a scream from the first floor, and a cry of, 'No! Please! No!'

Henry took the stairs three at a time, and Seth saw him pass through an open doorway. He arrived in time to see the dorsal view of a man with his trousers down to his ankles. Little Rose lay across the bed, still screaming and struggling.

Grabbing a handful of the man's hair with his left and his scrotum with his right, Henry hauled him backwards. It was now the abuser's turn to scream, but in agony. Unimpressed, Henry thrust him through the doorway and hurled him down the wide staircase.

Seth paused long enough to say, 'Cover yourself up, Little Rose. You're safe now,' before joining Henry downstairs, where he recognised the attempted rapist as the wall-eyed man with the broken nose. He was clutching his private parts and still howling with pain.

'Let's find him a seat, Seth,' said Henry.

Seth stood aside to let Marie and Carrie upstairs, and then took a chair from an empty table, setting it down conveniently for Henry to thrust Fewster on to it.

Hesketh asked, 'Whaddayer gonna do to him?'

'You'll have to wait an' see,' Seth told him, taking the belt from Fewster's concertinaed trousers and using it to tie his hands to the chair.

'Now, Seth,' said Henry, 'You're the skilful one with the sabre. I expect you'd like to do the gelding.'

Fewster screamed, 'No!'

'What was that, Fewster?' Seth cupped his ear and bent to listen.

'No! Please! Not that!'

The crowd in the saloon were staring, motionless, at the spectacle.

However they felt about Fewster's crime, they seemed uniformly fascinated by his predicament.

'Now, isn't that strange, Henry? I'll swear that's what Little Rose was saying. Didn't she say just that?'

'That was what she said, Seth.'

'I thought so, an' he took not one bit of notice of her.'

Henry nodded in agreement. 'Why should we take any notice of him? Go on, Seth, cut his balls off.'

'I'm not sure, Henry. Maybe I should cut his tassel off an' all.' He peered at the place where the threatened member appeared to be making every effort to retreat within itself. 'That's if I can find it.'

'No,' pleaded Fewster, now tearful. 'Not that. Please!'

Seth made a practice cut in mid-air and asked, 'Why not? You didn't ask Little Rose why not when she said that.'

'I didn't mean no harm,' sobbed Fewster.

'Did you hear that, Henry? He didn't mean no harm. He tried to force himself on to a little girl, and he would have done just that if we hadn't stopped him. As it happened, he terrified the poor child out of her wits and gave her a terrible experience that she'll remember for the rest of her life, but he didn't mean no harm.'

'I didn't mean no harm, I tell you!'

'Fully clothed, you'd scare any child, but half-naked, you must have been a living nightmare, Fewster.'

'Just geld him, Seth.'

'Not in here, Henry. It's best done outside. Do you remember the man we found in the Punjab?'

'The adulterer?'

'Yes, him. It was too bad we didn't get to him before the villagers did.'

'Too bad as far as he was concerned, Seth.'

'I would never have believed a man could bleed like that, an' all through his... where his manhood used to be. It had just gushed out like pump water.'

'No,' sobbed Fewster, 'please, no. I'll do anythin'.' His terror had robbed him of any control, and a stream of urine was creating a pool on the floor.

'You're right, Henry. Let's just string him up.'

It was too much for Fewster. 'You can't do that,' he pleaded. 'That'd be murder. They'd hang you for that.'

'Not by your neck, Fewster,' said Henry, 'although you can't say you don't deserve it.'

'What then, Henry?'

'Let's tie his bits and pieces up with thin cord an' then tie it to a stout rope. Then, we'll just let him dangle from the nearest tree.'

'I beg you! No!'

'That sounds like a good idea, an' it wouldn't be as messy as gelding.'

People were still watching, open-mouthed. Hesketh had even stopped chewing.

Fewster was alternately whining and sobbing.

Seth asked, 'Do you think you deserve mercy, Fewster?'

'Yeah, an' I'll never do it again, I promise. Honest to God, I promise I won't do it again.' He spoke the words with difficulty through a torrent of sobbing.

'You'd do well to have a care with the Lord's name, Fewster. That's the third commandment you're breaking.' He gave the impression of being in deep thought, and said finally, 'All right, we won't castrate you or hang you by your bits an' pieces.'

'I'll thank you for all time,' sobbed Fewster.

'You've little to thank me for, as you'll find out in a minute. Henry, let's untie his hands and bend him across that chair.'

When the rearrangement was complete, Seth stepped back, wielding his sabre and drawing a gasp from the onlookers. He made a couple of practice passes and then a massive swipe, landing the flat of his blade across Fewster's naked buttocks. The loud smack brought a gasp from the crowd, who might have expected a bloodier result, but who were no less impressed by the punishment. For his part, Fewster simply screamed with pain.

'I could always geld you if you'd rather,' offered Seth.

'No! No!'

Five times more, Seth delivered his punishment. Then, when Fewster's howling had dwindled to a mere sobbing, he returned his sabre to its scabbard. 'Now, listen to me,' he told the crowd. 'You can put the word out, that any man who touches Little Rose, either in lust or in anger, will answer to us.'

'What exactly did you do to him?' Marie had called at the stable with the news that Little Rose was now calm and coherent.

'We scared him a bit. He thought I was going to separate him from his bits and pieces, but I turned soft in the end, and settled for cracking his arse.'

'What?'

'Smacking his rump,' he translated. 'He'd never had it smacked with a sabre before, an' he wasn't at all suited. Mind you, he'll think twice another time before putting his *luleh* where it's not wanted.'

'Is that the Indian name for it?'

'One of them.' Memories of Fewster's come-uppance made him laugh again.

'What's so funny?'

'He really thought we were going to geld him.'

'He must have been terrified.'

'No more than Little Rose was.' Serious once more, he said, 'The poor little scrap's not even close to womanhood.'

'I know. If she'd been a grown woman, it would have been a crime, but a child like her....' She left the rest unspoken.

Seth broke the mood by saying, 'I'm going to escort you back to the saloon, and then I have to keep a lookout for Henry.' He buckled his gun-belt.

'Be careful, Seth. I mean it.'

Leaving Marie in the security of her room, he crossed the street and stepped into the shadows to keep watch. The night was cold, but the passageway afforded shelter from the wind, and he was aware of the benefit. He just hoped Henry wasn't set for a late night.

A moment later, he realised that the thought was unworthy. Henry had most likely saved his life, and he should be allowed to take as long as he wanted, anytime. It was just very cold out there. To warm himself up, he walked a little way down the passageway and then back again. It did no good at all, so he walked further. Then, as he turned to walk back, he saw the side door of the saloon open. There was light for a moment, and then it was dark again. He hurried across the street and stopped at the corner of the saloon. With nothing but moonlight, he could still make out Henry's checked shirt and red bandana. He could also see shadowy movement behind him. He took out his revolver and cocked it carefully, keeping the noise to a minimum.

It seemed he wasn't the only one with that in mind, because he distinctly heard more than one pistol being cocked. Henry had also heard it, and he turned to face the threat, but Seth shouted, 'Get down, Henry!'

There was a muzzle flash and the sharp crack of a revolver, and then, with Henry no longer impeding his view, Seth fired twice and heard the resulting cries of pain from the unknown gunmen.

'Are you all right, Henry?'

'I'm all right,' confirmed Henry. 'I think you got 'em.'

'I'm not sure.' Seth was pointing his revolver in the direction of the assailants. As he listened, he thought he could hear panting. Then there was a groan.

'Keep 'em covered,' said Henry, opening the side door of the saloon to shine some light on the passage.

In the dim light, Seth saw two men on the ground. One was moaning and nursing a leg wound. The other was still. He asked, 'Is he dead?'

'Mos' likely.' The voice was unmistakeably that of Nat Fewster.

'Give me your gun, Fewster, butt first.'

As he took the revolver, he heard the other man moan.

'You must have winged him,' said Henry.

'Let's have his gun an' all.' He took the gun and said, 'You two need to see the doctor.'

'You mean you ain't gonna kill us?' Fewster sounded incredulous.

'Not now you're unarmed. I'd have been happy to geld you this afternoon, but I draw the line at shooting an unarmed man.'

'Thank the Lord for that.'

'I've told you before,' said Seth. 'Have some care with the Lord's name. Anyway, if anybody's watchin' over you, I reckon it must be

Satan. They say he looks after his own.' He offered a hand and said, 'Get up, and I'll help you to the doctor's place.'

'I'll bring the other one,' said Henry.

With help from Seth, Fewster got to his feet. He asked, 'What is it with you boys, anyway? We shot at you, an' you let us live.'

'It's not for us to take your lives,' Seth told him, 'but try again, and we might not be so kind-hearted.'

'You won't have no trouble with us again.'

'You'd better keep to that, Fewster, because I can't see you getting any luckier than you've been today.'

14

Time to Leave

Fewster surprised them by being as good as his word, and they were spared further attempts on their lives. In fact, Pentecost itself was enjoying a period of peaceful behaviour for which Seth and Henry were as thankful as the townsfolk, and the general feeling of security and wellbeing was about to be reinforced. The good news came one Saturday morning in early November, when the Mayor visited the stable. He was in the company of a man neither Seth nor Henry had seen in the town. He was tall, powerfully built and smartly dressed, with a full, but carefully-trimmed moustache. They stopped work to receive him and the Mayor.

'Good morning, boys,' said Edgar Silverman.

The two returned his greeting.

'Allow me to introduce Jeff Burnett, our new Town Marshall.'

'We're glad to meet you, Marshall,' said Seth, shaking his hand.

'Welcome, Marshall.' Henry added his greeting and shook the newcomer's hand.

'I hear you two boys have been keeping the peace,' said Burnett, smiling at the thought. 'To say you're British, the townsfolk seem grateful for your efforts.'

'Well, most of them,' said Henry.

'We only lent a hand when we had to,' explained Seth. 'We can take a rest now you're here, Marshall.'

The marshall smiled at that and asked, 'Won't you consider being sworn in as deputies? There's bound to be times when I'll need a hand, I'm sure.'

Seth and Henry exchanged looks and came to the unspoken

agreement that had been a lifelong feature of their association. As usual, Seth spoke for them both. 'We're not American citizens, Marshall—'

'I told you boys before,' said Silverman, 'that's a detail that can be taken care of.'

'I was going to say that we're not citizens, but if you're ever in need of reinforcement, you know where to find us.'

'That's good enough for me.' The marshall shook hands with them again.

'What have you been doing up to now, Marshall?' The question came from Henry.

'I was a deputy in Deadwood. Do you know the place?'

'We've never been there, but we've heard about it.'

'The area's full of gold prospectors. There's even more of 'em now that the Sioux are being driven out of the Black Hills.'

'Driven out?' Seth found it hard to believe.

'The Army's herding them on to reservations. If they object, they have to take the consequences. It's not pleasant, but it's government policy.'

Henry asked, 'What are the consequences?'

'Have you heard of the Slim Buttes?'

Some trappers mentioned it when they passed through,' said Seth, 'but we never find out what's really happening.'

'These boys came out here to join Custer,' the Mayor told him with a sly smile.

'We heard about him from an American reporter in India,' said Seth. 'He said that Colonel Custer was a good man with the interests of the natives as well as the white people at heart.'

The Marshall nodded. 'Whether that was the case or not,' he said, 'the Little Bighorn did the Injuns' cause no good at all.' He gave the sigh of a man about to impart unpopular news. 'I mentioned the Slim Buttes, but that was just one incident.'

'What happened at Slim Buttes, Marshall?'

Silverman offered Burnett a cigar, but he shook his head. 'General Crook came upon some Lakota Sioux who were hunting in the area, and he attacked their village at night. The soldiers killed women and children as well as braves, and burned their lodges.'

'Why?' It seemed senseless to Seth.

'Revenge, I guess. The Sioux have no friends in these parts.'

Seth and Henry looked at each other and then looked away. A fondly-held belief had just crumbled into dust.

'Marshall,' said Seth, 'there's a half-Sioux girl working in the saloon. She's been under our protection until now, but you're the Marshall, and we have to look to you to uphold the law.'

'What's been happening?'

'We've caught men abusing her because of her Sioux blood, and we've persuaded them to leave her alone, but there could be others. Only recently, we caught one man trying to force himself on her. She's only twelve, not even a woman yet, not that that would—'

'What did you do?'

'We pulled him off her,' said Henry, 'and I chucked him downstairs.'

'We scared him,' said Seth. 'He thought I was going to geld him. In the end, though, I just tanned his arse with the flat blade of my sabre. He learned his lesson.' He decided to say nothing about the attempted murder.

The Marshall smiled at the picture they'd painted. 'Rest easy, boys,' he said. 'She's under my protection now. However these people feel about the Sioux and the Cheyenne, they can't be allowed to punish a little girl for what the Injuns did to Custer.'

⊕⊢∃∘⫯⊹⋿⊢⊖

It continued to be a day of surprises and disappointments, as they found when they visited the saloon at mid-day.

They introduced Little Rose and the girls to Marshall Burnett, and that was a step forward, but what Burnett had told them about the deeds of the Seventh Cavalry had given them cause to think, and there was more to follow.

Marie waited for Burnett to leave before saying to Seth, 'We've got news as well, Seth.'

'Yeah?'

'We shan't be moving into the hotel after all.' She was unusually serious.

'Why not?'

107

'Because we're leaving Pentecost. We've been offered work in Bismarck at almost twice the money that old skinflint Forsberg's been paying us.'

Seth wished he hadn't got out of his bedroll that morning. Some distance away, Carrie and Henry were talking just as seriously, and it wasn't difficult to guess what they were discussing. He asked, 'When are you leaving?'

'Monday,' she told him, 'on the morning stage.' After a moment's hesitation, she said, 'You could come with us.'

'We came here from Bismarck because there was no work for us there,' he said.

'We'll keep a look out, and when something turns up, we'll let you know.'

He squeezed her hand because he could think of nothing to say.

'We're not working after tomorrow morning,' she said. 'We can say our goodbyes properly then, although it doesn't really have to be "goodbye", does it?'

<hr />

'When they start their new job,' said Henry, 'they'll meet new people and make new friends. Carrie told me the same thing, but I'm not going to stay awake waiting to hear from her.'

'It's time to take stock,' said Seth.

'What does that mean?'

'I'm not sure. I think it means looking at how things stand, and thinking about what we need to do next.'

Henry lit the stove to boil some water for tea while he thought. Eventually, he said, 'One good thing that happened today, was that the town got a new marshall.'

'It was the *only* good thing that happened today,' said Seth.

'All right, so let's look at what went wrong, and where we go from there.'

Seth asked, 'Do you think someone's trying to tell us something?'

'You never know.'

'The girls are leaving, the town has a new marshall, and that means....'

'This town has no more need of us, Seth.'

'And that means we're ready to take advantage of new opportunities.'

Henry nodded briefly. 'We just need somebody to chuck an opportunity or two in our direction.'

Seth was staring thoughtfully into his tea. 'I've been thinking about that massacre the Marshall told us about,' he said, 'the Seventh Cavalry killing women and kiddies. I can't recall a time when the Hussars ever did that.'

'Neither can I, Seth.'

'None of the folk we've met so far have had a lot to say about Custer,' he went on, 'other than that the Little Bighorn was a tragedy and an act of wickedness by the Indians.'

'Maybe they weren't quite as impressed with him as we were. At least, not in the same way.'

'They're not usually slow to speak their minds.'

'Well, he's dead now, and nobody's any right to speak ill of him. I just want to go on believing he was a good man.'

'Me too, Seth. What that American newspaper man said was good enough for me.'

As thoughts went, it was as positive as any they could muster at the end of a particularly trying day.

⊷⊰∗⊱⊷

Try as he would, Seth was unable to make that Sunday and the morning departure less miserable than they were always going to be, and he knew that Henry felt the same way. They just had to be philosophical about it and, as everyone knew, with all the sensible thinking in the world, it took time for disappointment to fade.

It is also a well-known fact that a distraction is helpful in time of sadness, and such a diversion occurred the following day, when Seth went to the General Store to buy some more salve for the horses.

The proprietor passed a tin of salve across the counter and took Seth's money. 'I've gotten something else for you,' he said, 'now I think of it. It came on yesterday's stage.'

Recalling his state of mind when the stage arrived, Seth wasn't surprised the shipment had passed his notice. 'What is it?'

'It's that tea-stuff you wanted. It's had to come from Winnipeg, over the border. I'll unwrap it for you.'

'Don't worry about that. We'll unwrap it. What do we owe you?'

'It's expensive,' said the storekeeper, looking at the invoice. 'It'll cost you three dollars.'

Three dollars was a lot to pay for a pound of tea, but it had come a long way, so Seth paid for it without complaint and took the package back to the stable.

Henry stopped grooming one of the horses that had been left at livery, to ask, 'What have you got there, Seth?'

'It's the tea we ordered from the General Store.'

'That's good news, for a change.' The second consignment of tea from Katherine in Boston was nearing its end, and that source was now no more.

Seth cut the string that bound the parcel, and unwrapped it. To keep the tea dry, the four quarter-pound packets had been sealed in waxed cotton, and a quantity of newsprint afforded extra protection for the journey. Henry took out the oilskin package, while Seth gave in to curiosity by unfolding the Winnipeg newspaper that came with it. It was two weeks old, but Seth knew so little about Canada that, whether the news was old or new, it was of little importance to him.

The news seemed generally to be less dramatic than the accounts he'd been used to reading in the *Bismarck Tribune*, but it meant nothing to a stranger, and he was about to discard the newspaper, when an official notice caught his eye. It read:

The Police Force for the North-West is Now Recruiting

We are looking for men of sound constitution, active and able-bodied, able to ride, of good character, able to read and write either the English or French language, and between the ages of 18 and 40 years.

The notice went on to say that the initial term of engagement was to be three years, and that the new police force was looking particularly for ex-cavalrymen, who must be prepared to swear an oath of allegiance to Her Majesty Queen Victoria.

'I can't see a cavalryman objecting to that,' said Seth to himself.

'Objecting to what, mate?'

Seth handed the paper to Henry, pointing to the notice, and said, 'Swearing an oath of allegiance to the Queen.' Nodding in the direction of the newspaper, he said, 'I reckon that notice found us for a reason. What do you say, Sergeant Fowler?'

Henry finished reading the notice and handed it back to Seth. 'I agree, Sergeant Campion. Let's head north.'

PART TWO

1

May 1877

Fort Walsh, Saskatchewan

The Next Stage

For the first time since their discharge from the regiment, Seth and Henry wore a uniform of which they could be justly proud. They had emerged from their training in Winnipeg as sub-constables, and each had received a special commendation. Welcome though the honour was, however, they saw it simply as an acknowledgement that they'd given total commitment, and that had always been a part of their template for life. Before long, they were to see some of it in action, and they learned rather more when Inspector Walsh paraded them and addressed them in the compound.

'Last December,' he told them, 'I took men from this fort to police the arrival on Canadian soil of a large number of Sioux Indians seeking refuge from containment and punitive action by the United States Government. I met their leader, Chief Black Moon, and learned that the Sioux Nation was weary of being hounded, and that they had come to seek Her Majesty's protection.'

At this point, Seth felt a glow of pride. He listened as Inspector Walsh continued.

'I set out the terms under which they would be allowed to remain on Canadian soil. I told Chief Black Moon that his people must obey Canadian law, that they must not make war against Canadian tribes, and that on no account must they use Canada as a base from which to attack the United States. He agreed to those terms on behalf of Chief Sitting Bull, who had not arrived, but who was expected at some future date.'

The assembled men waited to hear about the latest development.

'I have received information that Sitting Bull is now camped about sixty miles south of this fort. I intend to meet him, but not with a large force. I shall take one sergeant, three constables and two scouts. Their names will be made known. Thank you all. Dismiss.'

Seth waited for the list of names to appear, which it did the following morning. The chosen sergeant was McCutcheon, an excellent man; Seth knew one of the constables only slightly, but he was delighted to learn that the other two on the list were Constables Fowler and Campion. He heard later that Sergeant McCutcheon had recommended them both for the assignment.

＊<|৪-३|¢-3|-৪|৪＊

The party left Fort Walsh on the fifth of May and approached Sitting Bull's trail from Montana. It seemed he was heading for Pinto Horse Butte, a name that puzzled Henry, who asked Sergeant McCutcheon, 'What's a butte, Sergeant?'

'It's a flat-topped rock with sheer sides, Fowler. You'll see one of 'em soon enough.'

'They're formed by wind erosion,' said Inspector Walsh playfully. 'If you stood there long enough, you'd get an idea of how it works, but I don't think you'd get a flat top and sheer sides.'

'I hope I'd have the sense to get out of the wind, sir.'

After a few days, they noticed that they were being watched by Sioux braves, who made no move to conceal themselves, but simply sat, mounted and ever watchful. So far, however, the Indians remained in position, simply keeping an eye on the detachment.

After some time, they found themselves completely surrounded by Sioux, but they rode on until they reached an encampment, where they stopped and waited for someone to come out.

For Seth and Henry, it was a new experience. All the time they'd been in Pentecost, the Indians had kept well away from white people, mindful of the ill-feeling against them, but here they were, surrounded by Sioux braves and squaws. Inspector Walsh was speaking with a man in a glorious headdress of eagle feathers, who introduced himself as Spotted Eagle.

'There's a hierarchy of chiefs,' explained Sergeant McCutcheon. 'Spotted Eagle is one of the lesser kind.'

Walsh said, 'I wish to speak with Chief Sitting Bull.'

Spotted Eagle sent a brave to Sitting Bull's lodge, and within a very short time, the celebrated Chief appeared.

Seth had no idea what to expect, but only a look of natural dignity marked Sitting Bull out as the people's leader. In all other respects, he seemed very ordinary, quite tall, possibly middle-aged and visibly lame. He had a large nose, high cheekbones, and two dark plaits ended somewhere beneath his shoulder blades.

After dismounting and shaking hands with him, Walsh asked, 'Why have you come to Canada?'

'We come in search of peace and protection,' said Sitting Bull in surprisingly good English. 'My grandfather fought on the side of the British in the second war.'

'The War of Eighteen-Twelve?'

'Yes. After the war, the White Father told the Sioux that they could come to Canada when they no longer wanted to live in the United States. My grandfather said that to find peace we must go north to the home of the redcoats.'

'And that is what you want?'

'Yes, we wish to be British citizens.'

As they walked to Sitting Bull's lodge, Walsh explained gently that he couldn't promise citizenship, and that the likelihood was that they would have to return at some date to the USA. Sitting Bull showed no reaction, neither disappointment nor anger, but asked about the terms under which the Sioux might be allowed temporary protection.

'Everyone must respect Canadian law, you must not make war on Canadian tribes, there must be no stealing of horses or other possessions, and you must never use Canada as a base to attack the USA.' He went on to give a concise description of Canadian law, which obviously pleased Sitting Bull.

The chief nodded solemnly. 'What you tell me about the Great White Mother's law is good,' he said. 'Justice for all people. That is good.'

His remark set Seth in mind of the disgraceful way some of the inhabitants of Pentecost had treated Little Rose, and he agreed entirely with Sitting Bull.

The conference continued, with Seth's admiration for both Walsh and Sitting Bull reaching new heights. If only the latter's request could be granted, and they could be allowed to stay indefinitely. In that matter, however, Walsh's hands were tied.

In the morning, Seth and Henry were packing their bedrolls, when they became aware of a commotion. They could hear Inspector Walsh's voice very clearly. He was challenging someone, so they hurried to his side. It appeared that one of the scouts had seen three American Assiniboine braves enter the camp with five horses.

'Those horses are stolen, sir,' he told Walsh confidently.

'Are you sure, Elijah?'

'Yes, sir.'

The other scout, whose name was Lavalle, said, 'Three of them belong to Father de Corty, the local priest. One of the thieves is White Dog.'

'I've heard of him,' said Walsh. 'I gather he has quite a reputation as a warrior.'

'He's a favourite of Chief Sitting Bull,' said Elijah.

'Sergeant McCutcheon,' said Inspector Walsh, 'take the constables and demand that the thieves hand over the horses.'

Seth, Henry and the other constable, a man called Isaacs, joined the sergeant, ready to apprehend the horse thieves. Sioux were now gathering to watch the proceedings.

'White Dog,' said Sergeant McCutcheon, 'I call on you either to surrender these horses or face arrest.

White Dog muttered some message of defiance and spat on the ground in front of McCutcheon's feet. More and more Sioux joined the watchers, eager to observe the outcome of the confrontation. As far as Seth could see, their number was running into hundreds, and they were jostling with one another to gain a better view.

Inspector Walsh took charge. 'So you refuse to surrender these horses or be arrested, White Dog. In that case, I'll arrest you for theft.'

White Dog said nothing, but leered defiantly at Walsh. With so many Sioux around to take his side, he must have felt supremely confident that he could evade arrest.

'Tell me how you came to have these horses in your possession, or I'll put you in irons immediately.'

White Dog looked around him, still expecting the Sioux braves to support him. When it became obvious to him that he was alone, he said, 'I find loose. I take.'

'Even if that were true, you would have been wrong to take them.'

'Keep loose horses in America.'

Walsh looked unconvinced. 'That's not the case in Canada,' he told him.

'I not know that.'

'Well, you do now. Listen, White Dog, I'm going to be generous and say I believe you, because thousands wouldn't. Be on your way, and try to stay on the right side of the law.'

As White Dog moved off, he muttered something very darkly in his own language. Clearly, it was a threat or an insult, and Walsh was naturally angry, having just given him the benefit of the doubt.

'Say those words again with the interpreter present, White Dog.'

White Dog stared insolently.

'I'll tell you once more to say those words so that the interpreter can hear them.'

White Dog remained silent.

Angrier than ever, Walsh said, 'Withdraw those words, or I'll arrest you for threatening a police officer, and you'll return with me to Fort Walsh.' To add force to his challenge, he took a pair of leg irons from Henry and dangled them in front of the miscreant's eyes.

Eventually, White Dog spoke sullenly. 'Not mean threat. Take back words.'

It was clear that Walsh knew he was lying, but he said, 'All right, off you go, but leave the horses behind.'

Seth watched White Dog and his cronies leave the camp, bested and humbled, and he suspected that Inspector Walsh had just won the respect of Sitting Bull and the entire Sioux community. It had been a valuable lesson for the party from Fort Walsh, and an important message had gone out.

As they rode back to the fort, the inspector told everyone how pleased he'd been with their conduct, and that word of praise seemed like riches to Seth and Henry. It had been a worthwhile time, and on their arrival at the fort, they rewarded themselves again, this time by paying a visit to the store, where they each acquired, at their own expense, a Stetson with a circular, flat brim and a four-finger-pinched crown. Such headgear was yet to be approved by the high command, but on a trek such as the one from which they'd just returned, it was a big improvement, and would perform much better in sunshine, rain or snow, than the white, pith helmet issued to them.

'Them helmets are just like the ones the foot soldiers wore in India,' said Henry as they sat drinking tea, one of the many benefits of being on British soil.

'Aye, and they're welcome to 'em. Besides,' said Seth, 'it's good to be different.'

'There's one thing that's not so good.'

'What's that, Henry?'

'Being called "Constable".'

'Give us time,' said Seth. 'We'll get there. We've a way to go, yet, mind, but we'll do it, just see.'

Henry took out his boot-polishing kit and began work on boots that hadn't seen polish in days. The next day was Sunday, with church parade taken by an Anglican priest, a real bonus, even if he didn't use the Reverend Nicholls' special dismissal.

Seth joined him, working up a shine that wouldn't have been out of place in their old Punjab barracks. His thoughts, though, were not of the old days in India; he thought less often about them nowadays, and more about their new allegiance to the North West Mounted Police, as the force was, as yet unofficially, known.

As he spat on his boots and worked his pad in tiny circles to drive the polish into the leather, he wondered what their next task would be.

2

A Matter of Trust

Seth and Henry were on orderly duty and had almost finished cleaning the barrack room when Sergeant McCutcheon walked in.

'You're to report to Inspector Walsh immediately,' he said.

Seth asked, 'Both of us?'

'That's right. Everybody knows you two do everything together.'

'What's it about, Sergeant?'

'He didn't say. You'd better go and find out. Don't keep him waiting.'

To be summoned by the officer in charge of the fort was more than unusual, but he'd given an order, and it had to be obeyed. Accordingly, they lost no time in presenting themselves at his office. Seth knocked and waited.

'Come in.'

Henry pushed the door open, and they entered to find Inspector Walsh hatless, so they removed theirs and came to attention.

'At ease.'

They relaxed. Looking around him, Seth could see that the office was remarkably plain, considering the importance of its occupant.

Seth said, 'You sent for us, sir.'

'Ah, Constables Campion and Fowler. Yes, I've been very impressed by the way you've both gone about your duties since you arrived at the fort. Both Sergeant McCutcheon and I are satisfied that you're each able to act on your own initiative, so I'm giving you an assignment. You'll need a scout, so you can take Lavalle.'

'We're obliged to you, sir,' said Seth. 'We'll do our best.' He was confident of that, even though the nature of the assignment was still a mystery.

'I know you will, Campion.' Walsh got up and walked over to the large map of the province that hung behind his desk. 'Bruce McAlister, one of the trappers, was expected to return to the trading post last week,' he explained. 'One or two days overdue is not unusual, but not a week. He was on the McDonald Trail.' He traced the route with his forefinger. 'I want you to get along there and search for him. If he's alive, he'll most likely be sick or wounded, so bring him in. If you find him dead, give his remains a Christian burial and report back to me.'

Henry asked, 'What's the likeliest danger he'd face, sir?'

'Bears. Be on the lookout for them. Normally, black bears are only a problem when they're hungry, but you need to be wary of them. Have you any more questions?'

Seth looked to Henry, who shook his head. 'No, sir. We know what to do.'

'Very good.' He signed a chit for provisions and handed it to Seth. 'Draw your stores and be ready to leave by nine.'

'It's just like the old days in Calcutta,' said Seth as they left Walsh's office and walked to the storehouse. 'Campion and Fowler are back on the trail.'

'Aye,' said Henry, as ever the voice of caution, 'but it's early days yet.'

'Right enough, Constable Fowler,' said Seth, opening the store house door, 'we'll take each job as it comes.'

They drew food, water, bedding and ammunition, and saddled a spare horse for McAlister. When they mustered at nine o' clock, Inspector Walsh arrived to see them off.

'Good luck, all of you.'

'We're obliged to you, sir.'

They both saluted and made their departure with Lavalle in attendance.

They searched for the rest of the day, but when darkness came, they were obliged to pitch their tent for the night. Henry built a fire and set about frying bacon and heating pinto beans while Seth saw to the horses.

'I reckon we'll get plenty warning if there are bears hereabouts,' he said.

'Aye.' Henry served the food into three mess tins and gave one each to Seth and the scout. 'The horses will certainly let us know if anything comes calling.'

'Soon enough,' agreed Lavalle.

With that comforting thought, they scuffed out the fire and turned in for the night. As usual, a combination of a long ride and fresh air guaranteed sleep, and they spent a peaceful night. It seemed that the immediate area was not inhabited by hungry animals.

After breakfast, they broke camp and continued on their way, still hoping to find McAlister alive, if somehow delayed, and they'd ridden for most of the day through some of the most picturesque landscape the two Englishmen had ever seen, when Lavalle alerted them to a figure almost hidden in the trees.

'Blackfoot woman,' he told them confidently.

'Come out, all of you,' called Seth, 'into the open, where we can see you.'

Only one native came out of the trees. As far as Seth could make out, she was a girl or a young woman – it was impossible to guess her age – and she was certainly pretty, in a long, deerskin dress, although she seemed wary of the newcomers.

'Lavalle,' asked Seth, 'what language do the Blackfeet speak?'

'Blackfoot.'

'All right, it was a daft question. Can you find out what's worrying her?'

Lavalle spoke to the girl in a language that meant nothing to Seth, and her reply was equally obscure, but she was no less concerned.

'She was afraid at first when she saw us, Constable, but she knows where McAlister is.'

'Good. Can she take us to him?'

'Yes, I'll tell her to show us the way.'

Lavalle spoke again to the girl and she turned and pointed towards the trees. The party followed her through the forest for maybe half a mile, when they came to a small lake and a log cabin, where Seth and Henry dismounted. The girl opened the door, and Seth entered the cabin. The interior was dark, having only one, small window and the light from the opened door, but he saw the single occupant clearly enough. He was lying on the floor, and his foot and ankle were bound in cloth. He was clearly in a great deal of pain.

'Thank the Lord for that,' he said. 'Ah never thought Ah'd see a Mountie.' His Scottish accent was still prominent, and he was almost tearful in his relief.

'There's two Mounties and a scout here, Seth told him. 'We've come to find you and take you back to the post.'

'Ah'm certainly glad to see you, Constable.'

'What happened?'

'Ah put ma foot intae a gin trap, would ye believe?'

'One of yours?' It had been known to happen to careless trappers.

'No, I know where mine are. It was an old, rusty one.' Pointing to the girl, he said, 'Yon lassie's a savage, as ye can see, but she brought me here an' bound my wound with some native herb she picked.'

Lavalle spoke to him for the first time. 'You're a lucky man, McAlister. The Blackfoot girl put a herb on your wound to keep it clean and make it heal.'

'Yes,' said Seth, 'another time, you might think twice before calling her a savage.'

'Ah meant nothing by it. She wouldnae be my choice of a woman, it's true, but Ah probably owe ma life tae her.'

'It'll soon be dark,' said Henry, speaking for the first time. 'We'd best stay the night here and set off in the morning.'

'I agree,' said Seth. 'Night-time is no time for being on the trail. Lavalle, can you find out what this girl's story is, and how she came to find McAlister?'

While the two Mounties tethered the horses, and Seth built a fire in the stone hearth, the scout engaged the girl in conversation, so that, when Seth was ready, he was able to hear her story.

'Her name is Wapun. It means "Dawn". Her husband and her family turned her out because she brought disgrace on them and the tribe.'

'How on earth did she do that?'

'She is unable to bear children.'

'That's inhuman. Anyway, how do they know she can't?'

'All the time she was married, she was never with child.'

'But she can't be all that old. How long has she been married?'

Lavalle shrugged. 'Blackfoot girls are ready for marriage after their first lunar bleed.'

'They don't believe in wasting time, then. How old is she?'

The scout spoke to the girl again and procured the information. 'Twenty summers,' he reported.

'Well, I consider she's been very badly treated, so it's up to us to give her protection, and particularly after she saved McAlister's life.'

Everyone, including McAlister, agreed.

'You don't know how badly she's been treated,' said Lavalle. He spoke to the girl again, and she came to him. As she stood before him, he hauled up her deerskin dress as far as her shoulders to show them her back, which was criss-crossed with lacerations.

'Cover her up, Lavalle,' said Seth, shocked by the evidence of her ill-treatment and surprised by the crude manner of the scout's disclosure. 'She's entitled to the same respect as anyone else.' The girl crept away, ashamed of her brief nakedness.

'I'd like just ten minutes with the so-called brave who did that to her,' said Henry.

'And I'd be tempted to join in.' Seth said to the girl, 'Wapun, you've nothing to fear from us.'

She seemed not to understand, so Lavalle translated for him, after which she looked more at ease.

'Wapun,' said Seth, pointing to himself, 'Seth. Friend.' He took her hand and held it gently.

She stared at him at first, apparently at a loss to understand what he was doing.

He tried again, pointing to her and saying, 'Wapun' and then at himself. 'Seth.'

This time, she nodded. 'Sess.'

'That's near enough.' He pointed to Henry and said, 'Henry.'

'Hen'y.'

'Good girl.'

Henry took her hand as Seth had, and said, 'Friend.'

Lavalle translated, unnecessarily, as it turned out.

'Ah'm at the mercy of you all,' said McAlister, whose needs were more basic than friendship, 'but Ah havenae eaten good Christian food since Ah trod on that trap. The lassie meant well, Ah know, but a man cannae live on fruit. It isnae natural.'

'You're right,' said Seth, standing up, 'She meant well.' He left the cabin to fetch the cooking equipment and food from the horses, and then, taking water from the lake, left it for them.

McAlister was naturally delighted to be served with bacon and beans; for the other three men, it was normal camp fare, but Wapun shook her head vigorously.

'Don't give her bacon,' Lavalle advised. 'They only eat other meat when there is no buffalo, and they don't trust meat from the pig at any time.'

'How about beans, then?' Seth showed her the pinto beans, and she nodded. Everyone was satisfied, and supper continued until the horses suddenly made a familiar fluttering noise down their noses that alerted the men instantly. It was followed by squealing, the unmistakable sound of fear.

Henry asked, 'Where are the carbines?'

'Oh glory.' Seth remembered. 'They're still with the saddles.' He picked up his sabre and took his revolver from its holster.

'You won't kill a bear with revolver,' Lavalle told him.

'It's the only gun I've got.' He opened the door.

'Seth, you damned fool!'

Ignoring Henry's warning, Seth stepped outside, peering into the night. The horses were still signalling their terror, and it was his duty to protect them as well as the occupants of the cabin.

A few seconds later, he heard the sound that had scared the horses, and now, a large shape approached that was somehow darker than the night that surrounded it. Seth had heard tigers snarl in India, but the grunting and growling of the bear was no less disturbing. Its quarry was clearly the horses, and Seth placed himself between them, realising as he did so that he was no longer alone.

'I couldn't leave you to feed the bears on your own,' said Henry. 'It might have meant the end of a partnership.'

They both fired as the bear drew near, causing it to roar with agony, thus bearing out Lavalle's warning.

The bear reared up, enraged and maddened with pain, and Seth swung his sabre across its throat. Screaming, it launched itself forward with its claws extended and, as Seth lunged again, there was a deafening explosion, and the animal fell lifeless with a strip of red serge cloth between its claws.

'Sorry that were a bit close to yer ear'ole,' said Henry. 'I didn't have a lot of choice.' He held a smoking carbine in his hands. Lavalle held the other.

'That was quick work with the carbine, Henry.'

'Aye well, it's surprisin' how quick you can shift when you have to.'

'Let's move the horses closer to the cabin,' suggested Seth, belatedly aware that his left arm was wounded.

'Aye, let's get 'em away from the scent of death.'

They unhitched the horses and took them, calming them on the way, to the trees behind the cabin.

Henry picked up the carbines and took them inside.

'It was my fault,' said Seth. 'I left the carbines with the horses.'

'So did we all,' said Henry, 'so let's hear no more about it, an' let's get your arm dressed an' all.'

Seth looked down to see that his sleeve was soaked in blood.

'That's what happens when you wrestle with bears,' said Henry.

McAlister was momentarily unconscious, no doubt weakened by loss of blood.

'Sess.' Suddenly, Wapun was at his side, chattering urgently in her own language. She helped him off with his red serge tunic and tore back the sleeve of his wool vest to reveal two deep cuts, which were bleeding freely.

Henry produced a bandage, but Wapun waved it away for the moment, dressing the wounds instead with some kind of purple herbal substance that she must have laid in for McAlister's wound.

'It's what she put on McAlister's ankle,' confirmed Lavalle.

Wapun held out her hand for the bandage and used it to secure the stuff she'd placed on Seth's wounds, finally rigging a rudimentary sling.

'Thank you, Wapun.' He smiled, hoping she'd understand, and she returned his smile.

'We should take it in turns to keep watch tonight,' said Henry.

'Quite right, Henry. Bags I take the first watch, 'cause I could easily be out for the count later.'

'All right. Wapun can keep you company.' He loaded a carbine and left it at Seth's side.

'Wapun, come and sit with me.' Seth patted the bench beside him, and she understood well enough to do as he asked. 'You're a good girl, and I'm going to take care of you, but just for now, I want you to keep me awake.'

Lavalle translated, and Wapun nodded readily.

'Okay, Wapun, we'll keep watch, you and me.' He put his good arm around her and held her close. The poor girl was owed some gentle treatment. She responded by murmuring something in Blackfoot that meant nothing to him, but which sounded friendly enough.

'She says you are a brave man for fighting the bear,' Lavalle translated. 'I think you were stupid as well as brave.'

'Thanks, Lavalle. Anyway, it's sleepy time. Off you go.' He looked at the deep brown eyes beside him and relaxed as far as his pain would allow, knowing that his protégée was on hand to wake him if necessary.

❧❦❧

It was evident that McAlister's wound had rendered him incapable of mounting a horse, so Lavalle suggested they made a litter for him, to be dragged in the native fashion, behind a horse. It seemed worth a try, so they cut two long branches and created the required vehicle.

'But for my arm, I'd help you on to the spare horse, Wapun,' said Seth.

'Leave it to me.' Henry was about to help her up, but Seth checked him.

'Wrong side, Henry. Indians mount from the right.'

'Of course they do.' He took her to the right-hand side, where he gave her a leg up into the saddle.

'Right,' said Seth, holding the reins in his right hand, 'let's go.'

When they arrived at Fort Walsh, Seth was about to collapse, so Henry and Lavalle dealt with the horses while he took Wapun to meet Inspector Walsh.

'Congratulations on rescuing McAlister, Campion,' said the inspector. 'I see you've made a new acquaintance as well.'

'Yes, sir. This is Wapun. She guided us to McAlister. She'd been caring for him after his accident, and she used her native skills to treat his wound, as she treated mine.' He pointed unnecessarily to his bandaged left arm. 'Wapun has been rejected by her family and her husband, sir, because she's been unable to bear children. Not only that, she's been treated harshly as well. I decided she needed protection.'

Walsh smiled good-naturedly. 'Quite right, Campion. One of our duties is to extend Her Majesty's protection to the natives, and you're doing just that. Does Wapun speak any English?'

'Not really, sir.'

'In that case, I'll speak to the people at the trading post and ask them to give her a home there. I'm sure she'll make herself very useful.' Looking at Seth's arm, he asked, 'Tell me, what persuaded you to come to blows with a black bear?'

'It's rather a long story, sir.'

'Give me the short version.'

3

New Words, New Understanding

Two weeks went by before Seth was free to take Wapun out for a half-day. When he called for her at the trading post, she was difficult to recognise at first. Her hair had been washed and cut much shorter, and her worn deerskin dress had disappeared in favour of European clothes. If anything, though, she looked even prettier, and her beaming smile alone would have made his visit worthwhile. He held out his arms to her, but she didn't seem to understand, so he beckoned to her. When she approached him, he wrapped his arms round her and held her tight. Now she understood.

As they left the post, she looked around her in confusion.

'No horses today, Wapun. We're on foot.'

'No horses.'

'Good girl.' He took her hand as they walked, another custom that seemed unfamiliar to her, and which gave her some amusement. All the time they walked, she insisted on being as close to him as possible, even freeing her hand from time to time so that she could embrace him. The signs were that, with him as her protector, she saw herself as his new squaw, and that was no surprise at all. His heart ached at the thought of what she'd endured at the hands of her people, so that, motivated by that feeling alone, he stopped and hugged her as he had at the trading post, and she, being an astute learner, hugged him too.

After a while, the river bank narrowed and, as prospects seemed brighter on the other side, they descended to a place where nature had created a series of stepping stones. Taking her hand from his, Wapun walked easily across and waited for him, laughing when he tottered uncertainly in his field boots.

With some difficulty, he landed on the other side to be greeted by the broadest of welcoming smiles. It was almost too good to be true.

He gathered her in his arms and held her, finally kissing her on both cheeks, a gesture that clearly won her immediate approval, because she insisted on doing the same to him, leaving him to wonder exactly what the Blackfoot tribe did to demonstrate affection, if they ever did it at all.

They continued along the riverbank until the path became overtaken by the encroaching forest. There, they sat down to eat the fruit Seth had brought, and it occurred to him that he would have to do something about Wapun's table manners, the Blackfeet being somewhat basic in that respect, but he would address one task at a time.

The weather was too cold for snakes, so they were safe enough on the grassy floor of the forest. He lay down, and Wapun lost no time in taking her place beside him. 'Sess,' she said. 'Nice.' It was one of the new words she'd learned at the trading post.

'You're very nice, too, Wapun, in fact, you're lovely.' He felt a wave of protectiveness mingled with desire as he put his arm around her and kissed her forehead, her cheeks, the tip of her nose – which made her giggle – her chin and her neck, all of which gave her obvious pleasure.

'You like that, don't you?'

'Like that,' she said. 'Nice.' It must have borne no relation to her experience with her own people; in fact, he doubted that she'd ever known affection with her husband. He kissed her cheeks again. 'You're a lovely girl, Wapun,' he told her, 'and no one's ever going to hurt you again.' Gently, he let his lips touch hers. She seemed surprised, but no less compliant. Her lips parted, and he kissed her more deeply, earning a response that surprised him for its sheer wholeheartedness. Their kissing continued with her enthusiasm unabated. It was a fresh and wonderful experience for them both.

He unbuttoned her blouse, but struggled with the tight buttons of her bodice. Deftly, she took over from him, completed the task, and laid the two garments aside. Finally, she pulled her shift over her head, leaving her surprisingly generous breasts exposed.

'You're a dream, Wapun.' He kissed each breast and its neat, brown nipple and areola while she gaped in wonder at a kind of courtship that must have been akin to a new world. Her breath quickened, and she hugged Seth's head to her bosom, as if she were laying her claim.

After a while, she wriggled away to free herself of her skirts and, having rendered herself completely naked, took her place obligingly beside him again. He kissed her lips and breasts, stroking her silky thighs, until temptation afforded no further delay, and he let his fingertips explore the fine, sparse triangle of hair that beckoned enticingly.

Suddenly, she stiffened and gasped.

'Do you like that?'

'Like that,' she confirmed with another gasp. 'Nice. New sing.' It was another bit of English she'd learnt at the post. Considering her inability to pronounce his name, he could only imagine that 'sing' was meant to be 'thing'.

He played for a little longer, to her evident delight, before getting up to shed his boots, tunic and breeches, a task she made more difficult by kissing him repeatedly and impatiently. Eventually, however, it was accomplished.

'Lie down again, Wapun,' he invited her. 'Good girl.' He kissed her slowly on her lips and moved gradually downward, kissing her breasts and the cleft between them, and then her flat tummy, journeying on to her pubic mound and the fine growth that graced it, emerging briefly to ask, 'Do you like this?'

'Like this!' It was a gasp followed by several more as he indulged her further.

After some time, he retraced his journey, gradually as before, finally enjoying her delight as well as his own when he entered the luscious embrace of her vagina.

She chattered excitedly while they moved together. Her language meant nothing to him, but its sentiment was unmistakable, and her chatter became increasingly animated after a while, until she clung to him, gasping and sobbing.

He asked her, 'New thing?'

'Yes… new sing.'

'Let there be many more.' He kissed her slowly and deeply, trying not to twitch while her senses were at their most heightened.

When she was settled, he began moving again while she continued to express her wonder, using her recently acquired vocabulary. Her world was now packed full of new things.

Eventually, it was necessary for Seth to report at the fort, and for Wapun to return to the trading post. Before leaving her, he kissed her and said, 'Don't worry. I'll come again soon.'

'Soon?'

'Maybe a week or two, but I'll be back.'

'Nice.'

'As nice as nice can be, Wapun.' He kissed her again and left. Like her, he was experiencing a 'new thing', something he'd never known, but it had everything to do with her.

※※※※

He found Henry in the barrack room, polishing his boots. He looked up when he heard Seth's footsteps, and said, 'You look fair suited, Seth.'

'I am.' He looked questioningly at the boot that was currently receiving Henry's attention. It was already pristine.

'You'd best get to work on yours. We've to parade before Inspector Walsh in the morning. Something's afoot, although I don't know what, exactly. Something to do with the natives, I fancy.'

Seth removed his boots and took out his polishing kit. 'Do you remember Lakshmi in Calcutta, Henry?'

'Aye, I'll say I do. You fair lost your head over that one, I seem to recall.'

'I've lost a lot more than my head this time,' he confessed.

'It's as bad as that, eh? I could see you'd plenty on your mind this last couple of weeks.' Henry was as quick to notice such things as he was slow to mention them.

'She's under my protection, Henry. I'm responsible for her wellbeing as well as her safety, and she sees herself as my squaw.'

'How do you see yourself/'

'I'm happy with that. I keep thinking about when we met her. She'd suffered badly – the scars on her back were fresh, if you remember – but she still thought about others.'

'Aye, she looked after McAlister all right.'

'She looked after me an' all.' He remembered her dressing his wounds with something that looked like a purple daisy. She was

133

unbelievably gentle and caring. The memory of her deep-brown eyes, the windows on her soul, returned to him unbidden.

Henry gave the boot a final buffing, squinting at his handiwork. He said, 'It's a funny thing, Seth, but I keep hearing wedding bells.'

'Aye well, I'll need permission from Ottawa before that can happen, but I can't see them objecting. Can you?'

'I don't know why they would, Seth.' Henry considered the question for a moment and said, 'One thing occurs to me, though. I reckon you'd be wanting a Christian wedding?'

'Of course I would.'

'The only problem I can see is that Wapun's not a Christian.'

Seth had considered that. 'Not yet, she isn't,' he agreed, 'but that can be set in order.'

4

A Lesson From the Past

The garrison mustered in the compound and waited for Inspector Walsh to address them. Beside him stood a native chief they'd never seen before.

'As some of you know,' said the inspector, 'Chief Little Child arrived here late yesterday afternoon. He'd ridden fifty miles to tell me about an incident involving American Assiniboine warriors, who'd crossed into Canada to hunt buffalo. They set up their lodges in Little Child's Saulteaux camp and told him he answered to Crow's Dance. Little Child told them quite rightly that he answered only to me.'

As if that assertion required confirmation, Little Child nodded gravely.

'There's been some violence, property has been damaged and sled dogs have been killed. Clearly, those Assiniboine are in need of correction. To that end, I shall take a detachment of fifteen officers to make Crow's Dance see the error of his ways.' Smiling involuntarily, he went on to say, 'Crow's Dance's parting message was to the effect that if the redcoats turn up, he'll cut out my heart and eat it. I shall remind him of that when I place him in irons.' His last sentence resulted in hearty laughter from the entire garrison.

The men were dismissed, and the list of officers chosen for the assignment soon appeared on the wall of the orderly room. Seth and Henry scanned it eagerly, jostled by several of their colleagues who were equally keen to be involved. The names Campion and Fowler appeared near the top of the list.

⊕⊷⊰⧈⊷⊱⧈⊷⊕

To keep the horses fresh, the detachment broke the journey after twenty miles or so, resting them until morning.

When they reached Wood Mountain, they halted by a small butte. Darkness had already fallen, but in the moonlight, Crow's Dance's camp was clearly visible in the valley beneath them, a little over a mile away. Walsh counted a dozen men and gave them his orders. 'Remain behind at this butte, in case I need you. The rest of you, load your ammunition now and follow me.'

A narrow ravine led down to the camp, and the detachment proceeded carefully and quietly to the bottom, where Walsh gave the order, 'Trot!' He led the others to the Assiniboine war lodge, which they surrounded.

Alerted by the sudden noise, braves stumbled out of their tepees to be faced by Mounties with loaded carbines.

Walsh asked, 'Which of you is Crow's Dance?'

'I am.' The surly chief stood defiantly before him.

'Constable Fowler, put this man in irons. He's under arrest.'

Henry moved forward to manacle the prisoner. As he seized Crow's Dance's arm, he snatched it away. Henry responded by punching him hard in the midriff, causing him to jack-knife. Seth held one arm while Henry manacled the other, saying to the gasping prisoner, 'That's what happens when you forget your manners.'

Another chief, Crooked Arm, had witnessed the incident, and he chose to co-operate, so the party took the two chiefs and the men who were with them back to the butte. Instead of returning immediately, however, the detachment spent the night at the butte. Incredibly, the majority of Assiniboine had heard nothing, and slept through the night.

In the morning, Walsh sent for Louis Lavalle. 'Go down to the encampment,' he told him, 'and tell the other chiefs that I want to speak to them, here.'

'Very good, sir.' Lavalle rode down to the camp to inform the remaining chiefs about the night's events and the fact that the White Chief wanted to see them. He returned with several of them and a collection of braves, who seemed particularly angry.

Inspector Walsh stood in front of them and spoke. 'I'm taking Crow's Dance, Crooked Arm and some of the others back to the fort to stand trial. As far as the rest of you are concerned, you must never again force your will on a Canadian tribe.' He waited for Lavalle to translate his message so far, before continuing. 'You must not attack other tribes.

Under the laws of the Great White Mother, all people are free to roam. You must not stop them.'

While the scout was relaying the inspector's words, Seth saw one of the natives furtively lift a carbine. His finger was already on the trigger when he pointed it at Inspector Walsh. In that instant, Lavalle's translation was interrupted by a shriek of pain. The Assiniboine's carbine fell to the ground and he clutched his hand, which was bleeding heavily.

'I'm obliged to you, Campion,' said Walsh as Seth returned his sabre to its scabbard. 'Someone bind that man's hand, and we'll take him to stand trial with the rest.' Speaking to the Assiniboine again, he said, 'You saw what happened to the brave who was about to shoot me. You can make this as easy or as difficult as you like, but there will be only one winner, and that will be the law of the Great White Mother. Now, return to your camp and fold your tepees. You're going back to the United States.'

Lavalle finished his translation, and the natives looked to one another, still surly and resentful, but less inclined to offer resistance. The injured brave allowed himself to be manacled, his hand now bandaged. The prisoners were relieved of their weapons, and the detachment moved off.

After a while, the sergeant informed Seth that Inspector Walsh wanted to speak to him, so Seth made his way to the front of the column.

'Campion,' said Walsh, 'I haven't thanked you properly for preventing that fellow from cutting short my career.'

'There's no need for thanks, sir. In any case, someone else would have spotted him.'

The inspector gave him a grown-up look. 'You and I both know that's not true,' he said. 'What puzzles me is your deftness with that sabre. How did you learn that?'

'My what, sir?'

'Deftness, your expertise.'

'I'm sorry, sir. It was the first time I'd heard the word. I suppose I'm just used to this particular one. That's why I asked if I could keep it instead of the one that was issued to me.'

'I'm glad you did, Campion.' It was clear that he meant it.

Something had also been puzzling Seth, and now he had an

opportunity air his curiosity. 'Do you mind if I ask you something, sir?'

'That depends on what it is. Ask me, and I'll tell you.'

'Well, sir, when we've had to deal with natives who've broken the law, it seems to me you've dealt with them quite lightly, and I've wondered why that was.'

'I don't mind at all. I'll tell you, but first, let me ask you something. Why are so many of them keen to escape from the USA and to come to Canada?'

'I think it's because of the way they're being treated over there. I was very sad to hear about the Little Bighorn – Colonel Custer was our reason for being in America – but it seems the Seventh Cavalry just want to massacre them wherever they find them. To take revenge that way is wrong, but killing women and children is unforgivable.'

'I agree, Campion. We want a country where everyone feels included and where the only natural enemies are the climate and the terrain. If we punish the natives and the visitors too harshly, we'll store up resentment that will fester for generations, and we'll never achieve that dream. That lesson was taught centuries ago by Machiavelli, and some people have still to learn it.

It made perfect sense, and it was a policy that Seth could live with quite happily.

'You mentioned Custer, Campion. How did he bring you to America?'

Seth told the story yet again, ending with their arrival in Bismarck on the day the Tribune reported the massacre at the Little Bighorn.

'What did you do then?'

'We worked as farmhands and then as stablemen, and then we saw a copy of the Winnipeg newspaper and a recruiting notice for the Police Force. It was just what we'd been looking for, only we didn't know that until we saw it.'

They rode on for a few hundred yards, and then Inspector Walsh said, 'You know, Campion, you and Fowler joined for all the right reasons. I think you both have a future.'

They arrived back at the fort, where they locked up the prisoners, made sure the horses were cared for, ate and finally came to rest, tired and satisfied with their achievements over the past few days.

Seth had just removed his boots when the Orderly Sergeant came to the barrack room with a large envelope.

'One of you, take this to the trading post, will you? It's important.'

Seth held out his hand and said, 'I'll take it.' His readiness to volunteer and the obvious reason for it provoked laughter among the others, but he didn't mind them knowing about Wapun.

He fastened his boots and walked to the trading post, handing the envelope to an important-looking man in the office, after which he went in search of Wapun.

He found her in the kitchen, washing dishes, so he surprised her by greeting her with a kiss, and then removed his red serge tunic, pushed back the sleeves of his vest, and joined her at the sink.

The idea of a man performing domestic tasks clearly amused Wapun as well as catching the attention of a woman who appeared to be a supervisor of some kind.

'What are you doing, Constable?'

He turned to face her, noticing at the same time that Wapun seemed nervous of her. 'Where I come from, they call it "washing-up". What do you call it?'

'But why are you doing it at all?'

'I'm just lending a hand.'

His answer failed to satisfy her, because she said, 'These people can be lazy enough without encouragement from... others.'

'Let me tell you about Wapun. To begin with, she found a trapper with his ankle in a gin trap. Do you know what a gin trap is?'

'Not really.' She was no less defiant.

'It has jaws and teeth that come together when something or someone steps on it. It's both agonising and dangerous.'

'All right, but what has this to do with Wapun?'

'She opened the trap to free him and then took him to a cabin, where she dressed his wound and cared for him. When we came looking for him, she took us to him, and later, when I was injured by a bear, she tended my wounds as well. That's how lazy she is.'

'I didn't know that. Mind you, there's no reason why I should.'

139

'There is now, because I've just told you, and I'll tell you something else. Wapun is under my protection. If I ever hear of you treating her harshly, you'll be in very serious trouble. Do you understand?'

'All right, there's no need for that.'

'There's better not be.' He pointed a finger at her to emphasise his warning.

Clearly unable to back down completely, she shuffled her feet and said, 'She'll be all right if she behaves herself.'

'So will you. Just bear that in mind.' Passing a towel to Wapun so that she could dry her hands, he beckoned to her to follow him outside, where she embraced him joyfully.

'Sess. Lovely.' She'd learned another new word, and she followed it quickly with two more. 'No horses.'

'That's right, Wapun, but not now. I have to go, but I'll come tomorrow and we'll go for a walk.'

''Mo'ow.'

'Tomorrow.' He thought about how to explain it and fell back on sign language, feigning sleep and then wakening. 'Tomorrow.'

'Tomo'ow.' Her features relaxed into a big smile. Now that she knew what it meant, she was happy again.

'Kiss, Wapun.' He held her close and kissed her on the lips.

'Kiss.' She returned his kiss.

'Good girl. Tomorrow.'

She beamed. 'Kiss tomo'ow.'

5

A Bitter Choice

They walked along the riverbank as they had earlier, but when they came to the crossing and Wapun pointed excitedly, Seth said, 'No.' Pointing ahead, he said, 'This way.'

'Sis way.' The 'th' sound was clearly a problem for her, but it didn't matter. Nothing mattered as he led her along the bank. Henry had told him about a place further along that he'd seen. If it had been anyone else, Seth would have suspected mischief, but Henry was incapable of anything even related to it.

He saw the cabin from about five hundred yards, although it was half hidden by the trees. 'I can see it,' he said. 'Come on, Wapun.'

As they approached it, it became apparent that it was in some disrepair, although it wasn't as bad as Seth had imagined. No one knew who its owner had been. All Henry knew was that, when he'd not been seen for a while, the police had investigated and found the place empty. The man's body was found some distance away and in such a state that it had been buried almost immediately.

'Cabin.'

'That's right, Wapun.' He opened the door and looked in, thankful that it seemed habitable. The old man must have left it in a sound state before going off on his last journey.

Wapun immediately sat on the bare, wooden bed. The Mounties who'd discovered the old man must have disposed of any furnishings, although for what reason, he'd no idea, except that such items harboured fleas and germs. Now that he thought about it, he'd seen the remains of a long-dead bonfire outside.

'Kiss.'

'That's just what I had in mind, Wapun.' He bent and kissed her on the lips.

Looking at him enquiringly, she touched her lips.

'Lips.'

'Lips.' She was quick to pick up new words. She would be speaking English before long. For the present, though, she responded eagerly to his touch, and they played for some time.

When he entered her, she threw her arms around him for sheer joy. Some time had passed since his efforts were appreciated to such an extent, and it added to his already colossal pleasure. He kissed her repeatedly, saying, 'I love you, Wapun.' In all his thirty years, he'd never told anyone that, even Lakshmi in Calcutta, but he'd never really felt so deeply about anyone until now.

'I love you.' It sounded odd, the flat, northern vowel on the lips of an exotic flower of Saskatchewan, and he wondered if she had any idea what she was saying. Then she spoke again. 'I love you, Sess.' She said it with such conviction, she must have known what it meant.

'I love you, Wapun.'

'I love you, Sess.' Language wasn't really such a problem.

※⊱⊰⁂⊱⊰※

Time was an unyielding force. All too soon, it was time to return, time for them to be parted again. He really had to do something about that.

At the entrance to the trading post, he kissed her and whispered, 'I love you, Wapun.'

She whispered the same message, and that was where they had to leave it until the next time.

When he returned to the fort, he looked up Sergeant McCutcheon, who was in a hospitable mood.

'Come in and take a seat, Campion. What's on your mind?'

'I'm wondering what the drill is for getting married, Sergeant.'

McCutcheon was only a little surprised, if that. 'So you want to marry your Blackfoot girl. What's her name?'

'Wapun, Sergeant, and yes, that's what I want to do.'

McCutcheon appeared to give the matter some thought. Eventually, he said, 'You'll need permission from Ottawa.'

'Yes, I realise that, but it shouldn't be a problem, should it?'

'Well, that's not all. Before you can apply to Headquarters, you'll have to see the Chaplain and get his approval.'

'The Padre here, at Fort Walsh?'

'Yes.'

Suddenly, Seth felt more confident. 'The Padre seems like a reasonable kind of bloke. I can't see him objecting, can you?'

McCutcheon was reluctant to be drawn. 'You'll have to speak to him yourself, Campion.'

⊕⊷⊢3⊶⊳|⊰⊱⊰⊢⊷⊕

The first opportunity Seth had was after Church Parade that Sunday, and he went to the Chaplain's door and knocked.

'Come in.'

Seth opened the door, removing his pith helmet as he entered.

'Ah. Who are you? I've seen you at Holy Communion, of course, but I don't recall your name.'

'Constable Seth Campion two four eight, Padre.'

'Well, Constable Campion, why do you want to see me?'

'I want to get married, Padre.'

'In that case, take a seat.' He indicated a bare wooden chair, and Seth accepted his invitation.

'Do you really *want* to get married, or do you feel that it is expected of you?'

'I beg your pardon, Padre. I don't understand.'

'I'm asking you if the girl in question is with child.'

'No, there's no question of that.'

'Good.' The Chaplain looked cautiously relieved. 'Who is the potential bride?'

The word 'potential' meant nothing to Seth, but the Padre's question was clear enough. 'Her name is Wapun, and she's a member of the Blackfoot Tribe.'

'I see.' The look of relief on the Chaplain's face evaporated, and he asked, 'Is she a Christian?'

143

'She doesn't even know what the word means, Padre, although her English is improving.'

'Oh dear.' He pursed his lips in thought before asking, 'If her English is rudimentary, how can you be sure of her feelings towards you?'

'Her feelings couldn't be more obvious, Padre.'

'Mm, and yours towards her are quite definite, also?'

'Yes, they are.'

'Hm.' The Chaplain felt in the pocket of his cassock and took out a briar pipe, which he proceeded to fill. Eventually, he said, 'This is a difficult situation, Champion.'

'Campion, sir.'

'Yes, of course. You see, I don't really see how I can approve of your plan to marry this, er, girl, and much less, perform the Marriage Service on your joint behalf.'

It was like a blow to the stomach. 'Why not, Padre?'

The Chaplain struck a lucifer and applied it to the bowl of his pipe, thus creating a delay that Seth found highly uncomfortable. When his pipe was alight, he said, 'Why not, indeed? I'll tell you why not, Campion. It is quite simply because she is a heathen.' For an elderly and feeble-looking man, he was surprisingly vehement. 'The Marriage Service is performed in the sight of God and the congregation. It contains a series of solemn vows which both parties must understand. They must also understand that they are making those vows before God, and I fail to see how a non-believer could possibly begin to do that.'

Seth was controlling himself with some difficulty. 'She will not be in ignorance for long, Padre. I'm sure I can convert her to Christianity.'

'You can? And what qualification do you possess that enables you to do that?'

'I grew up in the Church, Padre, and I'm familiar with the Bible.'

The Chaplain applied another lucifer to his pipe and shook it until it was extinguished. 'Utter nonsense. Your best plan, young man, is to forget this girl and find yourself a decent, Christian girl instead.'

'I shan't do that, Padre.' Seth took a deep breath to calm himself. 'Let me remind you of the parable of the Good Samaritan in the Gospel According to Saint Luke, chapter ten.'

The Chaplain looked up sharply at the biblical reference, but said nothing for the moment.

'Wapun was cast out by her husband and family because she was unable to bear children.'

'She has a husband, then?'

'The Blackfeet have no marriage ceremony. The squaw simply moves into the husband's lodge. I used the word "husband" because I can't think of a better name for him.' He continued, impatient to get to the point of the story. 'Wapun came across a trapper who'd caught his foot in a gin trap. Left alone, he would have bled to death very quickly, but Wapun freed him from the trap and dressed his wound. She cared for him until we came along, and then she led us to him so that we could bring him home.' Seeing that the Chaplain was about to interrupt, he carried on. 'During the night, a bear came to attack our horses, and I had to defend them. My arm was badly torn, and Wapun dressed that, too.' Before he could be interrupted, he said, 'She'd suffered the awful hurt of being cast out by her own people, but she took pity on two strangers. Let me ask you the question Jesus asked the lawyer in the Gospel, Padre. Who was the true neighbour?'

Clearly reluctant to answer the immediate question, the Padre said, 'But that doesn't make her a Christian, for goodness' sake.'

'And not being a Christian doesn't mean that she's not one of God's children.'

'Poppycock!'

By this time, Seth was no longer concerned about upsetting the Chaplain. He was simply determined to make his point. 'In Saint Matthew's Gospel, chapter ten, Jesus says, "Are not two sparrows sold for one copper coin? But not one of them shall fall without your father's knowledge." I was taught that God loves all living things, Padre, and that includes Wapun.'

'Enough, Campion! You would do better to confine yourself to policing and leave interpretation of the Scriptures to me. Suffice it to say, I will not sanction your marriage to that girl or to any other godless barbarian.'

'In that case,' said Seth, barely controlling his temper, 'I'll have to speak to a registrar.'

'Dash it all, Campion! You will still need my approval when you apply to Headquarters for permission to marry, and that will not be forthcoming. Now, I think you'd better go before you make me angrier than I am already!'

'I'll go, Padre, because you couldn't possibly be as angry as I am at this moment.' He got up and left the cleric to fume.

Henry heard him out and asked him, 'What are you going to do?'

'I'll marry Wapun in a register office and face the consequences. If I'm to be dishonourably discharged for breaching regulations, then so be it.'

Henry shook his head. 'There must be a better way than that,' he said. 'You should think hard before you go courting a discharge.'

As things transpired, Seth was left with little time to consider his next step, because, within a very short time, he was ordered to appear before the Officer-in-Charge.

He stood at attention with his hat under his arm and waited for the inspector to speak.

'I told you recently, Campion, that you had a future in the North West Mounted Police, and now I've had the Chaplain in here, breathing fire and....' He paused, possibly seeing the metaphor as inappropriate, so Seth completed it for him.

'Fire and brimstone, sir. I thought he would.'

'He tells me you were insolent towards him.'

'That's not true, sir. I spoke to the Reverend Burford respectfully and politely.'

Walsh referred to a written note on his desk and said, 'The Chaplain says you quoted the Holy Scriptures to him as if he were ignorant of them.'

'I thought it was necessary, sir.'

He referred again to his notes. 'All this, I understand, is because he refused to sanction your betrothal to the Blackfoot girl.' He looked up at Seth and said, 'You'll have to remind me of her name.'

'Wapun, sir, but that's not what the Reverend Burford called her. He said she was a heathen and a godless barbarian. Even so, I insist that I did not speak to him disrespectfully. If he chooses to bear false witness and, in doing so, break the ninth commandment, that's up to him.'

For the first time, Walsh sounded impatient. 'I'd advise you to guard your tongue, Campion. Now, without any further outbursts, tell me what you intend to do.'

'I understand that I need the Chaplain's approval before I can even apply to Headquarters for permission to be married by a registrar, sir. In that case, I intend to go ahead without official permission. If Headquarters want to discharge me for it, that's a matter for them.'

'They won't discharge you,' said Walsh angrily, 'but you'll probably find yourself in a prison cell, and you won't be much use to your bride there. For goodness' sake, man, think about the consequences before you do yourself and your intended bride a great deal of harm.'

Whichever way he turned, Seth faced a dead end. 'In that case, sir, I'll serve out the rest of my three years and then leave the force.'

'That would be a shame, Campion, but it would be your choice. Now,' he said, picking up his notes and depositing them in the waste paper basket, 'next Sunday, you must attend Church Parade as usual, and if the Chaplain speaks to you, you must respond civilly and respectfully. Is that clear?'

'Yes, sir.'

'I imagine you'll attend Holy Communion as usual?'

'It's... possible, sir.' Actually, he had no intention of receiving the Sacrament from the Padre.

'If you don't, you'll be turning your back on God and the Church.'

'I'm turning my back on neither, sir. My faith and my allegiance to the Church are as strong as ever.' He left the rest unsaid.

Inspector Walsh breathed the sigh of a man whose arguments are spent. 'In any case, Campion, you must put this setback behind you for now, because I'm sending you, Fowler and Lavalle on another assignment, hopefully to make an arrest.'

'What's it about, sir?'

Grimly, the inspector explained. 'While you were arguing with the Chaplain, two trappers arrived here with the body of Sergeant Stevenson of "B" Troop. He'd been killed trying to apprehend a man called Keiller, the murderer of Jean-Paul Duprés.'

'So Keiller killed Sergeant Stevenson as well?'

'I'm afraid so. Stevenson was an excellent sergeant and a sad loss. He also leaves behind a widow.'

'I'm truly sorry to hear that, sir.' Seth had known the dead man only slightly, being a member of 'A' Troop, but he also knew him by reputation. 'A widow is tragedy enough, but did he leave any children?'

'Thankfully, no. His widow will receive a small pension from the Canadian Government, but she'll still have to keep herself. I don't think you need worry, Campion. She's worked for the force in the past, and there'll still be a job for her.'

'I'm glad about that, sir, at least.'

'I applaud your concern, Campion.' He rose to his feet, indicating that the interview was over. 'Find Fowler and Lavalle, and bring them to me for briefing.'

6

Dead or Alive

Henry mused, 'Dead or alive, Inspector Walsh said. There's a lot of difference between them two.'

'He also said he'd prefer him to be taken alive,' Seth reminded him. 'He wants Keiller to stand trial. As a matter of fact, the reason he chose us and not somebody from "B" Troop is that they'd be only too ready to shoot him.'

'So they want to hang him instead.'

'That'll be the judge's decision, Henry, not ours.'

The party rode on through the now-familiar landscape of the McDonald Trail, and Henry said eventually, 'A cast in his right eye and a limp isn't much of a description to go on, is it?'

'I know him,' said Lavalle. 'I'd recognise him immediately.'

Seth asked, 'What can you tell us about him, Louis?' Since the search for McAlister, he and Henry had formed a friendly association with the scout.

'Disappointed and resentful is a fair description. He hates the French and he's none too keen on the English, either. Also, don't be fooled by the cast in his eye. He's a good shot with the revolver as well as the rifle.'

'As his two victims discovered,' said Henry pensively.

Seth slowed down to negotiate a low branch. 'The important question is, where is he headed? He certainly won't stay put and wait for us to arrest him. All the time we've been on this trail, he must have been making his own journey, but where?'

'My guess,' said Louis, 'is that he'll make for Reagan's Landing to pick up food and supplies and then he'll go up-river to avoid us.'

'On horseback, I image,' said Seth, thinking of the difficulty in overtaking him.

'Keiller always travels on foot,' Louis assured him. With a quick smile, he said, 'He doesn't get along too well with horses.'

'So there's still a chance we can catch up with him,' said Seth.

Louis nodded. 'And, hopefully, we'll see him before he sees us.'

◦◦◦◦◦◦◦◦◦

On the second day, they passed the cabin where they'd found McAlister, and Seth was freshly reminded of his current problem, but a word from Louis Lavalle served as a timely distraction.

'About an hour further along the trail, there's a fork and another trail that leads to Reagan's Landing.'

'If we can get there ahead of him,' said Seth, 'we can grab him as soon as he shows his face.'

'But be careful,' Louis warned him. 'If he's got cover, he can pick us all off.' He added dryly, 'A red tunic isn't the safest thing to hide in.'

'What about you?'

Louis looked down at his buckskin jacket and breeches, and said, 'I'd still be a target, but I wouldn't stand out like you two.'

They continued along the trail for a little less than an hour, until they came to the fork that Louis had mentioned. 'Take the right fork,' he said, which they did, dependent as they were on his knowledge of the trail.

Further along the track, they came across a party of Blackfeet, and Louis spent some time talking with them.

'They say Keiller passed them early this morning, soon after sunrise. It's impossible to get a proper idea of time from them.'

'Sunrise is at about five-thirty at this time of the year, now we're heading for the fall,' said Henry.

'Yes,' said Louis. 'He may reach Reagan's Landing before we do.'

It made sense to Seth. 'He's had time to cover a lot of miles since the murder,' he said. 'Who lives there, Louis?'

'No one. There's a trading post that's not always in use, but the landing and the cabin are used by travellers as a stopping-off place, that's all.'

150

With such disturbing thoughts foremost in their minds, they pressed on.

After an hour and a half, Louis said, 'Reagan's Landing is less than an hour away. We must take care.' As they had seen nothing of Keiller, they could be fairly sure he'd reached the cabin.

Half-an-hour later, Louis stopped them. 'I think you should remove your Stetsons and red tunics. If we tie up the horses and approach the cabin on foot, he's less likely to see us.'

They took off the conspicuous garments and left them with the horses while they crept towards the cabin.

For a moment, Seth thought he saw movement at the window. 'I think he might have seen us,' he said. His suspicion was confirmed almost immediately, when a rifle shot broke the silence, and a piece of bark flew off a nearby tree trunk.

A voice said, 'I know you're there, Mountie. Come any closer an' you'll get what the other one got.'

'He thinks there's only one of us,' said Henry.

'So much the better.' Seth took out his revolver. 'See if you can hold his attention while I go round the other side.'

'Be careful, Seth,' warned Henry.

'I think that goes for us all.'

'Don't be a fool, Keiller,' shouted Henry. 'Throw down your gun and give yourself up.'

'You're the fool, Mountie. I'm not going to give myself up to you.' He punctuated his message of defiance with another rifle shot.

As Seth crawled through the undergrowth, he heard Henry return the shot. With any luck, he would be able to keep Keiller fully occupied. He moved carefully through the grass and woodland, partly to avoid being seen, but also looking out for unfriendly wildlife.

Suddenly, Keiller shouted, 'So there are two of you. Well, I can shoot two as easy as one.' There was a rifle shot, and then he called out, 'How did you like that, Mountie?'

Seth pressed on as quickly and quietly as he was able, and soon drew level with the cabin. He waited for Keiller's next shot and used the distraction to make his way to the rear of the building. Happily, he found a door with an opening, through which he was able to see Keiller's every movement. He'd discarded the rifle for the moment and, curiously, he seemed to be relying on a revolver. He shouted, 'How about that? That's both of you. Next time, I'll shoot to kill!' He fired three times in rapid succession, during which Seth was able to identify the Adams revolver. Keiller had two rounds remaining. He fired again. 'That's for you, and this is for your friend.' He fired the fifth round, and that was when Seth opened the door and stepped into the cabin.

'Drop your gun, Keiller. I know it's empty.'

Keiller spun around and, realising his revolver was empty, threw it at Seth, who ducked in time.

'Give yourself up, Keiller. You've got no chance.'

Keiller hurled himself at Seth, reaching for his revolver, but meeting only Seth's fist. Maddened, he grasped Seth's gun hand and wrestled for the revolver.

'You're a fool, Keiller.'

'And you're going to be a dead Mountie, like the other one.' He slammed Seth's hand against the doorframe, and the revolver fell from his fingers, hanging from its lanyard. Keiller reached down to pick it up just as Seth's boot connected with his crotch, and he screamed in agony.

'Listen to me, Keiller.' Seth pushed the revolver into his breeches pocket.

There was a roar of rage, and Keiller sprang at him again, pinioning him against the log wall and fumbling urgently with the pocket that held the revolver. Seth brought his knee up hard against Keiller's chin and followed it by grabbing him by the hair and hurling him headfirst against the far wall. 'Now, listen to me, Keiller.'

With another roar, Keiller came forward again, butting Seth in the stomach and then howling as Seth drove his knee into his face.

'Are you going to listen to me?' He seized Keiller again by the hair and swung him against the wall so that he collapsed, barely conscious and groaning, but with the fight drained out of him.

'Jurgens Keiller, I'm arresting you for the murders of Jean-Paul Duprés and Sergeant Edward Stevenson of the North West Mounted Police. You have the right to remain silent, but it is my duty to warn you that anything you do say may be written down and used in evidence against you.'

'Damn you, Mountie! It's a pity I didn't kill you as well as that other one.' The words emerged through a mask of blood and saliva.

'Very interesting, Keiller.' Seth kicked him hard in the solar plexus before taking out his notebook and recording the prisoner's words. Then, going to the window, he called, 'Bring the irons, Henry! Our prisoner's ready to go home.' He waited, and was surprised when Louis appeared, carrying the necessary hardware.

'Henry's wounded in the leg,' explained Louis. 'I've bound it for him, but he can't put weight on it.' As he spoke, it was evident that Louis had also been hit in the arm.

'When we get back to the horses, I'll dress that for you, Louis.' Returning his attention to Keiller, he handcuffed him and said, 'On your feet, Keiller.' Then, to Louis, he said, 'I'll watch him, Louis. Can you put the leg irons on him?'

'It'll be a pleasure, Seth.'

'Try anything at all, Keiller, and you know what you'll get.' He held him while Louis locked his ankles in irons. 'Right, Keiller, walk!'

Louis asked, 'What's the matter with his nose, Seth?'

'I think it's broken. If it is, it's no worse than he deserves.'

Keiller moaned as he shuffled beside Seth and Louis.

'You think you're suffering, Keiller. Think about the widows of the men you've killed. They're suffering a damned sight more than you are.'

He found Henry clutching his thigh where Louis had applied a temporary dressing. 'Stay there, you two,' he said. 'When I've strapped this hound of hell into a saddle, I'll bring up the horses for you.'

He dragged Keiller down the track to where the horses were innocently munching grass, and hoisted him on to the spare horse so that he lay on his stomach with his head overhanging on one side and his feet on the other.

'You can't take me like this.' Again, with the impediment of a broken nose and burst lips, he formed the words with difficulty.

'You're wanted dead or alive, Keiller. Don't put temptation my way.' Having rigged his prisoner, he untethered the other three horses and, mounting his own, took them to where Henry and Louis were waiting. Then, using proper bandages, he bound Henry's leg and Louis's arm. 'I reckon you'll be all right until the surgeon sees you,' he said.

Getting Henry into his saddle wasn't easy, but they managed, and Louis was able to mount his horse with a leg-up from Seth.

⊜⊷⊰⊹⊱⊱⊷⊜

Back at Fort Walsh, the first officer they saw was Sergeant McCutcheon.

'Well done, Campion,' he said. 'I'll get some men to take the prisoner to his cell.' He looked briefly at Keiller's face and said, 'I see he resisted arrest.'

'That's right, Sergeant.'

McCutcheon called for two constables and said, 'Get a stretcher for the constable and take both men to the infirmary.' He beckoned another two and ordered them to take Keiller to the cells. 'You'd better report to Inspector Walsh,' he told Seth.

'I will, Sergeant, but first I have four tired horses to bed down for the night. I'll report as soon as I've done that.'

'Good man.'

Seth led the horses to the stable block, where he removed their tack and made them comfortable, grooming, feeding and watering them before settling them in their stalls. Eventually, he was free to report to the inspector. He found him in his office.

'Well done, Campion,' said Inspector Walsh, shaking his hand.

'It wasn't just me, sir. Fowler and Lavalle played their part as well.'

'Yes, I've heard. I gather Keiller resisted arrest.' He smiled oddly.

'Seriously, yes, sir. He was like an animal, and I had to restrain him before I could caution him.'

'All right. If you were possibly a little thorough in restraining him, it's quite understandable, but don't make a habit of it.'

Seth was too tired to argue. Like the horses, he needed his bed. 'You'd better see my notebook, sir.' He handed the item to the inspector, who nodded understandingly. 'That will win him no favours from the judge,' he remarked. 'Before you go, tell me how you went about arresting him.'

'Fowler and Lavalle kept him occupied, sir, while I approached the cabin from the rear. I apprehended him, but he was most determined, as

154

I said, and I had to beat the fight out of him. I arrested him for the two murders and informed him of his rights, but he wounded both Fowler and Lavalle as well, so he needs to be charged with those offences. He told them he was going to kill them, sir. He only quietened down on the way home, when I threatened to finish him off there and then. I wouldn't have done that, sir, but he thought I might, and that was enough.'

Walsh laughed. 'Go and find something to eat, Campion, and then get off to bed. You've done an excellent job.'

7

Surprises

Henry's flesh wound proved more serious than Seth or Louis had thought; it required an operation followed by recuperation, and Seth was a frequent visitor to the infirmary. At other times, he took Wapun to their favourite place.

Three weeks after the arrest, they heard that Keiller was due to stand trial within days, but another piece of news affected him in a different way, however. He'd gone to the post to collect Wapun, and one of the women who worked in the kitchen took him aside. 'Keep an eye on her,' she advised. 'I found her with her head over the privy this morning, and you know what that usually means.'

Seth thanked her for the information, and spoke to Wapun about it when they were alone in the cabin. He said, 'Wapun, you were sick this morning.' By way of translation, he made a play of vomiting.

'Yes, eve'y morning.'

'When did you last bleed?'

She looked at him uncertainly. 'Last bleed?'

There was no help for it, and crudeness could not be avoided. Pointing to her lower abdomen, he asked, 'When did you bleed?'

After some thought, she answered him by showing two fingers and making a moon-shape with her hands.

'Two months, eh?' It must have happened shortly before they met, and now he thought of it, he'd been a little puzzled that nature had never interrupted their coupling. He'd supposed that it must have happened between their meetings, but now it looked as if he'd been wrong, and the morning sickness seemed to confirm the diagnosis. 'Wapun,' he said, touching her tummy gently, 'you've got a baby growing in there.'

She only half understood. 'Baby in sere?'

'A papoose,' he confirmed. It was the only word of Blackfoot he knew, but it had come in useful.

'Papoose in sere!' She was joyful, throwing her arms round him.

'Yes, you and I are going to have a papoose.' He kissed her ecstatically, experiencing the familiar ache that came when he was reminded of her vulnerability. He wanted to gather her up and hold her tight for ever, so that no one and nothing could ever hurt her again. Soon, as well, he would have two people to care for. The memory of Little Rose was a reminder of the troubles faced by half-native children, and he swore silently that no one would ever inflict their prejudice on his child.

The greatest irony, of course, was that Wapun had been excluded by her husband and her family because they believed she was unable to conceive, and now it was plain that the problem had been on his side all along. Well, it was his loss.

He would have to speak to Inspector Walsh again, but first, he and Wapun had to celebrate, which they did with great enthusiasm and for the remainder of the afternoon.

⊕⊢₃⊸│⊹Ɛ┝⊜

Inspector Walsh received him the following morning.

'Come inside, Campion.'

'Thank you, sir.'

'Stand easy. What's on your mind?'

'It's about Wapun, sir.'

'Oh? I thought we'd laid that question to rest.'

'So did I, sir.' He shuffled nervously. 'The fact is, she's now with child.'

The inspector nodded. If he were surprised, he showed little sign of it. 'Your child?'

'Yes, sir.'

'Are you sure it's yours?'

'Yes, sir. The evidence all points to me.'

The inspector relaxed his expression. 'You're not on trial, Campion,'

157

he assured him, 'and you've only done what a great many have done before you.'

'I realise that, sir. The thing is, you see, I desperately want the child to have my name, and the only way that can happen is if I marry Wapun, even in a register office.'

'I see.'

'I just wonder if you might be able to persuade the Chaplain to take a more compassionate line so that I can apply to Ottawa for permission. I'd be ever so grateful, sir.' Now that he'd thrown himself on the inspector's mercy, he waited for him to speak.

'The likelihood of the Reverend Burford changing his mind is too slender to contemplate, Campion. However, there are circumstances in which I can override his decision in such a matter, and in view of your past services to this fort and trading community, I feel that I can allow you to make that application to Headquarters. Moreover, I'll give it my wholehearted approval.' He opened a drawer and took out the relevant form. 'Fill that in,' he said, 'and return it to me.'

For a moment, Seth was unable to speak, but the words finally came. 'I'm very, very grateful to you, sir.'

'Let's just say that you've earned a little extra consideration. Carry on, Campion.'

'Yes, sir. I thank you again, sir.'

Seth's next visit was to the barrack room, to see Henry. The latter, still on crutches, asked, 'Did you have any luck?'

'Yes, I did. The inspector's given my application to Ottawa his blessing. I don't need the Padre's approval. All I need now is a ring.'

'That's the best kind of news, Seth, and a ring doesn't have to cost a lot. I don't think you'll have much bother finding one.'

'Ah well....'

'What's on your mind, Seth?'

'The ring isn't the only thing I need. I need a best man an' all. I think they call him a "witness" in a register office wedding, but he does the same job, at least as far as I can make out.'

'Oh, aye? Have you anybody in mind?'

Seth appeared to cast around for ideas, finally asking, 'You wouldn't consider doing it, would you?'

Also straight-faced, Henry said, 'Me? I'd have to think about that.

It's not the kind of lark I've got up to in the past, so I need to give it a bit of thought.'

'Let me know when you've thought about it.'

'All right.' He put his thinking face on and said, 'Seth?'

'What?'

'That was a turn-up, wasn't it, Wapun bein' with child? All that time, the Indian fella was firing blank ammunition, and he blamed Wapun for it.'

'Yes, she's like a kiddie in a hokey-pokey dairy.'

'Good. Oh, Seth?'

'What?'

'I'll do that best man thing, if you want.'

'I thought you might.'

⚉⊢⋺⊹⋉⋲⊢⊷⚉

As Sunday afternoon was a time for resting, Seth took Wapun along the river again. He'd been looking forward to telling her the news, and he couldn't wait any longer.

'Wapun, we're going to be married.'

'What is "married"?'

'I will be your husband, your *oom*. We will be *istto 't*, together.' He was delighted that he'd been able to memorise the words Louis had taught him, but he was no better pleased than Wapun, who demonstrated her happiness in her usual way.

'I love you, Sess,' she said, hugging him.

'I love you, Wapun, and I love that little mite that's growing inside you, as well.' In truth, Seth couldn't remember a time when he'd been half as happy.

When they reached the cabin, they undressed and played, as usual. After a while, Wapun knelt over him, enthusiastic about this 'new sing' she'd learned, and sighed happily as she lowered herself on to him. Seth wondered how much longer they would be able to do it without endangering the baby. He'd had no experience at all of pregnancy and was woefully ignorant of such matters. For the time being, though, he enjoyed it while he could, and each moment spent with Wapun was sheer delight, as it was for her.

159

All the time she moved on top of him, he kissed her lips and her warm, welcoming breasts, and the knowledge that, in about seven months' time, the baby would be feeding from them gave him an odd kind of added pleasure. At a rough calculation, its birthday would be in late April or early May. It was a good time to be born, with spring burgeoning all around and the warm weather reaching the province. The thought of it made him kiss Wapun again.

Before long, she grew increasingly excited. She was never reticent about her feelings and sensations, and Seth always knew when she was nearing the pinnacle of a climax.

When she was calm again, he leaned forward to kiss her, and she gasped.

'I'm sorry, Wapun. I twitched. I often do.'

'To-itst?'

'Twitch.'

'To-itst. A new sing.'

'I'm surprised you haven't noticed it before.'

'To-itst again, Sess.'

'Okay, if that's what you want.' He obliged her with a series of twitches.

'Aa-ah.'

'Is that nice?'

'Nice, yes. A new sing.'

He had to encourage her to form full sentences, so he tried, 'This is a new thing.'

'Sis is a new sing.'

'Good girl. Say, "I like it when you twitch".'

'I like it oen you to-itst.'

She was learning fast. He remembered the difficulty he'd had, learning the two words of Blackfoot that Louis had taught him. 'You're a quick learner, Wapun.' He started to move again.

'I love you, Sess.'

He drew her downward and kissed her with total commitment, because words alone couldn't express what he felt for her.

8

October

Success and Disaster

The request for approval went to Ottawa within the next few days, but Seth was destined to be otherwise occupied for a time. A detachment from the fort was to meet a column coming from the west to meet a force led by US General Alfred Terry. Together, they would meet Chief Sitting Bull and a large company of Sioux braves, who had crossed the border following the Little Bighorn Massacre. The Canadian force would be led by its Commissioner, Colonel James MacLeod. Seth was included in the Fort Walsh detachment, but Henry was still deemed unfit for active service.

The plan was to persuade the Sioux to return to the USA. The Canadian Government felt that the longer they remained in Canada, the more likely they were to come into hostile contact with Canadian tribes, and there was also the risk of their hunting the buffalo to extinction, so that they, as well as the native Indians, would have to be fed out of the public purse. It was widely known that the Sioux were reluctant to leave Canada, so it would be a delicate matter for the Canadian and US forces to handle.

The detachment left the fort on a cold and cheerless morning, when the breath of men and horses was marked by tiny clouds of vapour that dissipated quickly in the gentle breeze.

After an uneventful ride, they reached the border, where General Terry had camped with a large body of cavalry, and after some discussion, Colonel MacLeod ordered the Mounties to escort General Terry and his staff back to Fort Walsh, where the Sioux had already gathered.

Louis Lavalle, who had been privy to the discussion, told Seth what he'd overheard.

'The Americans wanted to know how such a small number of Mounties can keep our Indians in order. Colonel MacLeod told him that the natives respect the authority invested in us by Queen Victoria, and that they're generally law-abiding.'

'I reckon he must be feeling quite envious, Louis.'

'And nervous. The Sioux we're going to meet at Fort Walsh are the ones that massacred Custer and his men. He thinks they could be thirsty for more white men's blood, and his cavalry still feel that they have a score to settle with the Sioux. If the situation turns nasty, we could be caught between the two.'

With that disquieting thought, they rode with the escort back to Fort Walsh.

When they arrived, they were ordered to remain outside the fort, where the Sioux were camped. Just a glance and a guess at the number of braves told Seth that if they were to prove hostile the outcome would be too awful to contemplate.

'We're to stay here until we're relieved,' Sergeant McCutcheon told them. 'Just stay calm and don't look impressed when they start capering and posturing. I've been talking to one of the Sioux interpreters, and he says they put on quite a show when they want to scare the wits out of the other side.'

Seth asked, 'What's happening in Fort Walsh?' He'd seen the American generals enter the fort with a number of Sioux chiefs. They seemed a curious mixture.

'They're having a big conference. Frankly, I think the Sioux will need a lot of persuading to return to America, but that's what the Government wants them to do.'

A stranger with the unmistakable appearance of half-native ancestry rode up to them and greeted Louis Lavalle.

'This is Blue Jake,' said Louis. 'He's a Sioux interpreter.'

Seth and the sergeant shook hands with him and introduced themselves.

'You're going to see some war dances tonight,' said Blue Jake. 'They'll try to impress you with a show of force. Just keep a poker face and hope that the older chiefs talk some sense into them.'

Louis was watching some of them paint themselves in preparation. He asked, 'Do you think some of these braves really would be inclined to attack the fort?'

'Yes, they would. They'd really like to rid the continent of white people altogether, but the older chiefs know it would be a mistake to start a war against the whites.'

Seth was watching in fascination. One of the Indians was covering his body in black paint.

'That's Rain-in-the-Face,' Blue Jake told him. He had an old grudge against Custer, and he claims the credit for killing him.' Quite unnecessarily, it seemed, he added the information, 'He's a bad man. See that coup stick he keeps waving?' The Indian in question had broken off several times from painting himself, to show something to his nearest neighbours that resembled a knobkerry hung with objects that were hard to make out, although they looked quite grisly. 'That's his coup stick, and the things hanging from it are the scalps of his victims.' Turning his horse away, he said, 'I have to go into the fort and relieve the other interpreter.'

'It's been nice meeting you,' said Seth, and Sergeant McCutcheon voiced his agreement.

Louis was still watching Rain-in-the-Face, who was now applying white paint to his limbs, possibly with the intention of making himself resemble a skeleton. 'He's going to look like the very devil,' he observed.

'I think that's the idea,' said Sergeant McCutcheon. 'Anyway, I must leave you. I have to make sure the rest of the detachment is prepared for the spectacle.'

The Mounties had to be satisfied with pack rations for the time being, but they were able to boil water on their camp fires to brew tea, which always had the capacity to put fresh heart into them whether they needed it or not.

Soon, the drumming began, and with it the dancing. Each brave wore warpaint and carried a lance or a tomahawk, Rain-in-the-Face, now resembling a fiendish skeleton with the addition of buffalo horns attached to his headdress. He carried only his coup stick, which he held up for everyone to see, before brandishing it before the line of seemingly dispassionate Mounties. He looked, as Louis had prophesied, 'like the very devil', and it called for masterly self-control for the detachment to maintain its poise.

Eventually, the gates of the fort opened, and Sitting Bull, together with his most senior chiefs, re-entered the Sioux encampment. At the same time, a relief detachment took over quietly from Seth and the others, who returned to the fort to brush down their horses before getting some much-needed sleep.

The next morning saw the Sioux breaking camp, and the news from Blue Jake was that they were moving north to set up a more permanent encampment. Inspector Walsh paraded them to tell them more.

'The conference was unsuccessful,' he said. 'Not surprisingly, the Sioux have no intention of returning to the USA, at least for the time being, and that means that they will have to be watched carefully.' Taking a folded document of some kind from within his tunic, he said, 'Colonel MacLeod has asked me to read this letter to you, and let me say that I wish to be associated with his remarks. He says, "My Dear Walsh, I was both impressed and delighted by the conduct of your men last evening. They retained their composure in the face of blatant and deliberate attempts on the part of the Sioux visitors to intimidate them, and I cannot praise them highly enough. Unfortunately, I have to leave early this morning, or I should have communicated my approval to them directly. In this case, however, I have decided not to disturb their much-needed and well-earned sleep. Kindly read this letter to them on my behalf. You have a body of men of whom you can be justly proud." The letter is signed, "J. F. MacLeod, Lieutenant-Colonel, Commissioner of the North West Mounted Police." ' Returning the letter to his tunic and casting his eye around them, he said, 'Each of you behaved, as Colonel MacLeod said, with perfect discipline, and I am proud of you all. Dismiss.'

The Sioux set up their encampment at the foot of Old Baldy Peak to the north-west of Fort Walsh, and Seth's detachment, led by Sergeant

McCutcheon, naturally made camp a short distance away, from which they were able keep the visitors under scrutiny.

'I don't trust them, and neither does anyone else,' said Sergeant McCutcheon, handing his field glasses to Seth.

Seth had often seen field glasses used by officers in the Hussars, and then by senior officers in the NWMP, but this was the first opportunity he'd had to try them himself. He trained them on the Sioux encampment, surprised and impressed by the magnification.

'Turn the wheel in the middle to bring them into focus,' prompted the sergeant.

'This is a grand thing to have,' said Seth.

'Have you never used them before now?' The sergeant sounded surprised.

'This is the first time,' said Seth, surveying the encampment again and relishing the sudden advantage that the magnification offered.

'And you're an old soldier, too.'

'Field glasses were like watches, Sergeant. Only officers could afford them.'

'These belong to the North West Mounted Police,' he said. 'Let me know when you want a closer look at the Sioux. I prefer to keep those hell-hounds in the distance.' He turned to peer to the south-east and said, 'We've been here fourteen days to the day. Our relief should be here soon.' Taking the field glasses from Seth, he said, 'Now, that's one body of men I'd like to see at close quarters.'

His wish was granted that afternoon, when the relief detachment arrived, and McCutcheon was welcoming them when Sergeant Nairn interrupted him.

'I'm sorry, McCutcheon, but I have to ask if your men have been vaccinated against smallpox in the last three years.'

'I'll find out, but what's the problem?'

'There's an outbreak at the Trading Post. So far, Fort Walsh hasn't been affected, but we can't be too careful.'

Accordingly, Sergeant McCutcheon gathered his detachment and asked, 'Is there any man here who hasn't been vaccinated against smallpox in the past three years? If you haven't, raise your hand now, so that I can see you.' He waited, but no hands went up. He went on to say, 'While we've been away, there's been an outbreak of smallpox at the Trading Post. So far, it seems, they've managed to contain it, but no one will be allowed to visit the post until the Surgeon has pronounced it safe.'

Seth's fears were naturally for Wapun, who couldn't possibly have been vaccinated, and his first inclination would have been to isolate her by taking her to the cabin and bringing food to her there, but if he wasn't allowed near the post, he was helpless.

He rode back to Fort Walsh with the detachment, in a torment of fear and suspense.

❦

He'd groomed Dan, his horse, and was picking his hooves when Henry limped into the stable block and found him.

'Na then, Henry.'

'Na then, Seth.' It was the way they'd always greeted each other, without fuss, but in complete accord.

'They say nobody's allowed near the post.'

'That's right, Seth.' Henry seemed unusually subdued.

'How can I find out about Wapun?' He didn't expect Henry to know that any more than he did; it was no more than an expression of the utter hopelessness he felt.

'I'm sorry, mate.'

'I know, Henry. Nobody can answer that question.'

'I'm saying that I'm truly sorry for your trouble, Seth.'

Seth looked at him blankly. Eventually, in an tortured whisper, he asked, 'Are you saying she's...? Are you saying... I've lost her?'

'Yes, mate. That's why I'm sorry. She was among the first to go.'

Seth closed his eyes and lowered his head in the indescribable agony of grief. Wapun had been under his protection, but he couldn't protect her against smallpox.

After some time, Henry said gently, 'You'll find her on this side of Fever Hill. One of the burial detail told me. Her grave's marked, but the Padre wouldn't let her have a cross. The ring you gave her is with her belongings at the post.' Almost as an afterthought, he added, 'I picked some flowers and put them on her grave.' Receiving no response, he said, 'Give me that hoof pick, Seth. You can leave the rest to me.'

166

'No, Henry.' Seth patted the horse's fetlock, the prompt for him to present his hoof. 'I won't neglect Dan. None of this tragedy is of his making.'

When he was satisfied that the animal was comfortable, he fashioned a cross, using timber from the old stable railings, perforating two pieces with a red-hot iron and fastening the horizontal to the upright with a wooden peg. With that done, he took the path to the starkly-named Fever Hill, where, after a little searching, he found a mound of fresh earth marked with a crude wooden plaque that read, *Wapun, Native Worker.* Henry's flowers lay beside it, as if in innocent apology for such a casual dismissal.

For some time, although he had no idea how long, he knelt beside her grave, at first in hopeless misery and then, as he gradually assembled his thoughts, in prayer. Eventually, he took out his clasp knife and worked on the cross, painstakingly carving his own tribute. The sun was almost set by the time he'd completed his task, but he could still read the message clearly. In any case, he knew it from memory. It read, *Here lies Wapun, 1856 – 1877, beloved of Cst. Seth Campion. Now in the arms of Jesus.* If the Padre wanted to raise his objection to that or to the cross itself, he would find the process unpleasant indeed.

Slowly and with a leaden heart, he bade farewell to Wapun and returned to the fort.

9

Two Years Later

Care and Respect

As the west was opened up to settlers, 1879 saw a massive recruiting drive by the North West Mounted Police, and the influx of so many new constables prompted the promotion of many serving officers.

'Inspectors have become superintendents,' Walsh told Seth and Henry, 'sergeants are also being promoted and, as experienced and valued constables, you are both promoted to the rank of sergeant. Congratulations, Sergeants Campion and Fowler.' He shook hands with them both.

'We thank you, sir,' said Henry. 'This means a lot to us.'

'We're very thankful, sir,' said Seth. 'May we congratulate you on your promotion? If I may say so, sir, it's highly deserved and popular with the men.'

'Hear, hear, sir.' Henry was quick to associate himself with Seth's good wishes.

'Why, thank you both. Now,' he said, referring to a document on his desk, 'your exemplary service as constables makes it all the harder for me to release you, but I must. You are both posted to Lower Fort Garry as instructors with immediate effect.' He corrected himself by saying, 'Well, almost immediate. You have the remainder of the day to take your leave of old friends and colleagues, but then you will be taken to the railway station in the morning. Congratulations again, and the best of luck to you both.'

The journey to Winnipeg occupied several days, but they were familiar with the route, as they had received their training, like many others, at Lower Fort Garry prior to their posting to Fort Walsh. The journey was picturesque in the April sunshine.

They were approaching Winnipeg when Seth felt prompted to say, 'When you think of it, Henry, we've travelled a lot further than most Englishmen.'

'I suppose we have.'

'We must have. I mean, fair enough, a lot of men have been to India and back, but we crossed the Atlantic, we travelled as far west as Bismarck and Pentecost, then north to Winnipeg and… everywhere else, all inside three years.'

'And we've used the time well,' said Henry. 'At least, we've no call to be ashamed of anything we've done.'

Seth nodded. 'We did what we could.' He lapsed into memories of Pentecost, of Mrs Norton and her family, of their contribution to law and order in Pentecost, of Little Rose and, more recently, Wapun.

'Don't brood, Seth,' said Henry, 'if brooding's what you're at. It never did a scrap of good.'

'How did you know what I was thinking?'

'You had that look. You have to remember I've known you a long time. Anyroad, just keep telling yourself that you brought a lot of joy to Wapun's life before the smallpox took her. After all her troubles, just knowing she was with child must have been happiness enough, an' you gave her a lot more besides.'

'Aye, right enough.' Henry was the only person allowed to mention Wapun, and his rough wisdom was never out of place.

Before long, the train pulled into Winnipeg Station, jolting both of them back into the present. They took down their kitbags and joined the other passengers, ready to alight and begin a new episode in their lives.

Outside the station, they looked around at the unfamiliar townscape. Any town or city was a novelty, although a disconcerting one, and they were relieved when they saw a single constable holding the reins of a horse-drawn brake. Seth hailed him.

'Are you going back to Lower Fort Garry, Constable?'

'Yes, Sergeant. That's if you are Sergeants Fowler and Campion. If you are, I've been ordered take you to the fort.'

'I'm Campion, this is Sergeant Fowler, and who are you?'

'Constable Garvey, Sergeant.' They shook hands, and Seth and Henry climbed aboard the brake.

On their way to the fort, they learned that their predecessors had been posted unexpectedly elsewhere. It was happening all the time.

Seth asked, 'What's your job at Fort Garry, Constable?'

'I work in the Orderly Office, Sergeant. It's an important job, but it's easy to be overlooked in there.' Clearly, Garvey was nursing a grievance.

'What's that on your back, Garvey?'

Garvey hesitated, but he'd been asked a question and he had to answer it. 'It's only that two sergeants, such as Snell and Barnes, stand a good chance of being promoted, while I can work as hard as I like and be forgotten, Sergeant Campion. That's all.' His expression was quietly defiant.

Henry spoke for the first time. 'You don't seem to rate those two very highly, Garvey.'

'It's not for me to comment, but you're taking over from them, Sergeant. You'll see for yourself how they've left things.'

The conversation went no further, which was just as well. In any case, they had arrived at Lower Fort Garry, where they thanked Garvey for his services and climbed down.

'The Orderly Office is across the Parade Ground, Sergeants,' said Garvey helpfully.

'Thank you, Constable. We can remember it.' They crossed the Parade Ground to report to the Commandant, Superintendent Russell, whom they found conveniently in his office, next to the Orderly Office. He was about forty, and very serious. Both men came to attention and saluted.

'Sergeants Campion and Fowler reporting for duty, sir,' said Seth.

'Good. Which is which?'

'I'm Campion, sir.'

'I'm Fowler, sir.'

'Glad to meet you.' He shook hands with them both. 'I hope

you're going to be an improvement on Barnes and Snell. I had them posted as soon as I could, but you two come strongly recommended by Superintendent Walsh.'

'We try to give satisfaction, sir,' said Seth.

'That's what I've been told.' Eyeing them both sharply, he asked, 'What have you noticed since you arrived here?'

It seemed an odd question for two new arrivals, but Seth was ready, as usual. 'The tack on the horses that brought us from the station hadn't seen saddle soap for quite some time, sir.'

'The sentry on the gate was improperly dressed, sir,' said Henry.

'In what way was he improperly dressed?'

'His boots were in need of blacking, sir, his buttons lacked brightness, and his creases lacked sharpness.'

'Excellent.' They were evidently the right answers. 'Sergeant Fowler, you will be responsible for drill and weapons training. Sergeant Campion, your remit will be horsemanship and horse husbandry.'

'Very good, sir.'

'Very good, sir.'

The superintendent called, 'Garvey?'

'Yes, sir?' The constable's head appeared in the doorway.

'I want you to show Sergeants Campion and Fowler to their quarters and then show them around the fort. I'm sure you can answer any questions they may put to you.'

'Very good, sir.'

'Very well. Dismiss.'

They knew the layout of the fort from the time they'd spent there, but it was important for them to see it in use. They followed Garvey to the barrack block, where he pointed out two single rooms, each at the end of a long barrack room, and produced name cards for insertion into the brackets on the doors. Henry, however, was more interested in the nearest barrack room, which he inspected briefly.

'You know, Garvey,' he said, 'apart from the Commandant, you're the smartest thing in this academy. That barrack room is a disgrace.'

'Yes, Sergeant. Some men need a person in authority to remind them about self-pride. Happily, I don't.'

Seth asked, 'Have you served in the Army?'

'Yes, Sergeant,' he said proudly, 'the Twenty-First Lancers.'

'It shows.'

'Thank you, Sergeant.' He appeared thoughtful for a second or so, and then asked, 'May I speak plainly?'

'We hope you will,' said Seth.

'It's just that Sergeant Barnes and Sergeant Snell tried to be popular with the recruits, but they only succeeded in losing their respect. That's how I see it, anyway.'

'And that also shows,' said Henry.

Seth asked, 'Where are the recruits now?'

'They're in the classroom.'

'At least they're doing something useful.'

Garvey showed them around the fort, including the stable block, where Seth inspected several of the horses and their bedding. He asked, 'What's the building behind this one?'

'The Administration Block. They have women working there, so they keep it separate from the main part of the fort.'

'I wonder,' said Seth, 'if the women in the office have a keen sense of smell. If they do, I pity them.'

Henry nodded in agreement. The stench of badly-kept horses would be most unpleasant. He asked, 'How long have things been like this?'

'Only two months, Sergeant. That's how long Barnes and Snell were here.'

'It just shows,' said Seth, 'how quickly things can get out of hand.' Inclining his head towards the classroom, he asked, 'When's the class due to dismiss?'

Garvey peered through the doorway at the clock on the Chapel tower and said, 'In just a few minutes, Sergeant. It's almost four o' clock.'

'Good. Garvey, go over there and tell them that as soon as they're finished, they're to come to the stable block at the double. No arguments.'

'Very good, Sergeant.'

As he left the stable, Henry said, 'He's a useful man to have around.'

'Yes,' said Seth, 'but don't forget that a man who feels he can talk freely about those two might just as easily talk about us. I'm not saying he would, but it's worth bearing in mind.'

'As usual, Seth, you're thinking ahead of me.'

Seth smiled and said, 'That's what I'm here for, Henry.'

The sound of boots approaching at the double alerted them to the arrival of the recruits. Garvey stood aside from them, looking uncomfortable.

'All right, Constable Garvey, we won't keep you. Thank you for your help.'

'I'm pleased to have been of assistance, Sergeant.'

As Garvey retreated gratefully, Seth faced the recruits, who were exchanging looks and possibly wondering what was going to happen next. Seth was happy to end their suspense. 'Fall in, three deep,' he told them. He waited for them to shuffle into three ranks, and ordered, 'With intervals, by the right, dress!' At the appropriate moment, he ordered, 'Class, shun! Class, stand at... ease! Stand easy.' Surveying them bleakly, he said, 'That was as untidy as everything else I've seen since I arrived here. I'm Sergeant Campion and this is Sergeant Fowler. You can tell us apart quite easily, but one thing we have in common is our disgust at the state of this stable block, and for what it's worth, the horses agree with us.' There was a burst of hastily-stifled laughter, and Seth continued, addressing a recruit in the front rank. 'When was this stable last mucked out?'

'Yesterday.'

'Yesterday, *who*?'

'Yesterday, Sergeant.'

'That's better, but it's a terrible thing to own up to. Horses produce large quantities of alkaline air every day. It smells even fouler than the dung you've allowed to remain in their stalls.'

The same recruit said, 'We were told to muck out every other day, Sergeant.'

'Who told you to do that?'

'Sergeant Snell, Sergeant.'

'Forget Sergeants Snell and Barnes. They have been sent away in disgrace. Now, bring out the horses, and muck out the stable before I get really angry.'

He and Henry waited until the task was complete and each stall contained fresh straw, and then he paraded them again. 'None of these dumb animals can feed itself in a stable, muck out its stall, groom itself or check whether its teeth or hooves need attention. They need you and you and you and you and you....' He continued down the line, addressing each recruit. 'You are the only help they have. Treat your horse with care and respect, and he will serve you faithfully, but neglect him, and I will heap misery on your shoulders in a way you'll never forget. What?' He asked the question of a recruit who had raised his hand.

'Can we go to supper now, Sergeant?'

'No, you can go to supper when every one of these horses has been groomed and checked. Now, get on with it!'

When he and Henry had inspected the last horse and found its condition satisfactory, he said, 'You'll all have formed your own ideas about me, and I couldn't care less what you think. I was called every name under the sun in the Eleventh Hussars, but now I'm proud to serve in the North West Mounted Police, and I intend to make you just as proud. For that to happen, though, you must forget your slipshod ways and make every effort to become disciplined and thorough in your work. We've inspected the stable and the horses, and I have to say you've made a good start. Keep it up. Class, turning right, dis-miss!'

Henry watched them go and said, 'They're all in a state of shock.'

'Aye,' said Seth, smiling at the thought, 'and they've still to have their first session with you.' He took a final look at the stable, now transformed, and said, 'This place needs of a lot of attention, but what it needs most of all is you and me, Sergeant Fowler. I think we came at the right time.'

'I can't disagree with that, Sergeant Campion.'

10

A Fleeting Recurrence

The ability to ride was a prerequisite in recruitment, but the new men quickly demonstrated that they were not all accomplished in the skill. Moreover, there were those who knew dangerously little about horses. Such an example occurred on the third morning, when Recruit Bryant reported that his horse was lame.

'Bring him out here,' Seth told him, 'and walk him up and down.'

Accordingly, the recruit disappeared into the stable and was gone for several minutes, so Seth investigated.

'He won't come out, Sergeant.' Bryant was hauling on the reins, but without success.

'Stop that and come over here, out of the way,' said Seth, walking into the horse's stall. 'Now,' he said to the disobedient animal, 'what's all this about?' He patted each fetlock in turn, saying, 'Hup,' until he'd identified the problem. 'He's about to cast a shoe,' he told Bryant, 'nothing more than that.'

'He still won't come out, Sergeant,' insisted Bryant.

Seth spoke gently to the horse, saying, 'Na then, lad, let's go and get you a new shoe, eh?' Then slapping the animal on the rump by way of gentle encouragement, he said, 'Walk on.' The horse walked beside him and they left the stable. Seth halted him in front of the class and said, 'A quick look and a few paces will tell you whether the horse is lame or about to cast a shoe, but there are other things you must learn from this instance. The first is that you must never, and I mean *never*, let a horse learn that he's stronger than you are. Fortunately, it will never occur to him unless you challenge him to a tug o' war, as Bryant did this morning.' He waited for the laughter to stop, and said,

'Mind you, I don't think Bryant's horse learned that lesson, being as distracted as he was at the time by pain. Bryant was holding the reins here,' he told them, pointing to a place only two inches or so beneath the horse's mouth. 'When you did that, Bryant, the jointed snaffle would dig into the roof of his mouth. I shan't demonstrate it on you, because we haven't got a snaffle small enough, and I think you've learned your lesson, anyway. I'm sure I won't see you do it again.'

'No, Sergeant.'

'All right,' he told the shamefaced recruit, 'Walk him over to the forge and ask the farrier to shoe that hind hoof.' He was pleased to see Bryant grasp the reins at a reasonable length. At the command, 'Walk on,' the horse complied, earning the ironic applause of the rest of the class.

For the next six weeks, when Henry wasn't drilling the recruits or training them in marksmanship and use of the sabre and lance, Seth worked on equitation, improving their horsemanship beyond their own expectations and enabling them to form a solid working relationship with their horses. Finally, he was able to parade them before the Commandant, who watched them ride, arms folded, over the jump course, controlling their horses solely with the leg.

'A fine display, Sergeants Fowler and Campion,' said Superintendent Russell.

They thanked him, relieved and delighted that the men had performed as well as they had.

'Timely, as well,' said the Commandant. 'We're expecting a visit from a United States Senator next week. He's looking at how the North West Mounted Police are trained, and I know he's going to be impressed with the work you two have done.'

'The Americans would certainly benefit from a well-trained police force, sir,' said Seth.

'We lived there for a while,' Henry told him, 'in a town where the law was enforced by one man.'

'Until he died,' said Seth.

The Commandant was astonished. 'Who upheld the law then?'

Seth shrugged modestly. 'We did, sir, and then they got a new marshall. That was when we came to Winnipeg.'

'Amazing. Well, you'll be able to tell the senator about it.' As an afterthought, he said, 'He's bringing his wife, although I don't know what there is here that's likely to interest her.'

***

Preparations for the senator's visit began almost immediately. It was important to the Commandant that the American visitor gained the best possible impression, as Lower Fort Garry represented, for the purpose of the visit, the Dominion of Canada. For their part, Seth and Henry had no idea what a senator was or did, but he sounded important and, as smartness and cleanliness were second nature to them both, they set about ensuring that the fort would be immaculate.

They rehearsed the reception until it became as familiar as a lifelong habit. Consequently, when the American coach was sighted, the recruits were lined up at the main gate, dressed and ready.

As the coach pulled into the gateway, Henry, who had been responsible for foot drill, called the men to attention and ordered them to present arms to their visitor, who looked most impressed by the immaculate recruits and the line of gleaming sabres.

He was borne away by the Commandant, no doubt to be offered the fort's hospitality, but of his wife there was no sign.

The mystery was uncovered when Superintendent Russell brought the visitor to the stable block. Senator Haines was a young man with carefully-groomed whiskers and an expensive-looking suit with a frock coat. Introductions having been made, he said to Seth, 'You know, Sergeant, my wife would have loved all this.' He was looking at the plaited straw around the entrance to the stable. 'Is this a regular feature?'

'It is at this fort, Senator. Sergeant Fowler and I served in Prince Albert's Own Eleventh Hussars, and we finished our stables like this as a matter of routine.'

'I see.'

The Commandant asked, 'Is your wife unable to be with you, Senator?'

'No, she came along,' he said with a touch of impatience. 'She's at the hotel, trying to decide what she's going to wear when we dine with you this evening.'

'It was ever a lady's dilemma,' said Russell sympathetically.

'She wants to be with me when your trainees demonstrate their horseback riding skills, Captain.'

'Superintendent, actually, Senator, and I'm delighted to hear it.'

The visitor was apparently absorbing the correction, because he said, 'What strange ranks you British have, Superintendent.'

'As they say in the French community, Senator, *autre pays, autre moeurs.*'

'Do they really? Are they still allowed to speak French in this country?'

'It's their right, Senator.'

'You surprise me.'

Seth was still getting used to the American term 'horseback riding'. He wondered what other kinds of riding they got up to. In all, the American visitor failed to impress him as he continued to conduct a tour of the training areas, during which he was required to answer a number of questions that demonstrated the senator's ignorance of police training. As he turned in, that night, he wondered if Mrs Haines would be as condescending and ill-mannered as her husband. Those failings sometimes went hand-in-hand with privilege, although that was thankfully not always the case.

—————

On the following morning, Seth and the recruits were lined up in readiness beside the jump course. The senator and his wife were late, but that was no surprise. If one thing were certain, however, it was that they would be impressed by the display.

Eventually, the Commandant arrived with Senator Haines and, behind him, presumably, Mrs Haines, who wore a wide-brimmed hat that obscured her face at its current angle.

The Commandant nodded, and Seth signalled the recruits, by raising his hand, to make ready. When he was satisfied, he lowered his hand and the first rider entered the course, breaking into a canter. He took the first jump, and the second rider set off, to be followed by the third and the fourth, and so on. The whole class going over the jumps with their arms folded and in complete control was a remarkable spectacle, and occasional squeals of appreciation from Mrs Haines suggested that she was highly impressed.

With the ride completed, the jumps were dismantled and tent pegs were pushed into the ground in preparation for the next display. The recruits picked up their lances and waited for Seth's command. His hand descended, and the display of tent-pegging commenced, provoking yet more exclamations of delight from Mrs Haines.

At the end, the senator took her arm and made to walk away, but she shrugged him off. 'No,' she said, 'I want to talk to the man who trained them to do all of that.' She walked purposefully towards Seth, and was about to address him, when her mouth hung open in surprise. 'Seth,' she said incredulously.

In that moment, he recognised her. 'Katherine, I don't believe it.'

The senator was caught completely unawares, and he asked, a little unnecessarily, 'Do you know this man, Katherine?'

'Yes, Lester. Seth and I are old friends. We met when Ida and I were visiting Aunt Emily in Pentecost. Seth, how are you, and how did you come to be a redcoat policeman?'

'It's a long story, Katherine.' He felt a little awkward, addressing her by her Christian name, but she'd already explained that they were old friends.

'Sergeant Campion,' said the Superintendent, 'I think you'd better allow Mrs Haines to re-join the party.'

Seth was about to respond, when Katherine said impatiently, 'I've just met an old friend from way back, and I want to know what's been happening to him.'

'Perhaps if you walk back with us, Sergeant,' said Russell, no doubt reluctant to disappoint Katherine.

'That's probably the best idea,' said Haines.

Seth called to the recruits, 'Well done, all of you. Dismiss.'

Katherine took Seth's arm and waited until the rest of the party were some distance away.

'I don't think your husband's very pleased, Katherine.'

'Forget him, he's a stuffed shirt.'

'But are you happy with him?' As he spoke, he wondered if he'd gone too far, but Katherine seemed untroubled by the question.

'He's rich, and he gives me a lot of freedom. What have I to complain about?' She dismissed the subject out of hand and asked instead, 'But how did all this happen?'

'Henry and I wanted to do something different, and when we saw that the North West Mounted Police were recruiting, we came north and joined them. It's the perfect life for us.'

'So Henry's here as well.'

'We do everything together,' he reminded her.

'Oh, I can't wait to tell Ida.' Still overjoyed, she took in the red, serge tunic and the breeches with their gold stripe. 'You're every inch the knight errant I said you were. Do you remember that?'

'Yes, I do.'

'And has Sir Knight found his lady?'

'I thought I had. In fact, I did. Yes, I found her, but I lost her two years ago, to smallpox.'

'Oh, Seth, I'm so sorry.' She was clearly affected by the news, and Seth was reminded of her quick changes of mood.

'It's getting easier, Katherine.'

'Life can be so cruel. I remember how awful it was when we had to go home to Boston and leave you and Henry.' They were approaching the fort, and the others had stopped and were waiting. 'I'm not going home until I've seen you again, Seth. Where can we meet after dinner?'

'I'd normally be at the stables.'

'I'll see you there.'

'I don't want to make trouble between you and your husband.'

She made a dismissive gesture and then smiled sweetly at the senator as he approached her.

❋⊱⊰❋

'I'm so proud of you for training those men to horseback-ride like that, Seth.' She played with his tunic buttons as she spoke.

'We just call it "riding",' he said, keeping a watchful eye on the domestic block. 'What did you tell your husband you were going to do?'

'Oh, I just told him I wanted to see my old friend before leaving.

180

I can't tell you how wonderful it's been, seeing you again. I'll never forget the time we had together.'

'It was special,' he agreed, freshly conscious that he was at close quarters with a woman for the first time in two years. Her scent, her proximity and the sound of her voice were the greatest luxury.

'If only things had been different,' she said.

'I could never have given you what he gives you, Katherine.'

'He can't give me what you gave me.' She added hurriedly, 'I don't just mean what we did at the lakeside, although that's not his best thing, either. I mean he doesn't make me feel what I felt when I was with you.' Impatiently, she said, 'Kiss me before I go, Seth. Remind me of what it was like.'

He did, at some length, and she responded as she had at the lakeside. After a little while, he said, 'You'll get lipstick all over your face.'

'No, I won't, and neither will you. I washed it off before I came to see you.' Possibly in anticipation, she added, 'I'll put some on before I go in again.'

He had to admire a seasoned campaigner.

'Kiss me again, Seth. We haven't much time.'

He kissed her slowly and gently. 'You're right,' he said, 'it's been the greatest thing, seeing you again.'

They kissed once more, and she said, 'Be happy, Sir Knight. I hope you find your lady.'

'You be happy, too.'

'I'm happy enough. Goodbye, Seth.'

'Goodbye, Katherine.'

11

Breakfast and a Cautionary Tale

In addition to the real pleasure of seeing Katherine again, her visit had been good for Seth in another way. For the two years since Wapun's death, his feelings and responses in connection with women had remained so fixed in limbo, it was almost as if they had ceased to exist. Incredibly, and in the brief spell of her visit, Katherine had reminded him of the joys his broken feelings had forced him to bury for so long. He would never forget Wapun; in fact, he would always love her, but suddenly, he was conscious of a kind of release from the seemingly interminable numbness he'd experienced.

At around the same time, Henry had made the acquaintance of one of the staff in the Payroll Office. Esther was a first-generation immigrant, who had arrived two years earlier with her parents so that her father could take his place on the staff of the Winnipeg Branch of the Bank of Montreal. She was an attractive redhead of twenty-two.

'She was engaged to a man in Bedfordshire,' he told Seth. 'That's somewhere down south, isn't it? Anyway, he died of influenza two winters ago.'

'How did you meet her?'

'It happened on pay parade. You probably saw her, but you wouldn't take much notice.'

'You evidently did. Anyway, I wasn't paying much attention to women at the time.'

'Aye.' Henry laughed good-naturedly. 'Katherine certainly put the colour back into your cheeks.'

'I still can't believe how it happened.'

'Just accept the fact that you're back in the land of the living.'

A voice said, 'You two are sounding cheerful.'

Seth recognised the voice and turned to greet its owner, the Reverend Otis. 'Good morning, Padre. I hope you're well.'

'So do I,' said Henry.

'Very well, thank you both, and you're obviously in good health, too.'

'You can't keep two good men down, Padre,' said Seth.

The Chaplain was about to take his leave of them, but he stopped to ask, 'Will you both be at Eucharist in the morning?'

'You may depend on it, Padre.' Seth had made no mention of the fact that neither of them had taken Holy Communion at Fort Walsh since his disagreement with the Reverend Burford and, on this occasion, he had something more important to ask. 'Padre, do you know of a dismissal that begins with, "Go forth into the world in peace. Be of good courage...."?'

' "Hold fast to that which is good...." I should say so. Has it a special meaning for you, Sergeant?'

'For both of us, Padre. We were brought up with it, and it's guided our footsteps since we were lads, but we haven't heard it for a long time.'

'In that case, you shall hear it again, now that you've been good enough to remind me of it.'

'Thank you, Padre. It means a lot to us.'

'Yes, thank you, Padre,' said Henry, equally delighted. When the Chaplain was gone, he said to Seth, 'Esther attends the Fort Chapel. I'll introduce you to her.'

As expected, Esther was at Holy Communion at ten minutes to eight, so Henry made the introduction then, and Seth discovered that she was as pretty as he'd said, and as personable, which was much more important.

On being introduced to Seth, she said, 'I hope you'll both come back with me for breakfast.'

'Won't your parents mind?'

'Not in the least. They're expecting to see Henry, anyway, and one more upright citizen will be just as welcome.'

'In that case,' said Seth, 'thank you, I'd like that.' He and Henry took their places, one on either side of her.

They observed the rite of Holy Communion, relieved to be able to do so. Devout as ever, Seth had felt it was wrong to bring ill-feeling to the Lord's Table, and he'd steadfastly abstained from observance at Fort Walsh. Henry had done likewise, sharing his friend's feelings about the Reverend Burford, but now all that was forgotten.

Having read the Prayer After Communion, the Padre stood before them and recited the dismissal that for so long had been just a memory.

'…Render to no man evil for evil. Support the weak, strengthen the faint-hearted, show love to all mankind. Love and serve the Lord, rejoicing in the power of the Holy Spirit. Amen.' He then read the blessing, and the service was over. It was as if, after a long spell of misfortune and unhappiness, things were suddenly improving.

❦❦❦❦❦

Esther's father, Mr Hawthorn, was a dapper, fussy man, balding, but with mutton chop whiskers, who insisted on knowing everything about Henry while his wife sat patiently by. Seth's obvious course was to distract Esther from her embarrassment by engaging her in conversation.

She asked, 'Have you and Henry really known each other all your lives?'

'Yes, well, for as long as we can remember, anyway. We grew up together, we were orphaned together, we worked on the same farm, and we joined the Army together.'

'And the North West Mounted Police.'

'That's right.'

With a sidelong glance, she said, 'I just hope my father approves of Henry.'

'There's nothing for him to find fault with,' Seth assured her. 'He won't find a more honest, straightforward and dependable fellow than Sergeant Henry Fowler. I know him better than anybody.'

Lowering her voice, she said, 'Henry says you arrested the man who wounded him.'

'That was a long time ago, but that's how we work, you see. We look out for each other.'

Ray Hobbs

A maid appeared in the doorway and spoke to Mrs Hawthorn. A moment later, her husband announced loudly that everyone should join him in the dining room for breakfast.

'It's always served late on a Sunday,' explained Esther, 'because of early Eucharist.'

'Quite right,' said Seth, although he was encountering the process for the first time.

'Hello, young man,' said Mr Hawthorn. 'Has Esther been keeping you entertained?'

'Esther is the perfect hostess, sir.'

'I'm glad to hear it. Come and sit beside me when you've helped yourself to breakfast, and then we can talk. I've probably worn Henry out with my questions, but I do like to get to know Esther's friends.'

'Of course, sir.' Seth took a plate and helped himself to eggs, sausages and bacon, as everyone else was doing, and then took his place on his host's left, picking up the table napkin and draping it across his lap as he had.

Mr Hawthorn put his hands together in a way that alerted everyone to the fact that he was about to say Grace. 'For the bounty we are about to enjoy may the Lord make us humbly thankful. Amen.' His family and the two guests echoed his amen.

'The Reverend Otis surprised us with a new form of dismissal this morning, Father,' said Esther. 'At least, it was one I'd never heard. Maybe Henry or Seth knew of it.'

' "Go forth into the world in peace",' recited Henry, continuing, but pausing partway through so that Seth could take over, which he did.

'You both knew it, evidently,' said Mr Hawthorn.

'We grew up with it,' Henry told him.

'I'm delighted to hear it,' said their host, evidently relieved that his daughters friends were godfearing citizens.

As they ate, Seth maintained a careful eye on Esther, who was seated across the table from him. The Reverend Nicholls had taught Henry and him a great deal, but they still had much to learn about conduct and behaviour in society, and such things were best learned by observation.

185

The recruits also had something to learn, and their various instructors applied themselves to their allotted disciplines. Soon, it was Seth's turn to take them on a cross-country trek so that they could learn how to manage and care for their horses in the field. It was also the first time some of them would pitch a tent and camp in the wild.

When the horses were tethered and the tents were pitched to Seth's satisfaction, he addressed the subject of the camp fire, on which they would cook their supper.

'This is going to sound daft,' he said, 'but I'm going to tell you, all the same, how important it is that you choose a place where your fire can't spread.' Acknowledging the laughter this provoked, he said, 'You'd be surprised how often it happens.' He chose a site, pointing out its distance from any combustible material, and sent some of them to gather fuel while others cut kindling. When that was done, he asked, 'What's the best way of lighting a fire?'

Immediately, one hand was raised. 'You could rub two sticks together, Sergeant.'

Another said, 'I'd use a burning glass. It's a lot quicker.'

'But not as quick as this,' Seth told them, taking a lucifer from its box and striking it. 'You can take the pioneering spirit too far,' he said. 'The important thing is to keep your lucifers dry. If you don't, that's when you'll have to fall back on a burning glass or two sticks.' His observation earned more laughter.

When the fire was going well, he invited the recruits to join him in a circle round it while he set up the griddle and frying pan. 'Hopefully, you'll remember what I said when we were tethering the horses. It was about taking the saddles and everything that goes with them. Who remembers that?' He acknowledged the show of hands and said, 'I thought I'd mention it, because there was one time when I forgot to do that same thing. Yes, I haven't always been perfect.' He allowed the friendly laughter, and went on. 'Sergeant Fowler and I were constables at the time, and we'd been sent to search for a fur trapper who was overdue at the trading post. He'd caught his foot in a gin trap, and he was very lucky to be found by a young Blackfoot woman.' He was still surprised that he now found it quite easy to talk about Wapun. 'She opened the trap and bound his ankle with the purple daisy. I'll find some to show you, because it was thanks to her and the way she dressed his wound that he was still alive and walking on both feet more than two years later, when we left Fort Walsh to come to Winnipeg. These things are important.' He looked across at the scout, who was nodding sagely. 'All that is by the by, because the important part of this story is that I took the saddles off the horses and then I was distracted. I actually left the carbines with them and forgot about them. That was until the horses got excited, and we realised we had company in the shape of a black bear.' He filled the pan with bacon and pinto beans as he continued with his story. 'The black bear is normally quite timid, but this one was hungry, and when that happens, they can be nasty.' He could see that the recruits were now fascinated by his story. 'The trouble was, all we had were our revolvers and our sabres.'

One of the recruits was unable to contain his excitement. He said, 'Sergeant Fowler said you fought the bear off with your sabre.'

'Well, you see, the bear was playing to his own rules, and he wouldn't wait for me to pick up a carbine, so the sabre was all I had. As a matter of fact, it was Sergeant Fowler who killed it in the end. He grabbed one of the carbines and shot it between the eyes.'

'Were you injured, Sergeant?' The question came from a recruit who'd been spellbound from the beginning.

Seth removed his tunic and lifted the sleeve of his vest to reveal the scars left by the bear's claws. The gasps and murmurs of the class told their own story. 'Like the fur trapper,' he told them, 'I was lucky, because the Blackfoot girl dressed my wounds with the purple daisy, too, and they healed quickly and without the usual corruption.' Looking around the group, he asked, 'Why do you think I told you that story, eh? Why did I own up to a class of recruits that I was once daft and careless?'

The recruit who'd asked about his injury said, 'Presumably, so that we wouldn't make the same mistake, Sergeant.'

'That's right, and in case you're wondering, I'm not likely to make that mistake again, either.' He gave the beans a stir and turned the bacon over. 'It's a pity I'm better at fighting bears than I am at cooking, but at least I've warned you. Get your mess tins ready, all of you.'

12

Tea and Affinity

That summer, the course reached its conclusion, and each recruit passed out as a sub-constable and made his way to his first posting. A new class of recruits would arrive at Lower Fort Garry within the week, but Seth and Henry would be able to enjoy a few days' rest before that happened.

That Saturday, Henry told Seth that Esther was bringing someone next morning to Holy Communion, a woman who'd recently transferred from Nominal Ledger to Payroll, where Esther worked, and that she was keen to make contact with him. Seth was happy to be introduced to her, but thought no more about the matter until Sunday morning, when Esther and her workmate arrived almost as the Chaplain was about to process into the chapel. Introductions would have to wait until the end of the service.

From time to time, Seth glanced towards the row where Esther and her friend were seated, but he was unable to see the newcomer properly due to the impediment of a wide-brimmed hat that concealed most of her face.

When the service was over and everyone was gathering outside, Esther was quick to announce the arrangements. 'My parents are expecting everyone for breakfast, so you'll all come, won't you?' Without waiting for an answer, she went on to say, 'Mrs Stevenson, may I introduce Sergeant Fowler and Sergeant Campion?'

They greeted one another, and Seth was able, for the first time, to see that Mrs Stevenson was a fair-haired, attractive woman of around his own age, with blue eyes that seemed to hint, if a little cautiously, at friendliness. Her eyebrows appeared to be naturally arched as if in surprise or pleasure.

'Sergeant Campion,' she said, 'I read your name on the payroll, and I had to make your acquaintance.'

'I'm honoured, ma'am.' Her name was familiar in some way that eluded him, but there was every chance she would prompt his memory.

'Shall we talk as we go?'

Seth offered her his arm. 'I'm at your service, ma'am.'

They followed at a discreet distance behind Henry and Esther, who would doubtless have things to discuss.

'I'm sure you're wondering why I wanted to meet you, Sergeant, so I'll tell you now. You see, I believe you arrested the man who killed my husband.'

Now the mystery was made clear. 'If your late husband was Sergeant Edward Stevenson of the North West Mounted Police, ma'am, you're correct.'

She smiled in her relief. 'Thank goodness I didn't make an awful mistake, but it seemed unlikely that there would be more than one Sergeant Campion.'

'I've never been aware of another, ma'am, and there are those who would say that one Sergeant Campion is quite enough.' He steered her gently out of the path of a man who appeared to be searching for a landmark, and asked, 'Can I direct you?'

In a strong Irish accent, the man said, 'The Church of the Blessed Lady, Sergeant. That's what I'm looking for.'

'Continue along this street for a quarter of a mile and you'll find it on your left.'

'Bless you, Sergeant, and thank you.'

'You're welcome.'

Returning to their conversation, Mrs Stevenson said, 'That would be most unkind of them.'

'Whereas you are the soul of kindness, ma'am. I have to say, also, that I feel for you in your loss, as I did at the time.'

'You're very kind, Sergeant, but you helped me at the time, although you had no way of knowing it.'

Surprised again, he asked, 'How did I help you, ma'am when you and I were strangers?'

'I wanted the murderer caught,' she said, 'although not out of personal revenge. I've tried very hard to turn my back on base feelings, but there's no doubt that he was a dangerous man, and there was no telling what else he might have done had he remained at large. I have to say, also, and I find this impossible to explain, that his arrest was important in helping me cope with the initial horror.'

'There are some things we simply have to accept, ma'am.' However, he had to agree with her assessment of her husband's murderer. 'Keiller tried to kill two of my friends,' he told her. 'One of them was Henry Fowler.'

'In that case, thank goodness he failed.'

'Amen to that,' said Seth, recalling the event.

Apologetically, she said, 'Let's talk about something more cheerful, shall we? Where do you hail from originally, Sergeant?'

'Sergeant Fowler and I were both born in a village outside Beverley in the East Riding.'

'Oh, in Yorkshire. I couldn't place your accent, but now you've explained it. I was born in Bicester.'

That meant absolutely nothing to Seth, who said, 'I've travelled in India and America, ma'am, but I have to admit that there are parts of my own country that are unknown to me. Bicester is one of them.'

'Bicester is in Oxfordshire, to the north-west of London.'

'I'm obliged to you, ma'am.'

They stopped outside Esther's parents' house and followed them inside, where Esther introduced Mrs Stevenson to her parents.

'I must seem very presumptuous,' she said, 'turning up like this, but Esther insisted I came.'

'Not at all,' Mrs Hawthorn assured her. 'We're always happy to entertain Esther's friends, Mrs Stevenson. You are most welcome.'

The party gathered around the breakfast table, and the conversation that developed confirmed Seth's belief that Henry was now connected with a remarkable family. The Sunday gatherings at the Hawthorn household were their first experience of family life since their time on the Norton farm, and he was heartily pleased on his friend's behalf.

After breakfast, Mrs Stevenson and Seth made their farewells, leaving Henry to become better acquainted with Esther's parents, involved as he was in conversation with her father.

As they left the house, Seth asked if he might escort Mrs Stevenson to her home, and she accepted his offer gratefully. It transpired that they'd passed her apartment on the way from the fort, so it involved only a short walk, during which they resumed their earlier conversation.

'You mentioned that you'd spent time in India, Sergeant. Was that with the Army?'

'Yes, ma'am, we both served there for twelve years with the Eleventh Hussars.'

She smiled. 'You and Sergeant Fowler must be inseparable.'

'You could say that, ma'am. We were born in the same year and we've experienced everything else together.'

'You're the embodiment of loyalty, but tell me, what brought you to Canada?'

Seth smiled apologetically. 'That's quite a long story, ma'am, and I've no wish to bore you with it.'

'I can't imagine for a minute that I'd find it remotely dull, but let me ask you something. Do you have duties to attend to this afternoon?'

'None whatsoever, ma'am. Until the new intake arrives, I have little to do.'

'In that case,' she said, halting at her door, 'will you indulge me by joining me for afternoon tea, here, at my apartment?'

Taken again by surprise, Seth said, 'Gladly, ma'am, but shouldn't...?'

'Shouldn't what, Sergeant?'

'I was about to say, shouldn't you have someone with you...?' He was on unfamiliar ground, and he was struggling.

'I imagine you're asking me if I should have a chaperone.' She smiled. 'I have to remind you, Sergeant, that I am a widow, not a vulnerable spinster.'

'Of course not, ma'am, and I am pleased to accept your invitation.'

'Let's say at a quarter to four, shall we?'

'Yes, ma'am.'

'And now that we're agreed on that, shall we dispense with "Mrs Stevenson", "ma'am" and "Sergeant Campion"? It would please me if you called me "Selina".'

'It will be a pleasure, ma'am...Selina. My name, by the way, is Seth.'

'I know. Until this afternoon, Seth.'

'I'll be here, Selina.' Now that he was over the shock, her name rolled easily off his tongue.

❦

'I don't bake cakes very often. I hope this one's not going to be an embarrassment.' She cut a piece and placed it on Seth's plate. 'I was only joking. It should be all right,' she said, watching him stare at the cake.

'I'm sorry. This is the first cake I've seen for fourteen years or more.'

'Really?'

'The farmer's wife used to make them for Harvest Supper. It was always an important event for us, almost as important as the harvest itself.'

'I can imagine that.'

'I feel awkward,' he confessed suddenly, 'talking so much about my past.'

'You shouldn't. I'm fascinated, mainly because you've experienced so much, and I've done so little.'

'You had a proper education, Selina, and that's more than I've had.'

She smiled gently but reprovingly. 'I had a governess, a woman who taught me at home. I learned, among the rest, things that were of no importance to me, whereas you learned things that were vitally important.'

'I suppose so.' He wasn't convinced.

'You were taught to cope with the practical aspects of life, whereas I was brought up to take my place in middle-class society.' She sighed. 'Then things became difficult for my family, and they decided that the best thing for me would be to marry a suitable man, which I did. Edward and I sailed for Canada in eighteen seventy-three, where he'd been promised an important position in a company here. When we arrived, we found that the company was insolvent and that the position was no more. In the absence of anything more suitable, Edward joined the newly-formed Police Force for the North West, and I found office employment with the force at the same time.'

'I'd say you've experienced quite a lot,' he said.

'It must seem so. More tea, Seth?' She picked up the pot.

192

'Yes, if you please.'

She placed the strainer over his cup and poured. 'I find it remarkable,' she said, 'that you travelled four thousand miles or more, just to join Colonel Custer and his regiment.'

'We believed, at the time, in what he was doing, but I'm afraid the United States Cavalry lost favour with us when we heard about the massacres that followed the Battle of the Little Bighorn.'

'But you did remarkable things. You saved the American lady from the clutches of those drunken oafs, and you saved the Indian girl from a worse fate. As for capturing those fire raisers....' She blinked at the enormity of it all. After a little more thought, she asked, 'Do you know what you and Henry are?'

He smiled at the familiar response. 'Are you going to tell me we're like the knights of old?'

She laughed. 'Yes, that's just what I was going to say. I imagine you've been told that already.'

'It's been mentioned once or twice,' he confirmed, 'but there's nothing special about us. All we've ever tried to do is live according to the principles we were taught to believe in. That's why the dismissal that the Padre read this morning is so important to us. We were brought up with it as our pattern for life.'

'I remember now. Seth,' she said, 'don't tell me you're not special.' Her blue eyes shone with unaffected admiration. 'As far as I'm concerned, you're both knights errant. You found yourselves in the nineteenth century, but you're conducting yourselves just as you would if you'd lived in the Middle Ages.'

'This cake is very good,' he told her in an attempt to change the subject.

'I'm sorry. I didn't mean to embarrass you.' Looking at his cup, she asked, 'Have you always taken tea without milk or lemon?'

'Since we arrived in India. Cows are sacred there, so the Hindus became restless if we tried to milk them, and lemons were an officers' luxury. I must say I've never tasted one.' He smiled at a recent memory. 'We struggled to find tea in America. It's not popular there, but here.... Well, it's just one of the benefits of serving as a Mountie.'

She smiled sadly. 'You're very much like my husband. He was proud, like you.'

'I only knew what I was told, Selina. I hardly met him, being in a different troop from his, but I know he was a fine sergeant.'

'Thank you, Seth.' She blinked hard.

'I'm sorry. I didn't mean to upset you.'

'You haven't upset me. The hurt is in the past. All you did was make a kind remark, and they can be as rare as they are welcome.'

'They can,' he agreed. 'There was a time, until quite recently, when I resented any mention of the girl I was going to marry. Only Henry was allowed to speak her name.' Seth rarely spoke about Wapun, but incredibly, he found no difficulty in telling Selena about her.

'Oh, Seth.' She leaned forward in her concern, but then she checked herself. 'No, I mustn't pry.' Even so, her face betrayed her concern.

'You're not prying, Selena. Wapun was a native girl who'd saved a fur trapper's life, and in guarding me against the corruption that sets in after a claw-wound, she probably saved my arm, at least. The trapper's foot was caught in a gin trap – one of those spring traps with sharp, jagged teeth made of steel – but then she found him and saved him from bleeding to death. Later, I was mauled by a bear, and she treated the trapper's wounds and mine with a special herb known only to the Indians.'

'What a remarkable girl.'

'And an unhappy one at the time. Her people had rejected her because they believed she was barren. They'd treated her shamefully, so I placed her under my protection.' He paused, remembering. 'If they'd only known.'

'If they'd known what, Seth?'

'If they'd known that she was carrying my child when the smallpox took her.'

'I'm so sorry.' Her voice was no more than a whisper.

'You're very kind, Selena, but my hurt, like yours, has softened with the passing of time.'

'I'm relieved to hear it. We can both remember fondly, but without yesterday's heartbreak.' In a perceptible effort to change the mood, she asked, 'Will you visit me again?'

'If that's what you want.'

'I should like that very much.'

'Then I'll be happy to come again.'

13

Rejection and Acceptance

Seth and Henry began training the new intake in their usual way, demanding total commitment from the start, and voicing their approval when the recruits earned it. As usual, they came with differing equestrian skills, although that posed no problem for Seth, who insisted on them adopting his style of horsemanship, regardless of anything they'd learned in the past. His only concern was that the horses knew the drill better than their riders, having performed it many times, and unless they were checked, would anticipate a word or prompt, thus relieving the recruit of the effort and responsibility. Another equine reaction that had to be taken into account was the horse's practice of distending its belly when its rider was fastening the saddle girth.

'The horse tries to make room for himself inside the girth,' Seth told them. 'You can't blame him for wanting to be comfortable, but the girth needs to be tight enough for the rider's safety, so here's what you do.' As he took both ends of the girth, the horse visibly lowered his belly. 'Did you see that? At this point, you wait a few seconds for the horse to relax again, and that's when you tighten the girth.' He pulled the tongue through the buckle and secured it. As he did so, he caught the eye of a recruit who'd already shown himself to be careless, as well as making himself unpopular with instructors as well as recruits with his egotistical attitude. 'Recruit Lawson, did you hear that?'

'Yes.' His response was one of patient condescension.

'Yes, *who*?'

'Yes, Sergeant.' He inflected Seth's rank with something not far short of disdain.

'Good, because from where I'm standing, you didn't appear to be paying attention. For your own safety, you should.'

'Yes, Sergeant.' Again, Lawson's response lacked humility, but Seth decided to let the matter rest for the time being. He had a great deal to get through, and the whole class required his services, so he pressed on, little knowing that Lawson would soon demand his attention again, but in a more immediate and dramatic way.

The recruits had tacked up their horses, and each stood in readiness to the left of his mount.

'Class,' ordered Seth, 'class, mount!'

All but one of them lifted himself into his saddle and placed his feet in the stirrups. The exception was Lawson, who picked himself up off the ground, having fallen beneath his horse. His saddle hung to one side, and his horse shifted its feet uneasily.

'Get up, Lawson,' said Seth, 'and straighten that saddle. Your horse is embarrassed, and he has my sympathy.'

For the rest of the class, his order was the first intimation that something was wrong, and they all turned to see what had happened. Their laughter when they saw the crooked saddle and the disconcerted Lawson was spontaneous.

'So you were paying attention when I showed the class how to tighten the saddle girth, were you? What happened, Lawson? Did it just slip your mind?' His question prompted more laughter, much to Lawson's displeasure. Furiously, he unfastened the girth and threw the saddle on to the horse's back.

'It wasn't the horse's fault, Lawson. Don't punish him for your carelessness.'

Lawson muttered something darkly, glancing at Seth while he re-fastened the girth.

'Come here, Lawson.'

Lawson gave the girth a final tug, but made no move to obey the order.

'Come here, now, Lawson.'

Querulously, the recruit left his horse's side and walked up to Seth.

'What did you say, just then?'

Lawson glared at him. 'I'm tired of all this mindless drill. Why does everything have to be done your way?'

'I think you found the answer to that question when you fell off your horse.'

There was another burst of laughter from the class, and Lawson's temper finally deserted him. 'I suppose you find that amusing, too.'

'No, I'm not amused, Lawson. Don't forget that I'm the unfortunate instructor who's trying to turn you into a police officer, and you're making my job harder than it needs to be. Re-join the class, and if you'll make an effort to learn from instruction and follow orders, I'll disregard your outburst.'

Lawson's rage was now beyond control. 'I'm damned if I will!' He turned to go, but Seth caught his arm. 'In that case, you'll just have to keep falling off your horse until you learn some sense.'

The laughter that followed did nothing to calm Lawson's rage. He tried to wrench his arm away from Seth, but without success. Furiously, he lashed out with his free fist, at which Seth dodged sideways, still holding Lawson's arm.

'Let go of me!'

'You've gone too far, Lawson.' He turned the arm and forced it up Lawson's back. Then, addressing the class, he said, 'Dismount and stand easy. I'll be with you shortly.' With one hand keeping the captive arm in place and the other gripping Lawson's collar, he marched him to the orderly office, where he found Constable Garvey at his desk. He looked up in surprise.

'Is Superintendent Russell in his office, Constable?'

'Yes, Sergeant.' Garvey got up and knocked on the door marked *Officer in Charge*.

'Yes?'

'Sergeant Campion's here, sir, with a... a prisoner, sir.'

The door opened, and Superintendent Russell stopped in surprise.

'Recruit Lawson is guilty of refusing to obey an order, insolence, and attempted assault on a superior officer, sir.'

'That officer being you, I take it?'

'That is correct, sir.'

'And what have you to say for yourself, Recruit Lawson?'

Still angry, Lawson said, 'I'm sick of this damned place!'

'Perhaps you'll explain, Sergeant Campion.'

'Yes, sir.' Seth described the incident plainly and without

embellishment. Finally, he said, 'Lawson has been openly critical of our methods, sir, but this was the first time he was abusive or offered violence.'

'But he didn't actually assault you?'

'He tried to punch me, but I avoided the blow, sir.'

Lawson must have felt that it was his turn to speak, because he shouted, 'Tell him to let go of my arm!'

Russell called, 'Constable Garvey!'

'Yes, sir.' Garvey appeared in the doorway.

'Ask at the Payroll Office for someone to calculate Lawson's pay up to the end of today and to send it to me. Before you do that, though, escort him to the cells. He can spend some time there cooling down before he changes into civilian clothing and leaves the fort for the last time.' Turning to Lawson, he said, 'As you've no doubt gathered, Lawson, I'm discharging you from the course. The North West Mounted Police are looking for a certain kind of recruit, and you are nothing like it. You're a disgrace, and you can be thankful I'm not charging you with threatening a police officer. Take him away, Constable.'

⊕⊷⊱⊰⋇⋇⋵⊷⊶

'I feel that I've failed, somehow.' He broke off to accept a cup of tea from Selina. 'I'm obliged to you, Selina. The only comfort is that we'd never have made a proper Mountie of him.'

'That should be a great comfort to you, Seth. Also, Superintendent Russell approved your actions. You shouldn't worry about it any longer.'

'I think you're right, Selina. Lawson will be lucky to hold on to any job as long as he continues to think he knows more than the people who are trying to train him.'

She cut a piece from a cake and put it on his plate.

He asked, 'What kind is this?'

'It's a Victoria sponge cake, named in honour of the Queen, who is said to be particularly fond of afternoon tea.'

He broke a piece off and tried it. 'It's always been a pleasure to serve Her Majesty,' he said, 'but it's an even greater pleasure to eat the cake named after her, and the pleasure is greater still when you've made it.'

'Thank you, Seth. That was a lovely compliment.' She was wearing a long, olive-green skirt with a white, frilled blouse that seemed the perfect accompaniment for her gentle features, and even after so short a time, Seth was aware of the direction his feelings were taking.

'Compliments are important. I learned that in India, but it's just as true anywhere else.'

'What a lovely thought.' She asked, 'Do you ever have the urge to return to England?'

'Not really.' He remembered Katherine asking him the same question. It was the conversation that led to her sending tea from Boston. 'Now that tea is plentiful, I'm quite settled.'

She laughed gently. 'Tea was obviously important to you.'

'It still is. It was almost impossible to find in America. We had some sent over by a friend in Boston, and then we had some sent from Winnipeg. It was wrapped in a Winnipeg newspaper, which was how we learned about the Police Force for the North West.'

'Coincidence is a remarkable thing.'

'Do you ever feel homesick, Selina?' He hoped not; in fact, he found the very idea of her being at all unhappy acutely disturbing.

'Not now. When I lost my husband, I felt that I wanted to run back to my family, but that wasn't possible. Since then, I've come to think of Canada as my country.'

'I feel the same. Everything we were looking for when we left India is happening here.'

'More tea?' She noticed that his cup was now empty.

'Yes, if you please.'

She placed the strainer over his cup and poured. 'You know, Seth,' she said, 'I enjoy talking with you, because you're so genuine.'

'I can't see any point in being anything else. I'm the person I am, and people can either accept me or leave me alone.'

'I imagine most people accept you.' She looked thoughtful for a moment, and said, 'You said you'd learned in India about compliments. What did you mean?'

He gave a dismissive shrug. 'Oh, that.'

'I'd like to know, Seth.'

'All right.' He mustered his thoughts. 'I met a girl in Calcutta—'

'What was her name?'

'Lakshmi.'

'An Indian girl, then.'

'Yes, she was.'

Something in his tone prompted her to say, 'I'm sorry. I'll try not to interrupt you again.'

He was grateful for that. 'Most people in Calcutta are Muslims, although there are other religions. Lakshmi was a Sikh, and she'd suffered quite a lot of abuse, partly because of that and partly, I suppose, because she was a girl. She was a lovely girl, and I don't just mean that she was pretty, although she was. I mean in herself, the way she thought and the way she treated people.'

'You obviously knew her well. Did you have a full relationship with her?'

Seth was unsure what 'a full relationship' meant, so he took a guess and said, 'Yes.'

'I'm sorry. I interrupted you again.'

'It's no matter. Anyway, I told her something, the kind of thing girls like to hear, but I meant what I said, and she knew that. She said that compliments meant a lot to girls and women, because they made up for some of the unpleasant things that happened to them.'

'I know what she meant.'

'Of course you do.' Returning to his story, he said, 'I felt sorry for her, and I tried to balance those things by paying her regular compliments. If compliments are genuine, I find it's also a way of seeing... no, that's not the word. It's a way of *recognising* the best in someone, and that's important.'

'You're absolutely right, Seth.' For a moment, she seemed quite surprised, but then she went on to say, 'If only more men thought as you do, but they don't, so I'm just thankful I know you.'

'As I told you before, Selina, there's nothing special about me. It's just the way I was brought up.'

'By a vicar because you'd no family.'

'And the farmer and his wife.' It seemed only right to mention them.

'I'm just saying that there are people who've grown up with every advantage of family, education and opportunity, but you still leave them far behind when it comes to being a decent human being.'

'I suppose so.' It didn't seem all that strange to Seth, and he'd never considered himself particularly disadvantaged, but he wasn't inclined to argue with her. 'You know,' he said, 'of all the good things in life that I can think of, this is one of them.'

'This?'

'Sitting here and talking with you like this is like being a member of a family. At least, I think it is. It's so long since I was part of a family, it's difficult to remember what it was like, but I know this is good.'

'Just keep coming, Seth.'

14

January 1880

Fever and Alarm

Tea on Sundays soon became an agreeable habit for Seth and Selina, and they both looked forward to it. Seth could now relax more in Selina's company, because he no longer found the differences in their respective social backgrounds quite as inhibiting as he had at first. There were times when duty intervened, usually in the shape of a cross-country trek with a class of recruits, but otherwise his visit was a regular fixture, although it was not their sole activity. One new experience for Seth was the theatre, which he was learning to appreciate with Selena's gentle guidance. Those visits, however, were always made in the company of Henry and Esther, as Esther's parents appreciated the decorum that the arrangement afforded. At all events, though, Seth's meetings with Selena were frequent and regular, so it seemed, at first, quite natural when a constable handed him note, telling him that it had been delivered by a member of the office staff. He opened it, and was immediately surprised to find that it was from Esther. It read:

> *Dear Seth,*
> *Try not to worry too much when you get this note, but I have to tell you that Selina has just been taken to the hospital with a fever. We think it's influenza. At all events, she's in the best possible place, so keep that in mind.*
> *Yours with all good wishes,*
> *Esther.*

Henry saw him reading it, and asked, 'What is it, mate?'

Seth handed the note to him without a word, shock and worry having rendered him temporarily mute.

'She's strong and healthy, Seth. She'll fight it off.'

'I hope so.' They were both aware that Esther's fiancé had died of the disease.

'There's nothing you can do. You'll just have to wait until you hear something.'

'But how? They won't let me into the hospital because of the risk of contagion.'

Henry could only agree, at least for the moment, because something suddenly occurred to him. 'That new telegraphic thing they've got in the Orderly Office, it's just as likely the hospital will have one, too.'

Seth knew hardly anything about the new equipment, but it was worth considering. 'I'm obliged to you, Henry. I'll speak to Garvey.'

He found Constable Garvey in the Orderly Office, but he was unable to be of immediate help. 'You'll have to ask Superintendent Russell for his permission to use the telephone, Sergeant. He says it's rather expensive.'

'I'll do that. Is he in his office?' As he spoke, the door to the inner office opened.

'No, I'm here, Sergeant Campion,' said the superintendent. 'What's the trouble?'

'A very close friend of mine has been taken into hospital, sir, with a fever. It may be influenza, but no one really knows yet. I wondered if I could speak to someone at the hospital, using the new equipment, sir. I imagine they have the same thing there.'

'It's more than likely, Sergeant. When was he taken in, your friend?'

'Actually, it's Mrs Stevenson, who works in Payroll, sir, and she was taken this morning.'

'Ah.' The superintendent thought for a second and said, 'Come into my office, Sergeant.' He led the way, offering Seth a seat and closing the door behind him. 'There are two things to consider,' he said. 'One is that no one at the hospital will have any idea, as yet, of when the fever is likely to break, so they won't be in a position to comment. The other is quite simply that they're unlikely, busy as they are at this time of the year, to welcome enquiries by telephone.' Smiling sympathetically, he said, 'I can do nothing about the fever, but I can help you with the other problem.'

'I'd be very grateful for any help, sir.'

'Of course. You see, I am responsible for the Administration Block as well as the main academy, so I have a legitimate reason, as far as Winnipeg General Hospital is concerned, for enquiring after a patient who is employed here. I shall be happy to make enquiries on your behalf, but I would suggest that we leave it for at least one more day.'

It was a step forward. 'I'm greatly obliged to you, sir, and I thank you most sincerely.'

'You are welcome, Sergeant,' he said, looking up at the wall clock, 'but I imagine you have duties to attend to.'

<hr />

Seth spent the next twenty-four hours in the throes of suspense and anxiety. He forced himself to concentrate on his duties, but at other times, he was completely distracted, and, sensitive as ever, Henry gave him room to cope with his fears.

Still unsure to some extent of his ground, Seth had not confided in Selena about his feelings for her, which had grown ever stronger with their Sunday meetings, and now he was afraid he might be denied the opportunity altogether.

After waiting for what seemed an age, he saw Constable Garvey leave the Orderly Office. He seemed to be approaching the stables, so he evidently had a message for him. He felt the tension heighten, and then Garvey said, 'Superintendent Russell wants to see you, Sergeant.'

'I'm obliged to you, Constable.' He asked the class to excuse him, and accompanied Garvey back to the Orderly Office, where he knocked on the superintendent's door. Then, on hearing the invitation to enter, he pushed the door open and came to attention.

'You sent for me, sir.'

'Stand easy, Sergeant. In fact, take a seat. Yes, I did, because I've just spoken with the sister in charge of the ward where Mrs Stevenson is being cared for.' He smiled sympathetically. 'It is influenza, but she's in safe hands.'

'Was that all they could tell you, sir?'

'It was all they were prepared to tell me. They're always guarded, you know, and I can only imagine it's to avoid creating expectations, optimistic or otherwise.'

'I'm greatly obliged to you, sir.'

'I'll speak to them again, tomorrow, Sergeant. Meanwhile, remember your responsibility to your recruits.'

'I will, and I thank you, sir.'

⚜

By the following Thursday, Russell was able to give him better news.

'Mrs Stevenson is likely to be discharged from hospital within days, Sergeant. The current wave of influenza has created an unusual demand for hospital beds, but I'm sure they would not discharge her unless they're confident of her complete recovery.'

'Thank the Lord for that, sir, and please accept my thanks for your efforts.' In his relief, his words tumbled out.

'You're welcome, as always, Sergeant. Mrs Stevenson is a widow, I believe.'

'Yes, sir. Her late husband was Sergeant Edward Stevenson, one of the troop sergeants at Fort Walsh, who was killed attempting to arrest the killer of a fur trapper.'

'How utterly tragic.' Russell's reaction was clearly heartfelt. 'Do you know what happened to his killer?'

'Yes, sir. I arrested him and took him into Fort Walsh. He was taken to the assizes and tried for the two murders, although he came close to committing two more. Sergeant Fowler and Louis Lavalle, our guide, were both wounded. I imagine Keiller was hanged.'

'Without a doubt. You emerged apparently unscathed. You did well to arrest such a desperate man.'

Seth remembered the incident clearly. 'He was indeed desperate, sir. I was obliged to beat him almost senseless in order to tame him, but I was able, at length, to make the arrest.'

The superintendent nodded slowly. 'I'm obliged to you for telling me that, Sergeant Campion. It strengthens my already high opinion of you. Now, you may carry on with your duties, assured that you will soon see Mrs Stevenson well and hearty again.'

⚙╬╬╣╠╬╣⚙

Once more, the constable who had been relieved on the gate handed Seth a note, and again, it was from Esther:

Dear Seth,
I thought you'd like to know that Selena is at home again. She will be weakened after her illness, and influenza is usually followed by a heavy cold. However, I'm sure she will cope with that. Let's be thankful that she has survived.
She has been told to remain at home until Monday, 19th, when she must report for work again. Sick leave is without pay, but she has her widow's pension, so she shouldn't be in want.
Yours with all good wishes,
Esther.

It was typical of Esther that she'd considered everything, including Selena's financial situation.

⚙╬╬╣╠╬╣⚙

He arrived outside Selena's apartment with food he'd been able to scrounge from the fort kitchen. He kicked the snow from his boots, rang the doorbell and waited.

After a couple of minutes, the door opened, and he saw Selena as never before. She looked pale and exhausted, and she wore a dressing gown, presumably over her nightgown. 'Selena,' he said, 'I've been.... I'm.... I'm so relieved, I can't tell you.... Let's go inside, out of the cold.'

'Seth,' she said, 'you're quite beside yourself.' She moved aside to let him in, and closed the door gratefully.

'It's just the relief of knowing you've survived. Were you in bed when I arrived?'

'Yes, but it doesn't matter. What have you got there?'

'Food. Have you eaten, today?'

'Not yet.' She let him into the sitting room, where a fire had been laid but left for later.

He struck a lucifer and touched the screwed-up paper beneath the kindling. 'You must eat to regain your strength,' he told her, 'and I'm going to see that you do.'

'Do you want me to cook something?'

'No, just stay there and rest. I wouldn't normally enter a lady's bedchamber, but I'm going to find something to keep you warm.'

Her bedroom wasn't difficult to find, as it was the only other sizeable room in the apartment, and he returned with a sheet, two blankets and two pillows, which he arranged on her sofa. 'Now, come and let me tuck you in.' He hesitated. 'I think that's what they call it.'

'That's right,' she said, laughing for the first time. 'You really were concerned about me, weren't you?'

'Much, much more than that,' he admitted as he tucked the bedclothes around her. 'Superintendent Russell spoke to the people at the hospital every day, using the new telephone machine. It was kind of him to do that on my behalf.'

'Oh, Seth.' She reached for his hand, and on an impulse, he took hers and kissed it. She looked at him in surprise, but raised no objection.

He'd never lacked boldness in female company, but being with Selena was different. His old, self-assured ways were now in the past. Self-consciously, he asked, 'Do you like venison?'

'I like most things when I'm hungry, but venison is special. I was going to get something, but I felt too weak.'

'I've brought you venison stew, and there's bread and butter as well, in case you hadn't been to the shops.' He looked at her weakened state and realised how stupid he must have sounded. She couldn't possibly do any shopping. He said lamely, 'Stay by the fire while I cook.'

'Esther's going to bring me some things,' she said, but I can't believe this, a man cooking for me.'

'You should wait until you've tasted it before you get excited,' he warned her. 'Seriously, though, it was made in the fort kitchen, so it should be all right. I'm only going to heat it up.' He carried the stew in its container to the tiny kitchen, where he emptied it into a saucepan. Then, realising that the fire in the stove was out, he returned to the sitting room to place the saucepan on the hob.

'Of course,' said Selena, 'I haven't lit the stove.'

'It's no matter.'

When the venison stew was heated through, he found a plate and carried the meal to her on a tray, which he placed on the low table beside the sofa.

'It smells wonderful,' she said. Then, as an afterthought, she touched his hand and said, 'You'll probably catch an awful cold from me.'

He'd already noticed that her nose was pink and her consonants were impeded by congestion. 'I can cope with that,' he said. 'Just the relief and the pleasure of seeing you again are comfort enough for me.'

'You're an exception among men, Seth.' She picked up a fork and tried the stew. 'This is truly magnificent,' she said, 'but I don't know how much I'll be able to eat. I haven't much of an appetite.'

'I'll sit here and encourage you,' he said, drawing up a chair. 'You can't imagine how worried I've been.'

'You keep telling me that, so I'm beginning to realise the extent of your concern, and I'm quite touched by it.'

Selena actually finished the helping of stew with little encouragement.

'There's more,' he told her.

'I really couldn't eat any more, Seth.'

'The cook told me it would still be fit to eat tomorrow, so you can have it then. I've covered it.'

'You're very kind, Seth.' She took his hand again.

His eye fell on a book on the low table, and he read the title. ' "Far From the Madding Crowd." ' He asked, 'What does "madding" mean?'

'I suppose it means "behaving in a highly excited manner". The title's a quotation from a poem by Thomas Gray.'

'You know, other than the Bible, I've never read a book in the whole of my life.'

'I'd be surprised if you'd ever found the time,' she told him gently. 'I took this one down to read it, but I kept falling asleep.' She squeezed his hand and asked, 'Will you read it to me?'

'I'll do my best.' He opened the book and found the first page of the story. From the start, he found it surprisingly easy to read, set as it was in a farming community, albeit in a strange part of Britain, and he was well into the first chapter when he glanced at Selena and saw that her eyes were closed and she was breathing regularly. He closed the book and took the tray into the kitchen to wash the plate and cutlery. When he returned to the sitting room, he found her still fast asleep. Quietly, he banked up the fire to make it last, and tucked the covers around her as she slept. Finally, on an impulse, he bent and kissed her forehead before leaving the apartment.

15

No Knight is Complete

Henry did his best to reassure Seth. 'Esther looks in on her regularly,' he told him. 'You can be sure Selina won't be in want of anything.'

'It's good of Esther. It was kind of her to keep me informed, too.'

'That's Esther,' confirmed Henry. 'Kindness and her have never been strangers.' It was evident that he had other matters on his mind, as well. 'I've news to tell, and I'll tell you before anybody else, Seth, as you're my oldest mate.'

'What will you tell me?' He knew already, having seen Henry's request in the Orderly Office.

'About Esther and me. We're going to be officially betrothed, a week come Saturday, or "Saturday week", as Mr Hawthorn calls it, with her family present. You and Selina are invited to dinner.' He added confidently, 'She'll be strong enough by then, I fancy.'

'She will, Henry, and we'll be there.' He shook his hand vigorously. 'I wish you the very best, mate, and let me say, you've made a wise choice with Esther.'

'I'm obliged to you for those words, Seth, but listen, mate. You and I have always done things together. That's right, isn't it?'

'There's no denying it.'

'Well, then,' said Henry cryptically, 'get a move on and remember what they say.'

'What do they say?'

'He who hesitates… is… something or other.'

Seth considered that briefly and said, 'I've never heard anybody say it in just those words, but I can't very well argue with it.'

The street cleaners were clearing snow from the footpath when Seth reached Selena's apartment. One of them stepped aside for him, saying, 'After you, Sergeant.'

'I'm obliged to you, but listen. Would you like to earn a dime?' He was feeling generous.

'What are you after, Sergeant?'

'Just clear the snow off these steps,' he said. 'and I'll give you ten cents.'

'No sooner said than done.' The cleaner set to and cleared Selina's steps, accepting the ten cents gratefully.

Seth rang the doorbell, feeling unusually nervous, but when he saw Selena fully-dressed and cheerful, he could feel only happiness. 'It's good to see you dressed again,' he said, instantly regretting his choice of words when she gave him a look of mock-censure. 'I'm sorry,' he said. 'That must have sounded disgraceful. I meant....'

'I know what you meant. Come inside and give me your greatcoat and your gloves and helmet.'

Relieved of his outer clothes, he kissed her on the cheek and followed her into the sitting room, where the fire was going well.

'I put the kettle on the hob when I saw you talking to one of the street cleaners,' she said.

'I asked him to clear the snow from your steps,' he explained.

'You really are an exception, Seth.'

'I hope so.'

'Just let me scald the tea.'

'Let me carry the tray, Selena.'

She smiled broadly and said, 'I'm no longer feeble, but as you insist, I'm grateful for your offer.'

It was a genuine pleasure to see her dressed in a dark-blue skirt and white blouse. He watched her pour boiling water into the teapot, and he placed it on the tray, wondering what she would wear for the gathering at Esther's home. It was easier for Henry and him. They would be in uniform because that was all they had.

Quite conveniently, she asked, 'What news have you?'

'Mr and Mrs Hawthorn have invited you and me to dinner next Saturday.'

'I know.'

'I imagine Esther told you.'

'Yes.' She smiled apologetically and said, 'I shouldn't have spoiled your announcement. I'm sorry.'

'There's no need to be. Did she tell you the reason?'

'Yes. Isn't it wonderful?'

'They're a well-matched pair,' he agreed. 'Shall I take this into the sitting room?' He lifted the tray.

'If you please. I'm afraid I haven't baked anything this week, for obvious reasons.'

'Of course not.'

'Would you like to put it on the low table?'

'With pleasure.' He placed the tray on the table and waited for Selena to take her place before joining her on the sofa.

'I could find you some bread and butter, if you're feeling hungry,' she offered.

'I'm not at all hungry, but I'm obliged to you, all the same.' Suddenly, he felt awkward. He wanted to tell her how happy he was to find her well again, because that was how he felt, and it was so important to him that he wanted to pour his feelings out, but he'd told her that several times, and he had to move on. 'I think it's kind of Mr and Mrs Hawthorn to invite us. Don't you?'

'Well, yes. They're very kind people.'

'Of course they are.' It was awful. He was making banal conversation when there was so much he wanted to say to her.

'It will be a wonderful occasion.'

'Truly wonderful,' he agreed.

He hadn't been aware that his behaviour was at all worthy of comment, so he was surprised when Selena said, 'Seth, you're looking at me strangely. Is something the matter?'

Surprised that she'd noticed any change in his manner, he recovered quickly and said, 'Only something I've left undone for too long.' He was reminded briefly of the time he'd ridden with Marie to Red Wolf Creek, where she'd asked him the same question. This occasion, however, was infinitely more important. He nerved himself to say, 'I was wondering how you'd react if… if I kissed you.'

'Well, Seth, there's one way you could find out.'

He took her in his arms and touched her lips with his, scarcely able to believe that the intimacy was finally taking place. Then, sensing consent, he kissed her with increasing boldness, so that when he eventually broke away, she said, 'You were right, Seth. You left it far too long.'

'I… hesitated.'

'Am I correct in thinking that the brave Mountie was afraid to make his true feelings known?'

He nodded modestly. 'I've tamed drunken and violent troopers, I've fought bandits and fanatical tribesmen, I've faced hostile Indians, I've fought a hungry bear and I've arrested a dangerous and violent criminal, but yes. I was… anxious.'

'I never realised I was so terrifying.' Her smile was instantly reassuring. 'Would a cup of tea brace you up?'

'I don't need bracing now, but tea would be very pleasant, so yes, if you please.'

'Not pleasanter than kissing me, I hope?'

'It's not even in the reckoning,' he assured her.

'Good.' She poured tea into a cup for him. 'I'd hate to come second to a herbal infusion.' Returning the teapot to its stand, she asked, 'What was the obstacle, Seth?'

'The obstacle?'

'Yes, I mean the reason why you were so reluctant to let me know how you felt.'

It was easy, now, for him to explain. 'It was you being properly educated, while I learned only the basics at Sunday School. I felt like an intruder in your life.'

'I've already told you, Seth,' she said, reaching for his hands. 'You have qualities that transcend learning.'

He regarded her unsurely. 'I'd maybe feel better if I knew what "transcend" means,' he said.

'It means that they're higher and more important than formal education. The cleric who schooled you performed his task magnificently. In fact, I'd like to have known him.'

'He was a remarkable man,' he agreed.

'And so are you.' Smiling, she said, 'It must be the case, because I've said it, and although I say it as shouldn't, I'm rather good at assessing people.' Her eyes twinkled as she said, 'You're extremely good at kissing, too, not that I'm speaking from wide experience, of course.'

'Of course not.' He bent and kissed her again, encouraged by a new degree of participation.

'I was taught that a woman should always remain passive in intimacy,' she said, 'which bears out what I said about formal education being of questionable worth.' She joined him again in a lingering, questing kiss. When they drew apart, Seth said confidently, 'I love you Selena. I've felt that way for a long time.' It was as if the words were out before he'd assembled them properly, but he was glad, all the same, that he'd uttered them.

'So have I.' She kissed him briefly, as if underlining her somewhat unexpected admission, and then touched the teapot. 'It's still hot,' she said, and whilst I'd happily spend the afternoon in your arms, it's a shame to waste good tea. Don't you agree?'

As he watched her pour, he asked, 'Did you read your book after I left you, last Sunday?'

'Oh, *Far From the Madding Crowd*? Yes, I read it to the end, but not for the first time.'

'Do you often read books more than once?'

'Yes, if I like them enough. What did you think of it?'

'I felt as if I knew the people in it,' he said, taking the cup and saucer from her. 'It was like reading about the life I knew and about people I'd known on the farm in England. Of course, I didn't get very far with it. When you fell asleep, I thought I'd better leave you in peace.'

'I didn't mean to fall asleep.'

'You were weak and exhausted. I'd stayed too long.'

'Oh no, you hadn't,' she told him very definitely. 'I was glad of your company. Look, would you like to borrow *Far From the Madding Crowd*? You were so impressed with it, it would be a shame not to read the whole story.'

'I'd appreciate that.'

She got up to take the book from one of the wall shelves and handed it to him. 'I have many more,' she said, 'and you're equally welcome to borrow any of them.'

'You're very kind, Selena.' He meant every word, but his mind was still in a whirl after their unexpected exchange of confidences. After some thought, he said, 'When we met, you told me you thought that Henry and I were like the knights in olden times.'

'Yes, and I still think that; in fact, I'm convinced of it. What's suddenly reminded you of that?'

'It didn't happen suddenly. I've been thinking about it for some time.'

She leaned closer and kissed him lightly. 'Something's on your mind, Seth. Tell me about it.'

'All right.' He wrapped his arms round her because what he had to say was so important and intimate, there must be nothing, even daylight, between them. 'Somebody once told me that a knight isn't complete without his lady,' he said.

'I'd never disagree with that, even for a moment.'

'What I'm trying to say, to ask you....'

'What?' Her voice was warm and encouraging.

It would wait no longer. He had to ask her. 'Selena, will you do me the honour?'

'Yes, Seth, with absolutely no hesitation, I will.'

16

The Ideal

Seth called for Selena and was freshly captivated by the sight of her in a gown that was a delicate green, but which she told him was called '*eau de Nil*', explaining that it meant 'water of the Nile'. Whatever the colour was called, and whichever river it was named after, he found it entrancing and, having held her coat while she prepared herself for the outdoors, he helped her proudly into the cab that he'd left waiting outside her apartment. Climbing up beside her, he called to the driver, 'Twenty-two, Norwood Avenue, if you please, driver.'

The cabby cracked his whip over the horses, and the cab lurched forward through the thickening snow.

Selena was wearing the ring that Wapun had worn all too briefly, and Seth took her hand to remind himself that his dream had become reality. 'It's a modest offering,' he said, 'until I can find something more suitable.' He felt that 'find' was a more polite word than 'afford', although that was secretly his chief concern.

'Nonsense, Seth. It's a lovely ring, and it says exactly what it's meant to say.'

'And you say everything I need to hear.'

'I'm glad of that.'

The driver pressed on through the driving snow, the horses and carriage wheels making heroic progress through the fast-lying snow, and eventually drew up at the roadside. 'Twenty-two, Norwood Avenue, Sergeant,' he reported.

'Thank you, driver.' He climbed down and helped Selena out of the cab. Fortunately, the snow had been recently cleared outside the Hawthorn residence, and the latest fall was yet to create an obstacle.

'I thank you, Sergeant,' said the driver, taking the fare.

'That's right enough,' Seth told him, gesturing to him to keep the change for himself.

'You're most kind, Sergeant. Ten o' clock, I believe you said.'

'That's right. I'm obliged to you.' He offered Selena his arm, and they walked up the path to the front door, which was opened, in response to a pull on the bell rope, by a maid, who took their outer garments.

The Hawthorns' habitual welcome, from the moment they stepped across the threshold, equalled the warmth of the house after driving through the freezing snow, both causing the guests to glow with pleasure. Then, with everyone assembled, something called an aperitif was served. Seth had never heard of it, but it sounded like an excellent idea and, when it arrived, he was surprised to discover that it tasted remarkably like sherry.

'Raise your glasses,' said Mr Hawthorn, 'and drink to "The Great Occasion".'

Everyone obliged, and conversation was resumed, with Mr Hawthorn ensuring that everyone was involved; in fact, his general bonhomie prompted Selena to say privately that he was a pleasing reminder of Mr Fezziwig.

Seth asked, 'Who's Mr Fezziwig?'

'He's a delightful man who appears in another book that you might find entertaining.'

They chatted with everyone in the easy way that guests adopt when they gather for an event that gives equal pleasure to them all, and Seth found himself very much at ease in a situation he was experiencing for the first time.

When dinner was announced, the party took their places, according to Mrs Hawthorn's carefully-written place cards, at the large dining table. Mr Hawthorn said Grace, and dinner commenced.

Looking around and seeing everyone so happy and involved set Seth in mind of the few gatherings he'd known. There were the harvest suppers at the farm in Yorkshire and the rugged, kindly hospitality the farmer and his wife had shown to two orphaned urchins. Then there were mealtimes at the Norton farm, where goodwill seemed to flow with endless ease. Mealtimes with friends and family, the latter albeit adopted for the occasion, were the best times, and he would always remember dinner with the open-hearted Hawthorn couple, not to mention Esther, who gave every indication of having inherited her parents' finest qualities.

The excellent meal continued, until the port and liqueurs had circulated. At this point, Mr Hawthorn called for everyone's attention. As they fell silent, he began.

'Just over one week ago,' he told them, 'I gave my blessing most readily to the engagement of our daughter Esther to Sergeant Henry Fowler. That event made my wife and me very happy indeed.' He paused as everyone registered their agreement. 'Then, I learned of another happy development, this time between Mrs Selena Stevenson and Sergeant Seth Campion. Selena has asked me if, in her father's absence, I will give her, at the ceremony, to be married, and I shall be honoured as well as delighted to perform that duty.' Again, the company demonstrated its approval. 'The two gentlemen involved,' he went on, 'will be in no doubt that they are fortunate indeed in their future brides, but let me say this about the potential bridegrooms. It is my belief that the North West Mounted Police is the embodiment of that which is good in our society, and I could not be better pleased that Esther and Selena are betrothed to two such exemplary officers.'

There was enthusiastic applause from all but Seth and Henry, who were feeling quite self-conscious after such an accolade, but then came their turn to respond. Mrs Hawthorn, Esther and Selena called simultaneously for a speech, and Henry stirred uncomfortably, Then, finding that he was unable to make himself smaller, he stood to say, 'My thanks are due to Mr and Mrs Hawthorn as well as to Esther for accepting my offer of marriage. Beyond that, I am a man of few words, so I can only say that I agree with every word Seth is about to say.'

Seth rose to his feet. 'He always leaves the difficult tasks to me,' he said, 'but that means that I always know where I stand.' He delivered the quip with a friendly nod in Henry's direction. 'Mr Hawthorn,' he said, 'I thank you and Mrs Hawthorn for your many kindnesses, but chiefly for your open-hearted hospitality. I thank you, Mr Hawthorn, for agreeing to give Selena away at the ceremony, and for your most generous description of Henry and me.' The company applauded, and Selena squeezed his hand in encouragement. Seth had anticipated the need for a speech, but she'd realised that it would present him with a challenge, even with her help and preparation.

'Henry and I sailed from Bombay four years ago in pursuit of an ideal.' He was secretly grateful to Katherine for that description. 'We believed we would find that ideal in Colonel George Armstrong Custer and the United States Seventh Cavalry, but we arrived rather too late. Maybe that was just as well, as things turned out for them.' He acknowledged the meaningful murmurs that greeted his observation.

'It's fair to say that we did what we could to enforce law and order in Pentecost, but we had to hand over the task, eventually, to an official town marshall, and that was when our quest took us in a northerly direction, to Winnipeg. I'm proud to say that I agree wholeheartedly with Mr Hawthorn's description of the North West Mounted Police, and you could say that it was in joining the force that we eventually found our ideal, but that wouldn't be strictly true. We found a part of it, certainly, but not the whole of it. The missing element had yet to be realised.' He was rewarded by bemused glances from around the table, and he looked at Selena, grateful beyond his experience for her help in preparing his speech.

'In helping those in need, and in pursuing our ideal, Henry and I have sometimes been compared in times past, and very much to our embarrassment, with the knights of the Middle Ages.' He smiled self-consciously at the reassuring murmurs around him. 'Having said that, I have also been told that no knight is complete without his lady. Well, that deficit is now made good, Henry has Esther and I have Selena, which means our quest is fulfilled more surely than we could ever have imagined. If knights we are, then you see at this table the happiest knights that ever took to horse.' He paused finally to ask, 'Would you agree with that, Sergeant Fowler?'

Henry nodded assertively and with new confidence. 'I agree with everything you've said, Sergeant Campion.'

The End

www.ingramcontent.com/pod-product-compliance
Lightning Source LLC
Chambersburg PA
CBHW032143020726
47496CB00003B/684